# BEAUTIFUL STRANGER
## RUTH WIND

Published by Silhouette Books

**America's Publisher of Contemporary Romance**

For my sisters, Cathy Stroo and Merry Jordan,
who've each chosen to serve the teens of the world,
offering hands to hold, ears to listen, shoulders to cry on
and hearts so full of love no judgment can enter in.
I am *so* proud of you both.

 **SILHOUETTE BOOKS**

ISBN 0-373-27081-X

BEAUTIFUL STRANGER

This edition published by arrangement with Harlequin Books S.A.

® and TM are trademarks of Harlequin Books S.A., used under license. Trademarks indicated with ® are registered in the United States Patent and Trademark Office, the Canadian Trade Marks Office and in other countries.

Visit Silhouette at www.eHarlequin.com

**Printed in U.S.A.**

## "We are going to have to deal with this attraction sooner or later,"

Robert said roughly, holding her hand tightly.

"Maybe it would be better if we didn't see each other."

He looked at her mouth, closed his eyes. "We'll just…take it easy."

"All right." She pulled on her hand. He pulled back.

"Why do you think it happens like this?" he said, stepping closer. "Out of nowhere?"

It wasn't out of nowhere on her part. "I always saw you, Robert. You just never saw me before."

He moved even closer, until his hips and hers were nearly touching. "Yes, I did."

She rolled her eyes. "Right."

"You used to have this green dress," he said. "Your hair spilled all over it. And you wore red lipstick in those days. Bright red, like something sinful."

His eyes were intent, "You've always been beautiful, Marissa. You just didn't know it till now."

Dear Reader,

Once again, Silhouette Intimate Moments has rounded up six top-notch romances for your reading pleasure, starting with the finale of Ruth Langan's fabulous new trilogy. *The Wildes of Wyoming—Ace* takes the last of the Wilde men and matches him with a pool-playing spitfire who turns out to be just the right woman to fill his bed—and his heart.

Linda Turner, a perennial reader favorite, continues THOSE MARRYING McBRIDES! with *The Best Man,* the story of sister Merry McBride's discovery that love is not always found where you expect it. Award-winning Ruth Wind's *Beautiful Stranger* features a heroine who was once an ugly duckling but is now the swan who wins the heart of a rugged "prince." Readers have been enjoying Sally Tyler Hayes' suspenseful tales of the men and women of DIVISION ONE, and *Her Secret Guardian* will not disappoint in its complex plot and emotional power. Christine Michels takes readers *Undercover with the Enemy,* and Vickie Taylor presents *The Lawman's Last Stand,* to round out this month's wonderful reading choices.

And don't miss a single Intimate Moments novel for the next three months, when the line takes center stage as part of the Silhouette 20th Anniversary celebration. Sharon Sala leads off A YEAR OF LOVING DANGEROUSLY, a new in-line continuity, in July; August brings the long-awaited reappearance of Linda Howard—and hero Chance Mackenzie—in *A Game of Chance;* and in September we reprise 36 HOURS, our successful freestanding continuity, in the Intimate Moments line. And that's only a small taste of what lies ahead, so be here this month and every month, when Silhouette Intimate Moments proves that love and excitement go best when they're hand in hand.

Leslie J. Wainger
Executive Senior Editor

Please address questions and book requests to:
Silhouette Reader Service
U.S.: 3010 Walden Ave., P.O. Box 1325, Buffalo, NY 14269
Canadian: P.O. Box 609, Fort Erie, Ont. L2A 5X3

## RUTH WIND

is the award-winning author of both contemporary and historical romance novels. She lives in the mountains of the Southwest with her husband, two growing sons and many animals in a hundred-year-old house the town blacksmith built. The only hobby she has since she started writing is tending the ancient garden of irises, lilies and lavender beyond her office window, and she says she can think of no more satisfying way to spend a life than growing children, books and flowers.

# *Prologue*

The girl showed up on his doorstep, wearing nothing but an oversize windbreaker to protect her from the February cold. Her shoulders were painfully thin under the jacket. Her stomach bowed out in an unmistakable shape she tried to hide, a shape all wrong on a fifteen-year-old.

The long hair hadn't been washed in a few days, and Robert could tell she was wearing the same makeup she'd set out with. Whatever belongings she'd carried with her were in a very small backpack.

When the knock came, it startled him into breaking a fragile bit of red glass he'd been fitting into a small frame, edging it with heat to ease it. Tsking, he flipped his safety glasses to the top of his head and went to the door. The girl was standing there on his step, her chin lifted at that cocky teenage angle that was all bravado, yet hid a scared little girl heart. She popped a big wad of gum. Long earrings glittered against her tangled hair, and her eyeliner was smeared, as if she'd slept in it.

"Hey, uncle," she said, like she'd just come in from school. As if she wasn't five hundred miles from home. Like he expected her.

Robert met that I-dare-you gaze for one long moment, seeing, with painful memory, himself at fourteen, fifteen, wanting somebody to—

Without a word, he opened the screen door. He didn't yell or ask what the hell she was doing. He simply pushed the door aside, opened his arms and she fell against him, her twig arms fierce against his ribs, her relief an almost palpable presence. She didn't have to tell him she was in trouble, that she'd run away, that she had nowhere else to go.

When her tough-girl facade cracked, it cracked wide open, and his fifteen-year-old niece, five months pregnant if she was a minute, burst into tears and sobbed like a baby. He just held on.

There wasn't much room for her in his little house, and heaven knew he was the last man on earth who ought to be an example for anybody, but Robert held her while she cried, then sent her to take a shower while he made her a big bowl of soup. He made her eat, then put her to bed in his own room before he called his sister, Alicia, who responded pretty much as he'd expected—her new husband was more important to her than her daughter. Robert forgave her before he even hung up. They'd had the same mother after all.

He leaned in the doorway and watched Crystal sleep, a knot of pain in his chest. No matter how bad he'd be at the father thing, he was better than nobody. He'd managed to oversee a motley crew of soldiers through a war—how bad could one teenage girl be?

He set to work on cleaning up the back room, boxing up his tools and supplies so she would have a room of her own. Tomorrow they'd figure out the rest.

# Chapter 1

As her classroom of twenty-seven ninth graders filed out of seventh hour—her last class of the day, thank heavens—Marissa Pierce grabbed her purse out of the desk drawer and bolted for the faculty rest room. In ten minutes, she had an appointment with the parent of a difficult student, and if she didn't visit Mother Nature right *now,* she wouldn't have a chance for another hour. Intolerable.

She bustled through the throngs of high schoolers in their baggy pants, and took pleasure in the simple fact of being able to bustle—an act that had been purely beyond her for a long time. It was still a little shock to zip up a pair of size-twelve slacks, but the best part of losing eighty-five pounds was this: being able to move lightly and without trouble through a crowd.

Just like a normal person.

The rest room was blessedly empty. Marissa tended to nature, readjusted her belt and peered at it in the mirror. All day long she'd felt odd about this belt. She knew she'd fiddled with it, touching it with her hand every so often to make sure the belly beneath it wasn't sticking out a mile. But the mirror insisted the belly looked exactly the same as it had this morning—a little rounder than some, maybe, but ordinarily so. And there were no gobs of back fat pushing out her blouse in the rear.

It had taken eighteen months to lose the weight, and she still had a good fifteen or twenty pounds to go. They had been long, long months at times, sometimes very discouraging, and even now it seemed that a kind of ghost of her former self clung to her.

But there were moments like this one, when she saw herself in a mirror, with a shirt tucked into a pair of trousers, that she realized anew it had all been worth it. After fifteen years of being the fattest kid, then the fattest woman in any room, of ducking mirrors and dreading shopping malls, she took extraordinary pleasure in the simple act of not wincing when she bent to put a little fresh lipstick on her mouth.

Feeling much better, she went back to her room in the clearing halls and found Crystal already seated in her usual place, third seat in the fifth row, by the windows. And as she often did, the girl stared out that window as if some rescue was imminent—or at least, she wished it was. Kids this age were often a mass of tangled hungers and skewed logic, and pregnancy only made all of that about twenty times worse.

One of the reasons Marissa had chosen to teach this age group was because her own adolescence had been very difficult. To her surprise, she was very good at it. Her heart and soul were engaged by the delicate, topsy-turvy, exuberant and exasperating world of teens. Every so often, a particular child captured her—last year it had been a boy with such brilliance for math that she'd been challenged every single day to stay ahead of him.

Something about Crystal Avila had snagged Marissa hard. She found herself worrying about the girl at odd moments, just before she fell asleep, or in the shower. It wasn't just that she was pregnant. Sadly, Crystal was far from the first pregnant teen to sit in this classroom.

No, it was deeper than that. There was such a depth of yearning, such sorrow in those dark eyes that it was sometimes hard to look at her. She'd lost something big in her old life, something more than her innocence. It plucked at Marissa in some odd way she couldn't shake.

Dropping her purse back into the desk drawer, Marissa said casually, "Hey, kiddo. You can come sit up here if you like."

She just shook her head, the long strands of straight black hair sticking on the coat she wore every minute, probably to hide her belly. She was a pretty little thing, small and delicate, her face adamantly Native American with broad cheekbones and narrow chin.

Marissa started the process of tidying her desk. "How was your day?"

Crystal made a grunting, you-are-so-stupid noise, and rolled her eyes. "What do you think?"

"I don't know. That's why I asked."

"It sucked, as usual." She bent her head, ran her thumbnail along the pencil holder carved into the desk. "I hate this place."

It was a good opening. Marissa carefully focused on gathering scattered writing utensils and putting them in a square container another student had made for her in woodshop. "Did you like your old school better?"

"No." A singularly surly word. "I hated it, too, but my *mom* didn't make me go."

"And you're mad at your uncle because he makes you?"

She shrugged, probably not quite willing to be that disloyal with an outsider.

"Well, you know—" Marissa kept her body moving, unfocused and therefore unthreatening "—if you weren't as smart as you are, I might think there were better ways for you to spend your time." She erased calculations from the blackboard and turned around. "But anyone with a brain like yours really needs an education."

"Oh, yeah," she said, snorting, "I'm *so* smart. Can't you see how smart I am?" She gestured with anger to her belly.

"Getting pregnant is a mistake, but it has nothing to do with brains." When the girl only lowered her head, Marissa went on. "Lots of really smart women get pregnant by accident—even women who are trying to be careful, so you aren't alone."

Crystal began wiggling her foot, but she still didn't have the blinders up. A surprise, but Marissa wasn't about to waste a chance. "You really are smart, Crystal. I'd really like to help you see that, if you'll give me a chance."

The great dark eyes flickered up, flared briefly with hope, then lowered quickly again.

Oh, babe! Marissa thought, that familiar ache in her chest.

"None of my other teachers ever told me I was smart. What if you're wrong?"

Marissa laughed softly. "I'm never wrong," she said. "And I'm really smart myself. I know what I'm talking about."

A knock sounded at the door, and Marissa straightened, turning to welcome the girl's uncle into the room. But halfway to her feet, her heart slammed hard into her ribs and then settled into a painful thudding.

Red Dog.

That was what they called him, anyway, an army nickname. Marissa knew him through her association with the Forrest family—he was Jake Forrest's best friend.

And one of the most intensely sexy men Marissa had ever seen. It was less a particular feature or even combination of features that made it so—it was the essence of him, a dangerous combination of brooding darkness and an appreciation of women that was like some devilish cologne seeping from his pores.

Marissa quickly turned and snatched a paper off her desk, seeking his real name. "Mr. Martinez?" With a degree of smoothness she would have thought beyond her at just that moment, she crossed the room and extended her hand, smiling warmly. "Come in. I'm so glad you could make it."

"Please call me Robert." Not a single flicker of recognition crossed his face as he clasped her hand with a firm, honest kind of grip. "Thanks for asking me here. Sorry I'm such a mess—I had to come right from work."

"Not a problem." And it wasn't. His chambray shirt and jeans were dusty with a long day's work in construction, but his long, graceful hands were clean. His hair, thick and inky, was pulled back into a long braid, highlighting the hard, high cheekbones and wide mouth. His eyes were serious, very dark, but she knew from watching him at various gatherings that they crinkled up when he laughed.

She struggled back into a professional demeanor. As they moved toward the middle of the room, Marissa liked the way his attention honed in on Crystal.

"Hi, honey," he said, and raised a hand in a gesture of inclusion. "Why don't you come on over here with us?"

The girl reluctantly slid out of her seat and shuffled over, dwarfed by her coat and baggy pants and all that hair sliding forward to hide her face. Her uncle slid an arm around her shoulders and embraced her quickly before he let her go.

They settled into chairs Marissa kept close to her desk for unruly kids. "Mr. Martinez—"

"Robert," he corrected.

"Right. Robert, I was just telling Crystal that I think she's very bright, and I'm worried about her."

Robert glanced at Crystal, then back to Marissa, and she saw his concern in the darkness of those uptilted eyes. "She is smart," he said. "But she doesn't seem to like school very much."

"Exactly. Maybe if we talk, we can get to the bottom of that. Make it better."

"All right," Robert said.

Marissa shifted slightly. "Crystal, can I ask you some questions?"

"I guess."

"Have you made some friends here yet?"

A shrug, a dull glance outside the window. "Yeah."

It was a lie and Marissa knew it, but she wouldn't push. With a flash of inspiration, she dropped her usual spiel about the missing homework assignments and asked instead, "Tell me, is there anything you're crazy about? I mean totally nuts. Like cats or horses or a book you've read?"

A small alteration in body language. Crystal's gaze slid toward her uncle. "No," she said.

Robert grinned. "You can tell her."

Long lashes swept down. "No."

Marissa glanced at Robert. He met her eyes, then reached out and put a hand on Crystal's shoulder. "She's not gonna use it against you, babe."

Crystal shifted away. "Everyone makes fun of me. Like I have a sickness or something."

"I won't laugh. I promise," Marissa said, crossing her heart and lifting a hand.

With a dark glare at her uncle, one that dared him to say a word, Crystal said distinctly, *"No."*

"It's all right," Marissa said. "You don't trust me, and you don't really have any reason to." She shrugged. "If you ever feel like telling me, I'll be glad to listen— and maybe I can figure out ways to connect school, which you seem to hate, to whatever it is that you love."

Crystal raised her eyes, and Marissa glimpsed something like surprise.

"Of course, that means we have to talk about the other things now." Marissa folded her hands. It was always hard to know how a parent would respond to the kind of news she was about to deliver. Some reacted defensively. Some turned their embarrassment into anger at the child.

"The reason I wanted to talk to both of you together," she said, "is because Crystal is doing very well on tests, but she's not turning in homework. In math, since she's obviously getting the concepts, I'd be willing to overlook the lack of homework, but I'm hearing about the same problem from other teachers, and they aren't going to be as willing to overlook that work."

Robert frowned, an expression of bewilderment more than anger. "She does her homework. I check it every night." He turned to her. "Aren't you turning it in?"

"I forget."

Marissa carefully did not smile. Crystal wasn't forgetting. Or if she was, it was a passive-aggressive kind of forgetting, a way to get what she thought she wanted. She'd discuss some ideas with Robert once Crystal left the room, but for now she let it go. "Crystal, I'd really like to help you get some good patterns going, so school is more fun for you. It would be criminal for you to waste that great mind." She paused. "Do you have any suggestions?"

A sudden wash of tears filled the dark eyes, and she looked away sullenly. One hostile shoulder lifted and fell.

"How about if you come here for an hour after school, and I can help you with your work—not just math, but whatever you're having trouble with?"

"I'm not *having* any trouble."

"Well, maybe it would just be a case of you turning the homework in to me, then, so I can see that it gets to the right places." She looked at the uncle, resisting that little zing of awareness he gave her. "Would that be okay with you?"

"What d'you say, Crystal? Maybe try it for a week or two, see how it goes, eh? It's only an hour. What the heck?"

Heartfelt shrug, both shoulders. "I guess."

Marissa smiled. "Good. I'll see you tomorrow, here, then. And since you've been tortured long enough, how about giving me a few minutes with your uncle? You can get a soda or something, maybe?"

"*Somebody* here won't let me drink pop."

Robert chuckled, and reached into the pocket of his jeans. "I saw the Sno-Kone man out there. Get some ice cream. It's good for you."

"How come it's good and pop is bad?"

"Because ice cream is made from milk, silly girl." He winked at her. "Get me a couple of ice-cream sandwiches, will ya? I'll be out in a few minutes."

Crystal took the money and gravely shook her head. "Someday, Uncle, you're going to be as fat as a house. Or my uncle Gary."

He laughed. "Probably." He patted her shoulder and inclined his head. "Go on."

Crystal shuffled out, and Robert turned back to Marissa, his face wiped free of amusement. "She's not doing real well here, is she?"

"No." Marissa, acting on a hunch, stood up and closed the door, then returned to her seat. "She's been here...what? Four or five weeks? And I've never seen her even talk to another student. Other kids try, you know, to include her, and she's not having it."

He sighed, and then, as if he couldn't think while sitting, stood up and paced to the window. "I'm not too good at this father thing," he said, turning. His arms were crossed. "I've never had a kid—but I gotta try. Her mom is useless, and there's nobody else. I've been trying to make her stick to regular hours and eat normal food—just, you know, normal." He gestured, shook his head. "Why am I telling you this?"

"Maybe because it's hard to go it alone," Marissa said. "It sounds like you're doing all the right things, and it's obviously a rough time for her." She frowned. "Is she doing any kind of parenting class, Lamaze, anything with other kids who are also pregnant?"

"She starts the end of the week. You think that'll help, maybe? Maybe she feels kind of isolated."

"Yeah." Marissa thought, fleetingly, of herself at fourteen—feeling like a hippopotamus in her flowing dress while all the other girls wore their skinny jeans.

"Trust me when I say this is a rough age for all the kids, but if there's anything to set you the tiniest bit apart, it's that much harder. She's pregnant, she's new and she's Native American, which sort of makes her exotic around here." She smiled. "In case you haven't noticed, it's not exactly a wildly integrated community."

Humor flickered over his eyes—eyes that crinkled upward at the corners just as she remembered. In detail. With a little ripple of despair, she decided he was just sinfully delectable.

"I noticed," he said. "I don't want to live in a city. Red Creek might have some flaws, but at least I don't have to worry about her getting on the wrong side of some gang."

"Do you mind if I make a suggestion?"

"No—please. I'm open to anything."

"I'll have her come in every afternoon and see if I can get her on track with school, maybe let her know there's someone else in her corner. We can start a check-off system to help her get her homework in. And it's probably going to help a lot to get her into her pregnancy class." She straightened. "But it also occurs to me that there's someone in town who would be more than delighted to help you mother this lost child."

He looked puzzled. "Mother?"

She chuckled. "Yeah. Louise Forrest—er, Chacon, I guess it is now. Jake's mother."

"You know Jake and his mother?"

He didn't recognize her at all. With a grin she said, "We have met, Robert. I'm good friends with Lance."

His body went soft with surprise, and she saw the knowledge and recognition dawn on his face. "Oh my God! I know who you are now. Marissa." His gaze moved with frank astonishment over her body. "My

God! You've lost…you're so much—'' He stopped, clamped his mouth shut, took a breath.

Marissa laughed.

"Sorry," he said. "That was really rude."

"Not at all. It's very common lately."

"You've lost a lot of weight."

"Almost a hundred pounds." She gestured like the Duchess of York. "And trust me, I love it when people are amazed."

His eyes made the journey over her figure once more, this time frankly appreciative. "You look terrific."

"Thanks. Now, about Louise…"

"Yeah." He nodded. "Yeah, Louise is a great idea."

"Day to day, it's just getting through. Sometimes just minute to minute." She smiled. "I teach them all day, remember. But when you run into something troubling, Louise might have good advice."

He nodded. "Thank you," he said, and held out his hand. "I can't tell you how much I appreciate the interest you've taken."

Marissa stood and clasped the long brown hand in her own, allowing herself at last to experience the slightly heady sensation of standing close to him, holding his hand and smiling up at him. "My pleasure," she said, and made to draw away.

But he held on, tightening his fingers slightly. "You were always beautiful, you know."

Marissa, stricken to the core, was afraid he'd see too much if she let him hang on a second longer, and she pulled away, hiding her emotions under a well-mannered smile. "Thank you. And thank you for coming."

At the door he paused. "Do you want to know what she loves?"

"I'll wait until she's ready to tell me."

He nodded. "All right. Thanks again."

He closed the door behind him and Marissa sank against the desk, swallowing the weird rush of emotion his simple, clear words had given her. *You were always beautiful.* Not exactly the words she would ever have expected to come from the lips of a jaded, brooding man who only crooked his finger and had women from thirteen to seventy flocking to his side.

Then she realized with a wry little smile that it was exactly what she *should* have expected. The great power of a ladies' man lay in his understanding of a woman's most private, most revered hungers.

Reaching for her purse, she chuckled. He'd certainly zeroed in on Marissa's.

There was a card from her sister in the mailbox when she got home, and Marissa laughed when she opened it. The front showed a beachy guy in worn white cutoffs, smiling hunkily, and the inside said, "Just wanted to send you something fun to break up your day."

Marissa had mailed out the exact card, for no particular reason, to her twin sister, Victoria, only three days before. They were identical twins, the only children of their obscenely wealthy and overly protective parents. What nature began in the womb, the isolation their parents had imposed had completed; the pair had an almost uncanny bond, as if they were one mind in two bodies.

When she walked in, still smiling, the phone rang.

"I just got it," she said into the phone, knowing by a twin's intuition exactly who was on the other end. "I should have known."

Victoria laughed. "I don't even know why we bother. Next time, just buy the card and keep it and so will I, and we'll both save the postage."

"Ah, what fun would that be?"

Victoria changed gears. "Enough of that. Who is he?"

It startled Marissa. "Who?"

"Some man. Don't lie. I felt it, right in the solar plexus."

Marissa chuckled. "Well, he's really no one. A cute parent, that's all. Sweet talker."

"Mmm. He must be hot, that's all I have to say. I'm going to come see for myself. Can I come visit? Maybe stay for a week. Or a month?"

"Really?" Marissa cried. She had not seen her sister in more than two years, largely due to Victoria's hectic and worldly schedule. "That would be *so* fantastic!" She smiled to herself. "I have quite a surprise for you."

"And I have one for you." She laughed softly. "I can't imagine that we'll duplicate each other this time."

Marissa thought of her sister's ultraskinny frame. "Nope. Not this time."

"All right, then. I'll see you in a week or two."

They hung up.

## Chapter 2

One of the best parts of Marissa's job was that her planning period fell just before lunch, so on those days that she was not required to be in the cafeteria or walking the grounds, she had a good long break in the middle of the day. She often went to a small café nearby to have a salad freshly made from a long list of menu items. Today she chose butter and radicchio and romaine lettuces, sunflower seeds, broccoli, tomatoes and shredded carrots and a bare sprinkling of pumpernickel croutons. They didn't even have to ask anymore if she wanted the dressing on the side.

Carrying her overflowing plate to a table near the window, she relished the salad slowly, along with a whole-grain roll and a thin spread of butter and the unsweetened raspberry tea they served, made with fresh lemons and raspberries. Outrageously good.

Gazing peacefully at the bright blue Colorado day, she felt sinfully satisfied. In her old life, she had rarely taken the time to enjoy food—eating had been a guilt-laden activity, something evil one was required to indulge, and she often hurried through it, almost inhaling a meal before others had made it halfway through.

It was a miracle to her now to really taste the butter on the bread, savor the small wheat berries in the soft dough. She dipped her fork in dressing and speared a pale green leaf of butter lettuce—it was one of her favorites at home because of the way the leaves felt in her hand, soft as suede—and took time to experience the combination of flavors. Before she had finished half the salad, she was satisfied—no, closer to stuffed.

Replete, and feeling virtuous from all the nutrients she'd managed to pack into a single lunch, she paid and headed back to campus, two blocks north. The walk was a particularly pleasant one, following a path through a park that ran through the middle of town like a long finger. The day was not yet hot, and a breeze lifted her hair.

A breeze that smelled of cigarettes. She glanced over, ready to smile; the few teachers who still smoked often slipped away to the park during lunch, and it was her habit to shake her finger at them cheerfully. But no one was sitting on the favored bench beneath a copse of aspens—instead, blue smoke wafted around the edge of a cinderblock building that housed rest rooms. Marissa spied a combat boot with a spot of pink paint at the toe peeking around the base of the wall.

With a sigh, she crossed the grass, shaking her head, and came around the building.

Crystal Avila hunched there, guiltily, and started so violently when she saw Marissa that she dropped the cigarette on the ground.

Marissa quickly stepped on it, grinding it beneath the toe of her shoe. "Bad idea, kiddo. And not just for you."

The girl ducked her head, pulled her coat more tightly around her belly. A fall of hair, taking up a thick reddish hue in the dappled sunlight, slid over her shoulders.

"Do you smoke a lot?" Marissa asked.

"No." She swallowed, dared to raise her eyes for a split second, dropped them again. "This is the first time since—" She burst into tears. "I don't know what I was doing!"

"Oh, honey." Marissa reached for her with one hand, ready to offer a shoulder for a hug if the girl needed it, but Crystal jerked away, hiding her face with her hands.

"Don't suspend me, okay? I swear, I'll do whatever you want, but I don't want my uncle to—"

"To what?"

"To give me that look, all sad and disappointed."

"Ah." She folded her arms, leaning as casually as she could against the wall. "Well, first of all, I can't suspend you for smoking because you're not on school grounds."

"Really?" Bright, hopeful eyes in a face streaked with tears.

"I could have you sent to study hall for leaving campus—"

"Oh." Deflated balloon. Shoulders drooping, head dropping.

"—but I don't see what purpose it would serve. You have enough study hall for fourteen people already." She sighed. "I want to help you, Crystal. I wish you'd let me."

Abruptly the girl put her back against the wall and slid down to sit on the ground, her elbows braced on her upraised knees, her hands over her face. "You can't do nothing."

"Anything. And you'd be surprised."

"You don't know," she said miserably. "You don't know what those girls say about me. I hate them."

Marissa knelt, trying to be as ladylike as possible in a straight skirt. That was one thing her old tent dresses had afforded that she'd never truly appreciated—freedom of movement. "You want to walk back to school with me? We can talk in my room. I don't have a class for an hour."

She shook her head. "I want to go home. Can you call my uncle?"

"Sure." She reached into her purse and took out a tiny cell phone. "What's the number?"

Crystal looked up. "It's a beeper." She gave the number and Marissa punched it in, then held the phone loosely as she examined the girl. "Someone hurt you today?"

She blinked. Nodded, her mouth tight. "I know how it looks, you know, but I'm not a slut. I never was." She raised her head. "I swear it on a stack of Bibles."

"I believe you." She hesitated. "Is it different people or someone in particular? If there's someone in particular, I can make sure it stops."

"Get real." She rolled her eyes. "Like I would rat someone out like that."

The phone trilled lightly in her hand. "Hello?"

"This is Robert Martinez," he said. That voice—it rolled over her in a wave of color, a rich sienna, like the skin on his arms. "You beeped me?"

"Yes. This is Marissa Pierce, Crystal's math teacher. She'd like to come home. Is that all right?"

"Is there something wrong? Is the baby okay?"

"They're both fine. She's just had kind of a bad day."

"A bad day? What does that mean?"

Crystal said, "Ask him if I can walk over to where he's working and I'll tell him what's going on."

Marissa repeated the information.

"That's fine. Look, I know she's right there, but is there something going on I need to know?"

"Yes," Marissa said.

"Can you bring her over? Or meet me somewhere?"

"Sure, I'll bring her." Crystal rolled her eyes. Marissa grinned. "Where are you?"

He gave her directions. It was only three blocks west, in the heart of the historical district. "We'll be there in five minutes."

Marissa stood, brushing her skirt down. "Come on, kiddo."

Crystal stood, wiping hard at her face with her sleeve. "Why are you always so nice? Don't you know people take advantage of you?"

"I'll take my chances."


When Robert's beeper had gone off, he'd been high on a ladder in the foyer of a Victorian ruin. His crew was working on the restoration of a mansion that had been built with mining money just before the turn of the century. Neglected for more than twenty-five years, rumored to be haunted, Rosewood would provide the centerpiece for a historical renewal project that the town of Red Creek hoped would attract summer tourists to replace the income lost when skiers looked elsewhere for entertainment.

Robert had been tearing out the plaster and lathe of a particularly rotten stretch of ceiling, his hair and face covered with dust and old spiderwebs, when the pager had beeped loudly.

He'd checked the number with a sinking feeling. He only wore the beeper so that Crystal could get in touch with him anywhere, anytime, and it could only be her paging him. He'd scrambled down, brushing off his face and arms as he went, then had called out to Tyler Forrest, in charge of the meticulous restoration of the wood, and Robert's direct superior. "Need to borrow your cell phone, man."

The number was one he didn't recognize, and when he'd called it and got Marissa Pierce, he'd felt a frisson of...anticipation over the sound of her voice. And then sadness that Crystal was still having so much trouble.

He handed the cell phone back. "I gotta take a break. Crystal is going to come here, and I'll need to take her home and get her settled. Shouldn't take long."

"Is everything okay with the baby?"

"Baby's fine."

Tyler nodded. "Take as long as you need. Kids come first."

"Thanks."

"Wait a second, man." Tyler reached into a leather satchel. "My wife found these. Why don't you take a look while you're waiting?"

He took the folder. "What is it?"

Tyler gestured to the boarded area above the landing of the stairs. "Photographs of the original window. Black and white, but at least it's a start."

Robert shook his head with a wry smile. "You're a damned pit bull, you know it?"

"So they say." Tyler grinned. "Just take a look."

He carried the folder out to the shabby porch, patting his shirt pocket for cigarettes in an automatic gesture. It

was empty, as it had been for three years. The habit of
reaching for them would probably be with him when he
was ninety. He took out a wooden match instead, stuck
it between his teeth and flipped open the folder.

The window was enormous, and it was not simply
painted glass, as had been fashionable at the turn of the
century, but the real thing—stained glass in lead. It was
also enormous, stretching from the base of the landing
to nearly a story and a half above. Robert whistled. It
was good work—no, better than that.

It was also well beyond anything he had attempted.
He'd done small restorations for private homes, usually
a small round in a door, a pair of matching windows
alongside a fireplace, things like that. He'd done one
large window for an Indian church, but not even it came
close to this in size. Tyler would have to find someone
else.

With a shake of his head, he closed the folder and
paced to the end of the porch and back again, peering
every so often down the sidewalk in the direction from
which they'd come.

Chill, man, said a voice in his head, and he exhaled
heavily, got rid of the match and forced himself to sit
on the wooden railing that surrounded the porch. A
breeze, smelling of pine resin and sunlight on a carpet
of old leaves, swept down from the mountains, as light
and clean as anything he could imagine. It was one of
the things he liked best about this place, that weightless,
scented breeze. It rattled the aspen leaves together overhead, startling a squirrel who skittered down the trunk
and nearly across Robert's feet before it realized its mistake and scuttled off in the other direction.

The tension in his chest eased. Whatever the problem
was, he and Crystal could figure it out. As long as they

had each other, a roof over their heads, food to eat, there would be an answer.

But when she appeared on the sidewalk, he wondered. Her head was bent in misery, her arms folded across her chest. She was too skinny. So miserable. She would not say a word about the boy who'd made her pregnant, wouldn't say anything about her life back in Albuquerque at all, come to that.

Next to her, Marissa provided such a contrast of healthy womanhood that Robert nearly resented her. Sunlight caught in the fall of her elegantly cut dark hair, hair that swung in a thread by thread flow that came only from a very expensive set of scissors. Today she wore a royal blue blouse, silk by the low luster, together with a simple straight skirt. Lush breasts and round hips, a complexion clear as a bowl of milk, teeth as straight and white as a picket fence.

He didn't move immediately, caught by a swift, sharp surge of lust, rare and surprising. He narrowed his eyes, wondering what kindled it, noticed the fine heavy sway of flesh beneath her blouse, the unconscious swish of hips—she had a very female kind of walk, one you didn't see much anymore. Like one of those old-time movie stars, Marilyn Monroe or Rita Hayworth. Yeah, she had a very Rita Hayworth look, a siren in silk.

It was only then that he realized how he must look himself, covered in hundred-year-old plaster dust. The recognition, couched as it was in the obvious wish to look better for her, annoyed him, and although he brushed a little at his shirt and face as he walked down to meet them, he dared her to look down on him for being a working man.

Anyway, it was Crystal who mattered, not her teacher.

As the two of them approached, Robert saw that Crystal's face was streaky and red-eyed. In the oversize jacket she insisted upon wearing, she looked like a refugee, especially in comparison to the elegance that came off Marissa in clouds, along with that rich-girl smell. For a moment, he hated the teacher and everything she represented—the entire power structure, the do-gooder mentality. Gritting his teeth, he resisted brushing dust from himself and said, "What's going on?"

They exchanged a glance. "I think I'll leave that up to Crystal," Marissa said with a soft smile at the girl. Even her voice was rich. Perfect vowels, perfect tone. He bet she never shouted, even when she was flat-out furious.

"Crystal?" he prompted.

She looked toward the tops of the trees, to the roof, at the ground, anywhere but at his face. In some way it wounded him. Why wouldn't she talk to him? "You tell him," she told Marissa.

"I'd rather you did, Crystal," Robert said. "Have I ever yelled at you? Have I done anything to make you think I'm judging you?"

"No." The word came out hoarsely. "It's not that."

"What, then? I don't get it. I want to help you."

Marissa touched his arm, just above the elbow, and when he looked up, she gestured toward a cluster of white buckets tucked under the shade cast by an old pine. "Why don't we go sit over there?"

He spared a glance at her skirt. "Mighty expensive clothes to go slumming in."

"They'll wash," she said, steel in her tone.

He knew better, but shrugged. "Whatever."

They walked across the neglected yard in silence and settled on the sealed buckets that contained plaster repair mix. Marissa, straight as a Victorian lady, waited for

Crystal to look up. "I really think this is in your court, kiddo."

"She caught me smoking," Crystal said, and dropped her face into her hands, hiding behind her yards of hair.

"Smoking?" He sat up, shocked in spite of himself. "Crystal!"

"See?" Crystal flung away her hair, threw out her hands. "That's what I mean. That shock thing you do. I hate it."

He felt like he'd been kicked, and before he spoke, he took a minute to breathe deeply, in and out, and tell himself that whatever Crystal did was just a symptom of her anger. He found himself touching a tattoo on the inside of his wrist, a memento of his own days of anger. "Crystal," he said quietly.

She looked at him finally, and there was so much misery in her expression that he reached out and took her hand. "Are you all right?"

Her fingers tightened around his convulsively. "Yeah."

"Do you smoke a lot?"

"No. I did sometimes, back in Albuquerque, but not since I came here."

"Why today?"

A shrug.

Marissa asked, "Do you want to get out of this school that badly?"

"No," she said, aggrieved. And to Robert's complete amazement, she started to cry again. "I don't know why I did it. It could be bad for the baby! But there was this girl and I just asked her for one, like to prove something, I guess. And—" She wiped her face with her sleeve. "It was stupid. I know it was. But, Miss Pierce, I'll do anything you want. Please?"

Robert let himself look at Marissa then, clenching his jaw to keep hope from showing on his face. The blouse made her eyes even bluer in her pale face, but it seemed like he could see goodness there. Not Rich Girl benevolence, but something real and honest.

And something more, too. In anyone else, he'd have named it street savvy, but he didn't know how this woman, with her three-hundred-dollar shoes and that million-dollar cosmetic smell, would have picked up street smarts.

But the bright blue eyes narrowed, her lips tightened and she leaned forward. "Listen here, Crystal. You got me the minute you walked in that door, and I know I'm a soft touch where certain kids are concerned. Fifteen was the worst year of my life, and I bet you're having an even more miserable time than I did, so I'm on your side in a way you aren't going to find very often. But—" she leaned closer, elbows on one knee "—I'm also smarter than I look, and if you play me, you'll lose me. Got it?"

Crystal, without a single atom of surprise about her—which was more than Robert could say—nodded. "I promise, Miss Pierce."

"Good." She looked at Robert. "Are you free to take her home?"

He hesitated, only a second. "Sure," he said.

Marissa inclined her head, and he found himself snared in a strange way by the measuring expression in her eyes. "There was no right answer to that question. Why don't you let me call Louise if you have to go to work? I know she won't mind."

"Who's Louise?"

He shot Crystal a silencing glance, and considered it. Louise Forrest Chacon was famous—almost infamous—

for her need to take care of not only her own children, but the children of the whole damned world. He had been the beneficiary of that loving attention more than once, the most memorable time being when he'd had to tell her that her son was in the hospital after falling down a cliff.

Something eased, all the tension and conflict he'd been feeling since they'd walked up, and he gave Marissa Pierce a smile. Rich Girl or not, she had something real that he liked a lot.

"Truth is," he said, "I got connections to my boss. He won't fire me. But maybe me and Crystal can take the afternoon and go for a visit." He stood and held out his hand, only realizing, when it was fully extended and she couldn't refuse without being rude, that it was covered with dust, making his dark skin look as if it had been plunged in flour.

But Marissa didn't even hesitate. She smiled—a true, deep smile that went all the way to her beautiful eyes—and she put her small, neatly manicured hand into his.

"Thank you," he said.

"You're welcome."

Robert knew, even in the few seconds that he allowed himself to want her, that it was impossible. She wasn't just well-to-do, not like an officer's wife or a doctor's daughter—but bloody rich. He recognized the difference from his days in the army, when he'd occasionally been called to provide security for a diplomatic function. It didn't matter what country the rich guests came from— an Arabian prince or a Brazilian rancher's wife or a Japanese royal—the details of that kind of money were always the same.

Clean. Impossibly well-groomed. Hair that looked as if it had been cut one strand at a time. Skin that had been perfectly fed and tended since birth. Toenails as well manicured as fingernails, clothes that moved invisibly, perfectly, of fabrics so fine they'd last seventy years.

But most of all, it was the smell. A smell that filled his head now, a scent of cosmetics, a particular combination of notes from products he couldn't even begin to imagine. Lipsticks and lotions and creams and shampoos that came in frosted glass containers to sit on marble sink-tops.

Never failed to get him, right in the libido, and it didn't fail now. Halfway hating himself for the weakness, he gave himself three seconds to inhale it deeply, allowed two seconds more for the desire that came with it to roll down his spine.

Yeah, he was weak. And it was a particularly dismaying weakness, that he was almost invariably attracted to such women, though he'd never actually pursued one. Logically, a poor Indian who'd spent his life fighting for every damned thing he had, ought to hate women like that.

But "ought to" didn't mean "did". *Above all things, know thyself.* What Robert knew was that smell could rip his heart out if he let it, because in some ways it represented everything he'd ever dreamed of as a boy—comfort and privilege and cleanliness. For that eight-year-old he'd been, for the fifteen-year-old shivering in a doorway, he savored the sense of her hand, her smell, her clean, orderly life, then let her go.

"Come on, Crystal."

She stood up and stopped in front of Marissa. "Thank you, Miss Pierce," she said with sincerity. She took a breath and said, "You know that thing you asked about?"

"Thing?" Marissa frowned a little, then remembered. "Oh, yes. Your passion?"

"Yeah. I'll tell you if you want."

"Please."

"Movies," she said, and that was all. She turned and started walking toward Robert's truck.

Robert lifted his head and grinned at Marissa before he could stop himself, and he saw a flash of something cross her face, a flicker of awareness, unmistakable. Instead of squelching it with a brisk word or a sharp glance, he found himself inclining his head, testing the sensation of that new, fresh lust of his own, and found that it felt pretty good, that he liked the almost forgotten and pleasurable sense of awareness in his thighs. Interesting.

"Movies?" she said.

Robert only nodded, giving her a faint smile. "Yep. The rest you'll have to get yourself." He followed Crystal to the truck, knowing that Marissa watched him. He felt her eyes on the back of his arms, his legs. He thought of her sexy, rolling walk, and let a single vision of his hands, sliding up heavy breasts covered in heavy silk, tease his libido, then brushed it away. He climbed into the truck. "You had lunch yet?"

Crystal shook her head.

"Want burgers and fries?"

"Really? Junk food?"

He grinned. "A little now and then won't hurt anything."

When she got home from work, Marissa changed into sweats and T-shirt and her now-battered walking shoes. She needed her work-out today more than usual. Pulling her hair into a ponytail, she stretched the backs of her thighs and calves as she'd been taught, then set out just as the sun slid to touch the top of Mount Evans, a craggy peak among many that lined the horizons of Red Creek, Colorado. The sun, she thought as she strode down Main Street, looked like a ball balanced on the tip of a seal's nose.

She loved the stillness of late afternoon and evening in Red Creek. April touched the air with the fragrance of new greenery and pine sap, but in the shadows, she could still feel the bite of the long winter, surprising and exhilarating.

As she moved, her heels hitting the old concrete of sidewalks poured in 1920, she felt the strain of the long day ease down her spine, flow through her legs and into the ground. Her shoulders shook loose, and she found her breath take a new, calm, deep rhythm.

Who knew simple walking could be such a life-changing experience? Eighteen months ago, a little blue over a failed romance, Marissa had finally tired of herself. Impetuously she'd set out on a walk around the town square to enjoy the sunset. Breathe the air. See something besides her own sorry face in the mirror.

That day she'd walked only five minutes, but it had been a five minutes that changed her life. The next day she'd done it again, just as an experiment, to see if it made her feel as good as it had the first time. It had.

It had gone like that for weeks—Marissa stepping out into the world at dusk to walk as far as she could, then come home, just to see what it was like. After a month, she could walk twenty minutes. After two, she was up to forty.

And after three months, people started to tell her that she needed to get some new clothes. Clothes that weren't falling off her. For the first time, she realized that she'd been losing weight by simply moving her body. When she stepped on the scales at the local grocery store—she didn't keep one in her house and still didn't—she discovered she'd somehow lost thirty pounds.

Thirty pounds.

As Marissa came around a corner, Ramona Forrest was waiting in front of the clinic where she worked. Short and busty, Ramona had taken up walking to rid herself of the extra layer of cushion she'd gained while pregnant, and she had begun to enjoy their evening walks so much that she'd enlisted Louise, whom they usually picked up on the next long turn.

Louise was waiting in the designated spot, but she didn't have on her sweats. "Hi, girls," she said. "I have a houseful and can't go, but, Ramona, your darling girl is up there, along with your husband, and I've got Curtis and Cody, too, so I'm fixing a big meal. Why don't you both circle back and eat with us when you're done?"

"Sounds good," Marissa said, and tucked a loose strand of hair back into her ponytail. "As long as you aren't doing the Southern thing and frying all of it."

"You know better. I've got plenty of skinned chicken breasts for my girls, and a salad with every green known to mankind. I even bought some of that raspberry vinaigrette." She said it "vinegar-ette" and Marissa smiled.

Ramona glanced at her watch, then the sky. "Half hour?"

"All right."

As they continued their walk, Ramona said, "She's up to something."

"Absolutely. She's so guilelessly obvious."

"With Louise, it's usually matchmaking."

"True. Wonder who it is." Marissa paused in horror. "Oh, I hope it isn't me!"

"Keep walking." Ramona tugged her arm. "Why you?"

Marissa groaned. "I sent Robert Martinez over to her today."

"Red Dog?"

"The very one." She squeezed her eyes tight. "Oh, good grief. I'll die of embarrassment if that's what's on her mind."

"I'm lost. Start over. Why would you even send him to—?" She interrupted herself. "Oh. Crystal."

"Right. I thought Louise might be a help to both of them."

"And she will, but she also got the bright idea to match the pair of you up." Ramona chuckled. In a Frankenstein voice, she said, "Be very careful," and shook her head. "She's a mule when she puts her mind to something."

"I know." She rolled her eyes and took Ramona's arm. "But I have to tell you that he's one devastatingly sexy thing, isn't he?" She grinned. "I even get kind of flustered when I have to talk to him. Me. Flustered."

"He's definitely gorgeous," Ramona said cautiously. They paused in their talking to take a hill that was particularly challenging. At the top she continued. "He's also a dog—hence the name."

Marissa felt a little pinch at the warning. "I know," she said aloud. "Not my type."

"Liar. The badder they are, the better you like them."

Marissa grinned. "I know. Isn't that funny? And my sister, who has made an art form of being the bad girl, loves the good guys. How weird is that?"

Ramona smiled, but her large brown eyes were serious. "I know he's gorgeous and wounded and mysterious, Marissa, but those wounds are deep. I don't think that man has ever had anyone in his corner. I'm not sure he's capable of making a connection with a woman.''

Marissa felt suddenly humiliated that anyone should think she would go after a man like that, or had any hope of him coming after her. Aware that her cheeks were red, she waved a hand and made a joke. ''I wasn't exactly thinking of marriage.'' She sighed. ''I'm not the kind of woman he'd go for anyway.''

''Uh, sweetie, have you looked at yourself in the mirror lately?''

She grinned. ''Oh, yes. I admire myself in the mirror at least seven times a day, for very long periods.''

Ramona laughed. ''So, why not you, then?''

''Do we have to do this? I'm embarrassed enough, okay?''

''Mmm,'' Ramona said, anchoring herself more firmly to Marissa's arm. ''I think we do. Maybe old Red Dog's just what the doctor ordered to build up that flabby self-esteem.''

Marissa laughed at a vision of lifting him overhead. ''Push-ups for the ego?''

''Sit-ups for the psyche!''

''Sex for the soul.'' It didn't have the same ring and she knew it, but she didn't take it back.

''Yeah, that's what he's about, all right. Sex.'' Ramona sobered. ''Is that something you could do? Take what he offers and walk away when it was done?''

''I could try.'' She laughed throatily. ''I mean, gosh, what's the worst that could happen? Not like I haven't had a broken heart once or twice in my life.''

''Haven't we all.'' They walked along the sidewalk, silent for a long moment. ''On second thought, Marissa, stay away from him. He's just…'' She lifted a shoulder.

''He's just what?''

"Wrong for you, that's all."

Marissa's antenna rippled. She narrowed her eyes and said, "Would you mind being a little more specific?"

Ramona didn't answer for a moment. She was a diplomat at heart, a doctor whose patients worshipped the ground she walked on. "Look, don't take this wrong—"

"Oh, I know where that always leads."

Ramona stopped. "You probably do. And I don't mean to hurt your feelings, Marissa, but you're clueless on this level. You think it doesn't matter that you're worth however many zillions it is now, but it does. You don't know anything about life the way he and Crystal had to live it. You don't even know about ordinary people's lives."

Stung, Marissa crossed her arms and looked at the last gilding on the edge of the world, a brilliant gold zigzag edging the tops of the mountains. "And how much do you know about it, Ramona? More than I do?"

A puzzled expression crossed her face. "Well, no, probably not, but—"

"But," Marissa added gently, "you might be less inclined to judge?"

Ramona winced. "Ouch." She raised her big, compassionate eyes. "I'm sorry. I'm the one being judgmental."

"It's all right. I'm used to it." She relented a little, rolling her eyes. "Let's not talk about it anymore."

"Labels," Ramona said with a sigh. "What a pain. We all get stuck with them. Red Dog is the sexiest, baddest, saddest. I was the brainy busty one."

"Richest, fattest, smartest."

Ramona laughed. "Ha! We could have duked it out for smartest."

Marissa laughed. "Thank heavens. I couldn't stand being the richest, the fattest *and* the smartest."

# Chapter 3

Crystal didn't like white people all that much. Back in Albuquerque, there never had been that many in her life, really, only the ones on TV and at school, but here, it seemed like nearly everybody was white. It made her feel lost, kind of, like she was in a foreign country and didn't know the language.

She had to admit the old lady was pretty nice, and she was married to a Mexican who still talked as if he hadn't been gone too long, and that made it easier to believe the lady was really that nice. She gave Crystal some Kool-Aid, and her house smelled like houses in Albuquerque, of onions and chili, which was for the Mexican husband, of course, but it still made it easier.

After a while, the house filled up so much that Crystal got kind of panicky, afraid all of them would want to make polite conversation with her. But Mrs. Chacon seemed to know the exact minute Crystal wanted to burst into tears, and took her into a room at the back of the house where there was a bed and a VCR. She had a ton of movies, too. "Your uncle said you like movies. Feel free to watch whatever you want, all right? And maybe you can have a nap. I'll save you some supper—don't worry about that."

It almost made Crystal cry. That was what she hated about being pregnant. She cried over everything, as if she had an underground well in her belly and it overflowed every day.

She looked through all the movies, and there were some pretty good ones, she had to admit. All the *Nightmare* movies, which she liked because they made her real life—no matter how bad it was on a given day— look pretty good since nobody was stalking her; and some goofy old movies such as *Gone with the Wind,* which Crystal had watched and didn't get at all. She thought Scarlett was a total bitch and deserved to lose a good guy like Rhett. There were also a couple of her absolute, tip-top favorites, such as *Ferris Bueller's Day Off,* which she'd seen at least a hundred times, and *Last of the Mohicans,* which made her cry and cry and cry, every single time. She didn't know if she wanted to do that right now. To get the full effect, it was best if she was all alone and could make all kinds of noise without anybody hearing what an idiot she was about movies.

There was no *Titanic,* which might actually have been too creepy for words. But there was one of the *Romeo and Juliet* with guns, the new one, with Claire Danes. Crystal put her hand on it, daring herself to look at it. But in the end, she just couldn't. Not without Mario.

For one minute, that hot feeling came into her throat—not tears, but something that burned a lot more—and she wanted to touch him, talk to him, *so bad* that she almost couldn't breathe. But that didn't do her or the baby or even Mario any good.

The only safe movie after that was *Ferris Bueller,* and she stuck it in the VCR and kicked back on the bed. In minutes she was sound asleep.

It wasn't as bad as Marissa expected, back at Louise's house. The rooms were bursting with Louise's three sons, their spouses and the grandchildren, who now totaled five with the birth of Anna and Tyler's second baby. Anna beamed tonight, looking like the ultimate Madonna as she nursed her black-haired boy, and she only smiled deliriously when people teased her about her three children, wondering if she planned on more. Tyler came to her defense. "We love babies. We're going to have twenty."

Anna laughed at that. "Or maybe five."

Robert was there, of course, quiet as he always was, laconically cracking dry jokes at odd moments, always eating whatever Louise piled on his plate. Often, Marissa noticed, Robert, and Louise's husband, Alonzo, could be found together, comfortably sitting side by side, exchanging a word now and then. And of course, he and Jake went way back, to Desert Storm. They talked in a kind of grunting guy shorthand, laughing at asides no one else ever got.

But Marissa didn't have to deal much with him directly, and Louise showed no overt signs of matchmaking, so Marissa relaxed and accepted the gathering for what it appeared to be: another of Louise's rollicking, impromptu suppers.

Marissa had never experienced such joyful family dynamics, and she loved being here. Filling her plate with the promised skinned, grilled chicken breast and a steaming pile of steamed summer squash, she settled in a corner near Ramona and tickled her baby's toes between bites.

But over and over, her gaze flitted toward Robert. Studying him covertly, she thought his face was kind of harsh, as if that difficult past Ramona hinted at had been etched into the shape of it. His mouth was stern and his eyes watchful, and he had a penetrating way of looking at people, unsmiling and direct in a way most people simply could not tolerate. He did not smile often, unless he was trying to charm someone.

Not someone. A woman. In spite of that dangerous aspect, or more likely because of it, he drew women in a way that amazed her. The first summer he'd lived in Red Creek, he'd worked in a little tourist trap near the grocery store, making tiny feather jewelry from carved rocks. Women did whatever they could to coax a smile from the wry mouth. Old women, young women, girls. All of them.

And he accepted it as his due, with a mocking little glint in his eye that might have made Marissa dislike him, if she hadn't also been able to sense the sadness behind it, the same vast longing that made Crystal stare so hard out the windows at school, as if looking for a knight on a white horse.

Dangerous, Marissa thought. She'd been doing pretty well these days at avoiding the lost men in the world, focusing instead on saving herself. And the odd kid.

Her sister, Victoria, would have charmed him instantly, Marissa thought suddenly. But not her. Not even now. She didn't have that femme fatale gene. She was exactly who she appeared to be: open, direct, honest.

*Fatty, fatty, two by four,* sang a nasally child's voice in her head. *Couldn't get through the bathroom door.*

Robert looked up, caught her staring and raised his chin in her direction, a simple greeting. She looked away, wincing inwardly over the fact that she had, this very afternoon, been thinking he might be slightly interested. Just for a fleeting second his mouth had turned up in a distinctly flirtatious little smile.

Standing, she pointed to Ramona's plate. "Finished with that? I'll take it in with me."

"Thanks."

Marissa retreated, dropping the paper plates in the trash, then heading for the sanctuary of the wide balcony attached to the back of the house, a wooden deck that overlooked a deep, long valley. At night, only the black zigzag of the mountains against the night sky could be seen. And it was a little cold, but Marissa breathed it in anyway—the stars, so bright and sharp and thick so far from the city, the utter silence of the land. She let go of a breath, relaxing.

Resting her hands lightly on the wooden rail, she looked down at them and smiled ruefully as she admired the new ring she'd had to buy when none of the old ones would stay on her fingers anymore. That had been a rich, rich moment, and she wore the antique circlet of garnets every day to remind herself how far she'd come.

Odd how those old tapes kept playing in her head anyway. She wondered, lifting her chin to drink in the crisp air, how long it would take them to go away.

The glass door slid open behind her, and Marissa turned to see Robert stepping outside. His braid fell over one shoulder. "Hi," he said, tucking his hands in his pockets. "You mind if I come out with you?"

"Not at all," Marissa said politely, though of course he was the one she had been escaping.

"I didn't have a chance to thank you for what you did for Crystal."

"Oh, don't mention it, please. Is she better tonight?"

"I think so." He joined her at the rail. "Bringing her here was a good idea."

"I'm glad." Marissa curled her fingers around the railing, willing herself not to look at him. But it didn't particularly matter—she was still very aware of him, a scent of something fertile, verdant. He was tall and lean, bigger than she had previously noticed. His cocked elbow almost touched her arm. He shifted, hands still tucked lightly into the pockets of his jeans, and said nothing.

But even in the silence, in their stillness, she could feel an electric hum between them, strong enough that she thought she'd see a faint blue light in the air between their bodies if she looked.

The silence stretched. He shifted again, and she half expected—half wanted?—him to go back inside. He didn't, though. Just kept standing there, radiating that electromagnetic field.

Finally she said, "This is such a peaceful town."

"Yeah," he said, and as if he'd only needed an opening he couldn't come up with himself, added, "I kept thinking I'd leave, you know. Tomorrow. Next week. Next month. Kept somehow waking up here again every day."

Marissa laughed. "I know the feeling. We used to come here to go skiing when I was a child, and I only came here to spite my father. Somehow I haven't managed to go anywhere else."

"How long have you been here?" He eased a little, leaning his elbows on the rail.

She had to think about it. "Seven years? No, eight. I

turned down Dartmouth and ran to the Rockies.'' She dared to look at him. No crackling blue electricity visible, but there was a nice glissando of light on the crown of his head and his nose. "How about you?"

"Three years. Didn't intend to stay more than a few weeks, really. But that was when Jake...uh..."

"I remember," she said to spare him. When Jake had fallen down a cliff and nearly killed himself. "Where are you from originally?"

He raised his head, met her eyes. "Albuquerque." He said it almost like a dare.

"Is there supposed to be some meaning there? If so, I didn't catch it."

"Are you disappointed?"

Startled in a chuckle, Marissa asked, "No, why would I be?"

A slight lift of one shoulder. "White girls always want to hear some romantic tale of the reservation."

"Ah." She inclined her head. "Little chip on your shoulder there. Might want to knock it off."

His teeth showed, just for a second, in the darkness. "I swear it's true."

"Well, my disappointment is much more basic. I think you should have a name like...oh, Johnny Blue Raven or something."

"Ravens are black." The smile broadened, and Marissa thought the air was definitely beginning to glow a pale blue, just right there around his head. "Where are you from?"

"A castle in Switzerland."

He laughed. "Touché."

Marissa liked the sound of that laughter, a little rough and hoarse, as if he didn't indulge very often. It made her wonder what it would be like to hear him laugh really hard—or if he ever did. "It's actually true. I was born in a castle in Switzerland." She smiled. "It was an accident—my mother was supposed to be home, but she had to see these friends."

"I see. So did you grow up in the castle, too, princess?"

"Not that one, sadly. A much gloomier castle in upstate New York, complete with ghoulish servants and guard dogs."

"No kidding?"

She rolled her eyes. "It was a mausoleum. My father was sure someone would snatch my sister and I if he let us out of his sight for three seconds, so we didn't even go to school—he sent tutors in to us."

He peered at her for a long minute. "No wonder you wanted to break out."

"Exactly." She brushed her hair out of her face. "Now you. Where'd you break out of?"

"Hell," he said without a single beat of hesitation.

Something told her to keep it light. "Pretty hot. I can see why you'd like the mountains."

She'd surprised him again. His head came up, and there was an expression of measuring in his eyes. "Yeah." He looked away again, clicking his heel on the deck, and Marissa focused on the long length of his back beneath a simple cotton shirt, a blue plaid. The fabric stretched tight across his shoulders. "Ever been to Albuquerque?" he asked.

"Once or twice. Probably not to the hell parts, though."

He laughed and stood up, turning to face her. "Now how'm I gonna be the poor beleaguered wounded guy if you keep making these jokes?"

Marissa raised her eyebrows. "I guess you'll just have to come up with another act."

"You're not at all who I thought you were."

"Neither are you," she said honestly, and somehow that was a lot more unnerving than that blue energy humming between them. "I didn't know you could laugh."

"It's been a while."

In the cool darkness, Robert did something he rarely allowed himself to do: he relaxed. Strange that he felt that freedom with this woman who was so far removed from his circle that she might as well have been a Martian, but there it was. Tonight she wore sweats and a long-sleeved T-shirt, and she smelled a little of soap and deodorant and sweat. It all made her feel more approachable, more real.

They talked, in that aimless way of people who want to keep each other company but aren't sure of the ground yet, of Red Creek and the historical project. Nothing important. But he found himself looking—almost helplessly—over her body now and then, discovering that he liked the ordinariness of it, too full across the bottom, still pretty solid in the thighs. A homey kind of body that made him want to sidle up to her, press himself close, feel all that giving terrain against the hard angles of his own shape.

Weird. He knew it was weird for him even as he thought it, but there it was. As she laughed, he surprised himself by wanting to laugh, too. When she lifted her chin to point out a shooting star, he looked instead at the underside of her jaw and wanted to press his mouth there.

Cool it. Obviously it had been just a bit too long since

he'd indulged himself in some good old recreational sex. He hadn't felt right about it with Crystal in the house. Not surprising he was getting a little hungry. Pushing himself away from the railing, he thought about going inside before he got any more bright ideas.

But Marissa said, "That hell you spoke of?"

Spoke of. It made him smile. "Yeah?"

"Is that where Crystal's from, too?"

He turned his lips down, crossed his arms. A serious question. He shook his head. "Hers made mine look like heaven."

"In what way?" The earnest teacher gazed out of bright blue eyes.

What could she possibly understand about Crystal's life? Or his, for that matter? But she was so damned earnest, he had to at least give it a shot. "It was poor when I was there. Lot of drugs and booze and gangs. But no one could get their hands on guns. They do now."

"The guns are the biggest difference?"

He shook his head slowly, struggling to find some way to quantify the difference, put it in terms she could understand. All the images he came up with—war and revolution and bad morale seemed too male to fit her experience.

"It's never quiet," he said finally. "Not ever. There's a siren or a party or a television or somebody's radio going twenty-four hours a day. It's never really clean. It's old and tired and forgotten."

He narrowed his eyes against the memory, as if squinting would blur it enough to take the sting away. "If you want to walk down to the corner for a soda, you've gotta look out on the street to see who's out there, first." He paused, still thinking, and raised his finger to indicate there was more. "If you want to open the window, you better have bars. If you want to keep a pet, you'd better make damned sure it never goes outside. And at night, when things are bad, it's a good idea to put the mattress on the floor."

A small, intense crease appeared between her eyebrows, but her eyes were steady and clear. "Thank you."

He nodded. "Probably lucky for her that her mother kicked her out of the house."

"She's pretty lucky to have you, that's for sure."

That caught him in the solar plexus. "Thanks."

"Do you know anything about the father of her baby?"

He sighed. Shook his head. "She's not talking, and I haven't pushed. I gather it was consensual—beyond that, I guess it doesn't really matter."

"I guess that's true." She seemed about to say something else, frowning into the distance. "It's just…"

"What?"

She shifted a little, brushed a wisp of dark hair from her cheek. "She stares out the window in class like she's waiting for someone to appear. Like she expects it."

Robert suddenly thought of Crystal's favorite spot in the house: an overstuffed chair in front of the big picture window, where she would curl up as much as her growing belly would allow. She could sit there for literally hours, just looking outside. He'd thought she was simply looking at the mountains. "Very observant," he said. "Maybe I'll see if she has more to say."

A nod. "Well, I guess we ought to go back in. I'm starting to get cold."

"Yeah, me too." But before she moved, he touched her hand. It surprised him that he did it, and he wasn't aware that he had until he felt the tiny bones beneath his palm. She looked up at him, a little alarmed, and he was alarmed himself, though he didn't pull away. There were a million reasons that starting anything with her would be a mistake, so he wouldn't, but he wanted her to know that the thought had crossed his mind. It was an offering, maybe.

He couldn't think of the right lightness of words to offer, so he only stood there, his hand covering hers, looking down into the wide dark blue eyes for a long, silent moment. "Don't let anybody ever tell you it's stupid to care," he said quietly, more fiercely than he intended. "You don't have to understand it to reach out."

She nodded, dipped her head and slipped her hand from beneath his. "Thanks," she said. "We should go back in."

Every Saturday morning, Robert and Crystal did their chores, and this day was no different. The routine varied little—they put loud music on the stereo, taking turns choosing CDs, and scoured the house top to bottom. She liked tackling the kitchen, something he hated with all his heart, so he let her. Robert dusted and vacuumed the living room, shook out the couch cushions, singing along with the classic rock Crystal rolled her eyes over. Her choices were even sillier—movie soundtracks, mostly, with a lot of very gentle, pop love songs that she knew every word to. None of the rap or blaring rock some of the younger laborers on his crew were so fond of.

Thank God.

This Saturday-morning ritual delighted the girl. She rose early, pulled back her hair, discarded her windbreaker and rolled up her sleeves. Singing, she scoured the sink and stove, wiped down cupboards and walls, practically spit-shined the floors. Every other week, she even washed the windows, something it had never occurred to Robert to do. When she finished, she tackled the bathroom and gave it a similar polishing, then stripped off her rubber gloves and walked happily through the house, lighting strategic sticks of incense that smelled of grass and fresh air.

Midmorning, he took a list—one that Crystal insisted on preparing every week—to the grocery store. When he returned, she popped her head out of the kitchen, grinning happily. "Hey, Uncle, come look what I did for you."

He followed, dropping his bags on the counter. The room was fairly large, with a big window looking out toward the mountains, and all the cupboards, stove and refrigerator on one wall. A small windowed alcove had previously held a small breakfast bar and two stools, where they usually ate. But she'd dragged the breakfast bar into the kitchen below the window and dragged the old Formica-and-chrome table into the alcove.

"You shouldn't have been moving this stuff, babe. I would have helped."

"I used my butt," she said with a grin. "Look at what I brought in, though." She opened the drawers set into the alcove one by one. "All your stuff, so you can have a good place to work."

"Ah, Crystal, this is so good," he said, putting his hand on her shoulder. The drawers had held miscellaneous kitchen junk before, which she'd sorted out and moved. From his bedroom, she'd carried all his jewelry and glass supplies, and carefully organized them by type, even fitting the drawers with cardboard dividers to keep things neat. Touched, he kissed her head. "Thank you."

"I know you gave up your workroom to give me a

place to sleep,'' she said. "This will work pretty good, don't you think?''

"It'll be even better. Look how much great light there is in here.''

"Okay.'' She slapped her hands together—*that's that.* "I'm going to get my sheets. Then will you show me again how to do those corners?'' Now that the weather had warmed up, she loved washing the sheets and hanging them out on the line to dry.

"Sure.'' He put the groceries away, then followed her to her room when she came in with an armload of sweet-smelling linens. On her narrow twin bed, he illustrated the army corner, tight and smooth, then pulled it loose. "You try.''

Adroitly she did it, but he saw her trouble was in the fact that she couldn't quite bend well enough to get it tight. "Let me help, babe.''

She straightened, laughing a little, her hand on her round belly. "It gets harder to do things, and I forget.''

It startled him, that happy, girlish laugh, especially in reference to her pregnancy. Trying not to make too much of it, he knelt and tucked the corners tight. "I don't want you to move anything heavy anymore, got it?''

"Yes, sir.'' She saluted.

"You really love cleaning, don't you?''

"My mother thinks it's crazy, too. She never stuck to routines—but it makes things so cheerful when they're clean, don't you think?'' She looked around with a little smile.

Robert straightened and looked at it through her eyes. Sunlight streamed in through the clean windows with their pressed, clean curtains. No litter of beer bottles or ashtrays sat on the coffee table, only a nice arrangement of plastic fruit that appalled him, but Crystal had picked out. She washed it every week and patted it dry.

He'd rented the place because it was the right size for him, a little box with a kitchen and two small bedrooms and a living room that opened on to a small wooden porch. It sat at the outskirts of town, so he didn't have to deal with neighbors much or any lawn to speak of, just the omnipresent meadowlands with their offerings of columbines and long-stalked grasses. "Yeah," he said. "It's a great house."

"You should have a cat or something." She plumped her pillows vigorously and slid one into a crisp pillow-case.

Aside from little requests like the feather duster she'd gone nuts for at Kmart, and the plastic fruit, it was the first time she'd even obliquely asked him for anything. "You want a cat?"

A shrug.

It struck him forcefully that he was no longer alone. After years and years and years of eating dinners by himself in front of the television, and getting up to everything exactly the way it had been the night before. He had somebody to talk to when he was blue. He had someone to say, "Hey, look at this," when there was something on the news. Somebody to share chores with, eat meals with.

He'd only done what was necessary when Crystal showed up; he'd made room for her, done the best he could. But now he realized how much she'd done for him. "Maybe we oughta go see if they have any at the pound."

Her face glowed. "Really?"

"Sure." He tugged on the end of her braid. "I like

cats. Maybe we can get two, one for me and one for you.''

"They have to be inside cats, though. No going outside. I don't like that."

"Okay." He wandered to the door, pulling his T-shirt over his head. "I'll jump in the shower, then you can have it. Maybe we could have lunch first somewhere."

"McDonald's?" she asked with hope.

"Ugh. No. Someplace better."

She grinned, looking impossibly young and pretty and sweet, the way she should. "Grown-ups are so boring."

He tugged the rubber band out of the bottom of his braid and shook out his hair. "Look who's talking." He threw his T-shirt at her. "McDonald's is not high cuisine."

"Yuck!" She threw the T-shirt back at him. "And don't use such fancy language."

"It's good for you."

The doorbell rang, and Robert picked up his shirt from the floor. "Get ready and we'll go." Probably the paperboy, who showed up at the dot of eleven every second Saturday. He stuck his hand in his pocket and found he only had a five. "Hang on!" he called, and went to the bedroom for a ten.

# Chapter 4

Marissa had a routine on Saturday mornings. She liked to get up early and walk downtown, pick up a latte from a café she liked, then walk through the pleasant side streets that branched off Main, to look at garage sales. It was a homey tradition in Red Creek, a homey tradition she enjoyed right along with everyone else. She also hit the big, three-county flea market that was held at the fairgrounds once a month, and although she enjoyed the social angle as much as everyone else did, her true purpose was related to her avocation: art glass.

She was a minor expert, specializing in Art Nouveau. She collected several items herself, and stayed in touch with an honest dealer who could sell the pieces in which she had no interest. It had amazed her at first, how often she found rare and not-so-rare pieces in Colorado, but there had been a huge amount of mining money here in Red Creek, and more in Denver. More than once she had spared a vendor from making a big mistake in sell-ing the 1908 Van Briggle vase they'd grown tired of for two dollars and fifty cents instead of the thousands it would command in the open market, or letting the Louis Comfort Tiffany inlaid bronze dish go as an ashtray.

This morning, she'd come out especially early, scenting possibility in an ''Attic'' sale on one of the oldest blocks in town. Three families had come together for the sale of an old woman's Victorian mansion. Tables had been set out on the lawns between two houses, and Marissa browsed happily among the old records and books, tickled when she found an old, hardbound Donna Parker she remembered, the one in which Rickie's mother died. So sad. She tucked it happily under her arm, and around the crotch of an old tree, spied the kitchen and glasswares and costumed jewelry, all spread on a huge Arts and Crafts buffet in exquisite condition. Aha!

Furniture wasn't her usual area, but she examined the piece intently, trusting her instincts. It was in perfect condition, save a very small chip on one corner, and she knew it was worth far more than the fifty-dollar price tag stuck on it. She took out a notebook she carried for this purpose and scribbled notes about it for future reference. The drawers were open, holding ropes of old costume necklaces and rhinestone earrings. The top was cluttered with extraneous kitchen supplies, among them an enormous collection of vases in every shape and form available, along with plates of carnival glass—that carried price tags commensurate with its value. Marissa didn't collect it, but was pleased to see that the sellers did know the worth.

Most of the rest of the glass was flawed or worthless—a fairly good example of milk glass was badly cracked, and a promising cameo glass proved to be an imitation. She was about to go find one of the sellers to let them know they needed to have the buffet appraised before letting it go when her eye caught on a soft glow in one of the drawers. Hesitantly she moved a tangle of Mardi Gras beads out of the way to reveal a small, opalescent statue of a woman in a circle of glass. Marissa's heart pinched as she reached for it, drawing it into the light—it was! She held it up to the sun, laughing at the glow it cast. It was a miraculously unchipped, uncracked and perfectly whole perfume bottle stopper by Lalique, with the design of a naked woman in a twist of branches.

''Oh!'' she said, turning to the woman in a jumper who approached pleasantly. ''Let me ask you a question.''

''Of course.'' A bright, tanned smile. ''Are you interested in the buffet?''

''No, but is it yours?''

''Yes, all of these came from my aunt's house. She died recently and we're remodeling.''

''Well, the vases are all junk and the jewelry, but the buffet needs to be appraised. It's worth at least a couple of thousand.''

Her lips turned down in surprise. ''Really? I have always hated this thing. So clunky. I don't much like anything from that era, so I won't keep it anyway, but I appreciate you letting me know.''

Marissa opened her hand, letting her treasure glow in her palm like a beacon. ''And how much for this?'' She held her breath.

A shrug. ''Pretty. How about fifty cents?''

Marissa smiled, and pulled out her purse and carefully set the piece down. ''I'm going to write you a check for this, but there's a rule. You may not look at it until I leave.''

''A check for fifty cents?''

"No." Marissa completed the check, tore it out and folded it in half. "Considerably more than that. This is," she said, picking it up with reverence, "a wonderful and rare antique. If your aunt has more of this kind of thing, I really want to see it, and if you have more glass in the house, you should have it examined."

The woman looked concerned, and waved toward some clothing on a rack to one side. "Do you want to wrap that in something?"

"Great idea." She took an old silk hair scarf from a hanger. A collection of soft, airy dresses in bright India cottons had caught her eye, one in a cranberry shade, one in a beautiful green. They were maternity dresses, with the tags still hanging from the sleeves, and very tiny. She pulled one out and thought of Crystal's dark hair against the fabrics. "How much?" she asked the woman.

"A dollar each."

Marissa bought them, and feeling buoyed by the little yelp of the woman when she opened the check, she drove to Robert's house. The happy mood carried her all the way up the steps and she gave a quick, strong knock to the screen door—then courage deserted her.

Suddenly she felt like an idiot. Women must think up excuses to see him all the time. How would this look? She frowned, looking at the dresses again, and worried that Crystal would never wear such things. Robert would probably be offended that she thought he wasn't taking care of the girl's clothes well enough.

Oh, bad idea. She nearly bolted, but a voice called from within, "Hang on a second!" and she couldn't move. Anxiously she looked down again at the dresses, simple summery things that would be so much more comfortable for Crystal over the last month or so of her pregnancy. The colors were still as beautiful as she thought, and she sighed.

"Marissa!" The word held surprise.

She looked up and saw Robert, dimly, through the screen.

Shirtless.

And his hair was down. "Hi," she said weakly.

He stayed where he was, pulling a long-sleeved T-shirt over his head and tugging it down over his flat, brown belly before he crossed the room and opened the screen door to her. A wicked twinkle lit his eyes. "You look like you've come to the wolf's door," said that slightly hoarse voice.

Marissa could not summon a single word to her lips, mainly because every thought in her brain evaporated, splatting like water on the heat he generated just standing there in a pair of very old jeans and a threadbare white T-shirt that clung to his torso like a layer of oil, showing every muscle, every sleek line, every indentation of his body. It was inside out, and she wondered vaguely why he'd been in such a rush to cover his chest.

But it was his hair that made him dangerous. She'd never seen it down like this. It streamed over his shoulders, each strand as glossy and healthy as every other, the mass of it not nearly as black as she'd thought, but laced with warmer browns and even a few glitters of lighter brown.

She didn't like long hair. She liked razor cuts and army styles, even crew cuts. Long hair said a man hadn't grown up. It said he didn't give a damn about what the world thought. In Colorado, it often said he was a redneck with a shotgun in his truck and a ready six-pack of beer.

On Robert, long hair was right. It was a rejection of

the mainstream culture, but he had that right, didn't he? She thought, suddenly, of the upside-down American flag on the jean jacket he wore sometimes.

"Cat got your tongue?" he said, and a slow, sly grin turned up the edges of that wide mouth. His eyes crinkled the slightest bit at the corners.

"Um." She looked at the dresses in her hands, and wished for a long, painful minute that she had never had a single impulsive impulse, and especially that she'd never had this one.

She felt her cheeks redden with total social humiliation, and flailed around for some explanation as to why she was here. Helplessly she lifted the dresses, as if they might tell him, and suddenly her tongue came unstuck. "You know, I had an idea, and maybe it was a bad one, and I'll just…um…" She backed away, her free hand fluttering up as if to grab some intelligent word from the air. "I'll let you go on with whatever you were doing."

He grinned, showing those straight white teeth, and kicked the screen door wider, propping it with one foot. A bare foot. His naked toes gave her a jolt. "Wow," he said conversationally, folding his arms casually over his chest. "Think the teacher's a little flustered." His eyelids fell just the slightest bit, lending him a suggestive, seductive aspect, and he wet his bottom lip with his tongue. "Scared of me, white girl?"

The answer was yes. He looked like a hot summer night. Like a motorcycle ride. Like two o'clock in the morning. She took a breath, blew it out, regained a little dignity. "I didn't think I liked long hair," she said.

He laughed. With exaggerated vanity, he tossed his head and sent the mass swirling over arms, chest, back. With an arched brow he said, "Want to brush it?"

She smiled. "Pass."

"So," he said, lifting his chin, "what d'you have there?"

"Oh." Still a bad impulse, but what could she do about it now? "I found these, and thought they might work for Crystal. I bought them at a garage sale, but they still have their tags—I know a lot of people don't like used stuff—and they were so pretty and it's going to get warm enough that she's not going to be able to stand that coat, and they just looked like her somehow."

He waited through the long spill of words. "That was a nice thing to do." One long brown hand touched the fabric. "I don't know if she'll like them—you know teenagers—but it's worth a try."

She relaxed. "Oh, well." She waved a hand. "They were only a dollar apiece, so I took the chance."

"Come on in." He cocked his head, pushed the door wider, led the way into a bright, clean, sweet-smelling room. "Crystal," he called. "You have a visitor."

"I do?" She came around the corner, perplexed, and halted dead. She wore a pair of jeans and a simple, over-size white shirt. The hair that usually hid her face was swept back. Marissa was struck by the very painful thinness of her body, except for her breasts and belly, and by the sweetness of the makeup-less features.

To Marissa's relief, she didn't look upset. "Hi, Ms. Pierce. What are you doing here?"

She almost started stuttering and explaining too much, but a single glance at Robert's amused face put her straight. In the same spirit with which she picked up the dresses in the first place, she held them out. "These made me think of you."

Instant wariness in the dark eyes. "Really?"

"If you don't like them, it won't hurt my feelings. I know I'm a boring adult and don't get the fashion thing, but I was at a yard sale and they were cheap, and brand-new. Couldn't stand to leave them there.''

Crystal came forward slowly, put a hand on the skirt, just as Robert had. "I could try 'em.''

Marissa let her take them, pleased when Crystal said, "Can you wait, tell me if they look good?''

"Of course.''

She slid away, holding the dresses up to her body. She almost skipped. Marissa let go of her tension and smiled at Robert. "You never know, do you?''

He lifted his eyebrows, a funny expression in his eyes. "I guess maybe I haven't thought too much about the clothes angle. Got her a few little things when she first got here.'' A rueful grin. "I forget about that girly stuff, you know?''

"You're allowed.''

"Can I get you something? Crystal makes really great limeade. She learned to make it in home ec.''

"I'd love some, thank you. I've been checking out garage sales this morning.''

He gestured for her to follow him into the kitchen. "Excuse me for saying so, princess, but that doesn't seem like your style.''

"You never know. I had an outrageously great morning.''

"Yeah?'' Moving efficiently, he put ice in three glasses and poured a pale green liquid from a glass pitcher. He gave her a glass, and carried two others into the living room and put them down on the coffee table. "Oh, damn. Forgot the coasters. She'll kill me.'' He turned, whipped three out and put them on the table, winking. "I haven't been that civilized before, you know.''

Marissa smiled around the tiny knot he put in her

chest. However she had imagined Red Dog living, this tidy hominess was about as far from the fantasy as it could get.

"So," he said, settling in a chair across from her. "What did you find, besides the dresses?"

A little burst of light filled her chest and she smiled as she reached into her bag to pull out the silk-wrapped prize. "Are you familiar with antiques?"

"Not really." But he whistled when she unwrapped the perfume stopper, his eyes going wide as he accepted it as gingerly as it deserved. "Very pretty. What is it?"

"A perfume stopper from the turn of the century."

"It's great," he said, and sounded sincere. He turned it slowly, admiring the shifting light, and Marissa found herself admiring his hands. They were beautiful, strong and lean and long fingered, but they were also scarred. Little white scars, most very old, tattoos, new marks from working. Letters marched across the middle joint of each finger, and she grinned. "What do your fingers say?"

"You don't want to know," He gave her the stopper.

She raised amused eyes. Her last boyfriend had been a biker, after all. "Bet I already do."

"I seriously doubt it."

Marissa only smiled. She did know, but she'd let him keep his secret.

Crystal came out, shyly. "Well, what do you think?"

"Oh, it's beautiful! I was right." Marissa stood up to admire her properly. The soft fabric draped lightly around the swell of belly, and swirled around her calves. "That color is perfect for you. It makes your skin look so warm."

"I like it." She twirled around. "Feels good—like

Ginger Rogers or something.'' She looked at Robert. ''You like it, Uncle?''

He whistled, low and long. ''Very pretty. Guess you womenfolk know stuff we guys don't.''

''Duh.'' Crystal sobered as she looked at Marissa. ''Thank you, Ms. Pierce. It was really nice of you.''

''Don't mention it.''

Robert chuckled. ''Yeah, Crystal, she got the pleasure of seeing me with my beautiful hair down.''

A ripple of recognition moved on Crystal's face. Uh-oh, Marissa thought.

''All the women like his hair,'' Crystal said. ''They all like him. But he doesn't like any of them back.''

''And we all cry in our beer every night over it, too, I can tell you,'' Marissa said lightly. ''I understand that every Thursday night, there's a special pagan dance in the woods where the single women throw herbs on a fire and sing special chants to capture his heart.'' She tsked, spreading her hands. ''So far, he's proven immune to everyone but you.''

Crystal knew she was being appeased, but she gave Marissa a rueful grin anyway. Rolling her eyes, she said, ''Thanks again, all right? I'm gonna take a shower now. I have a date with Mr. Perfect, you know.''

Marissa laughed. ''All right. See you Monday.''

''You're good,'' Robert said when the door closed. ''Didn't miss a beat.''

She turned. ''I've been teaching for a while. You learn.''

''Maybe.'' He shook his head. ''Not everybody does.''

''Well, thanks.'' She picked up the glass and drank down most of it at a gulp, only realizing when she stopped drinking that it was absolutely fabulous. ''Oh, my gosh!'' She held the glass up to the light. ''That's fantastic! I'll have to get her recipe.''

''The secret is simple syrup instead of sugar.'' He shifted, foot to foot, as if he were impatient, and she started to move away, when he said, ''You know, that's a very nice dress.''

Marissa instantly found her hand fluttering up to cover the flesh the scoop neck revealed, remembering for the first time that she wasn't draped in four yards of cloth, but a simple, straight, sleeveless sundress. Lazily and plainly, he let his gaze slide down her body, touching shoulders, breasts, legs.

And Marissa found herself standing straighter, thinking of the collarbone that showed beneath her flesh, of the dip of her waist. She grinned. ''Thank you.'' She put down her glass. ''And thank you for the limeade. I'll get out of your way.''

He walked with her, out on the porch, but somehow, when they landed on the porch, he was standing in front of her. She looked up at him, ready to say something polite, but their eyes sort of slammed together or something, and she forgot what she wanted to say.

He was close. Close enough that she could see a trail of tiny, teardrop scars below his left eye, close enough she saw there was variation in the color of his eyes after all. What looked like unbroken black from a distance was really a very subtle gradation of cocoas. A few sun lines had settled into the corners of his eyes, and he appeared to have no beard at all, or else he'd shaved very, very closely.

The teasing humor of a few moments ago was gone, and he regarded her gravely, his lower lip tucked under his upper. In the warm day, she suddenly felt that magnetic field crackling vividly between them again. Wind caught a long lock of his hair and it blew across his face, and she wanted to raise a hand to brush it away. He still didn't break that stillness, only looked down at her with fierce intent, as if he wanted to use X-ray vision to see into her head.

Finally she said, "What?"

His eyes slipped, touched her mouth. Her heart skittered, and for a long, long moment, she thought he was going to kiss her. She had enough time to imagine what it might be like—how his wide mouth might taste, what his tongue would feel like, sliding against her lips—before he stepped sideways, almost as if he were avoiding a collision. "Thanks again," he said roughly, and went around her and went inside.

When she got home, Marissa called her sister. Victoria picked up the phone on the fourth ring. "Gorram," she said in their private language. "I was dreaming about you."

"What was I doing?"

"I'm not sure," she said, and Marissa heard her rustling pillows. "Something to do with electricity." She yawned. "Blue. It was blue."

She wasn't surprised. Their connection seemed heightened in sleep—as children, they'd often dreamed each other's dreams. Now they seemed to dream each other's thoughts, at least now and then. "It's electromagnetic attraction. That man again."

"Really?" The word was guarded.

"It's nothing. It's not like we're dating or anything. He's just very sexy."

"Available?"

"Mmm. Not really." She knew she was soft-pedaling it and her sister knew it, too. Because of their intense connection, they'd made a pact in their teens to keep love lives totally private, an area where they didn't have to feel shadowed. It was hard, at times, but it was also necessary.

"Too bad."

"It is, kind of."

Victoria yawned. "Morrag," she said, their word for good night, as Gorram was good morning. Most of the language they'd made up as toddlers was gone, but a few code words remained.

"Morrag," she said and hung up, feeling better. Robert had unnerved her today. Or she'd unnerved herself. Restlessly she opened the fridge, scanned the contents with a frown and realized what she was doing.

Closing the door, she took a deep breath and closed her eyes. In an article on weight loss, she'd read that people, especially women, had programmed themselves to ignore their true impulses in order to please society, and often mistook a myriad number of emotions and impulses for hunger. The recommendation had been to stop and feel, take a minute to pay attention to the body and the emotions.

What was she really feeling? Physically, there was a restlessness crawling in her legs and up her spine. She wanted to run or scream or jump up and down. Her emotions buzzed and flitted, scurrying around each other like worried birds. Even her thoughts—usually the clearest thing—were whirling.

She inhaled slowly. What did she really want? An image of Robert, peering down at her as if he might kiss her, flitted over her vision. Then his hands, scarred and beautiful, and his teeth, white and straight, flashing against his lips.

Marissa chuckled. Well, that was pretty clear. Sex. She wanted to have sex with Robert.

Duh, as Crystal would say.

That was step one—figuring out the want. Step two was figuring out the reality. She couldn't really allow herself to indulge that wish. For one thing, he was obviously ambivalent.

No, that was his feelings, not hers. Why couldn't *she* indulge?

Reason number one: Crystal, who might be wounded and feel used. Good one, but it didn't feel authentic. It sounded like the Wizard's voice in Oz, booming out the obvious answer.

Sex with Robert. She let the visuals fill her—that hair touching her, his mouth and hers. Oh, yeah. She had a sudden vision of licking his throat and realized the urge was quite a bit stronger than she'd realized.

And then she tried to imagine herself getting to the naked part. Him, lean and strong and sculpted. Her—oh, yuck—white as a fish and soft and squishy. An exaggerated picture of her flesh spilling sideways from her bones appeared with evil intensity, and Marissa gritted her teeth.

Oh, no. Not even her imagination was allowed to steal her accomplishment. Her eyes snapped open and she marched into her bedroom, kicking off her shoes, then reached for the zipper on her dress. She pulled it over her head and tossed it aside, unhooked her bra and skimmed off her panties and threw them all on the bed. Tossing her head, squaring her shoulders, she marched to the long mirror she'd purchased when she'd hit the sixty-pound-loss mark, a celebration.

It was an antique, an oval floor mirror framed in

cherry. She stepped into the reflection, naked, and dared her imagination to make a mockery of her.

But there were other eyes looking with her, eyes of all those kids who chanted nasty names, all the men who'd tried not to look at her body even if they liked her, all the selves she'd been when she gazed in sorrow at the blob of herself over the years.

*You were always beautiful.*

The words came to her in Robert's voice, the very words he'd said that day in her classroom, and they gave her courage to see what was really in the mirror—not what *could* be or *should* be or *had* been. Just what was there now.

A collarbone, first of all, graceful and almost fragile looking. Arms that had toned up pretty well the past three months. Although they'd never be model slim, they were quite acceptable even in a sleeveless dress.

Breasts—A+. It had been a great concern that her breasts would be flabby, lifeless, when she lost so much, but they weren't. She hadn't actually lost there as much as the rest of her, which she understood was unusual. But at her heaviest, her breasts looked small; now in comparison to the rest of her, they were quite pretty. Happily she moved on.

Waist, better but not tiny. B. Belly…well, only a C. Maybe even a C–. It wasn't anywhere close to flat, and in fact, that was a target area for the next few months, now that her arms were looking so much better.

Hips, good enough. Thighs—well, kind of sturdy, but not bad.

She stepped back, narrowing her eyes, and turned from side to side, seeing herself, liking most of it, not blurring her eyes over what she didn't like.

A body she'd finally learned to treasure, to take care

of, to honor. If Robert ever saw it—if they ever got that far—she didn't have to be ashamed.

Was that what she wanted?

Yes. But see reason number one: she could not hurt Crystal just because she had the hots for the girl's uncle.

For that reason, she would sublimate her desire for him. She liked him a lot, liked his sense of humor, his wickedness. She often liked men with those qualities— Lance Forrest, for example, was one of her best friends. Robert could be her friend, too.

Healthy sublimation. Hmm. She had to attend a fund-raiser in Denver tonight. Maybe she'd go into town early and go shopping first. Or even better, see if her buddy Mark was free to fly her in and hang around to fly her back. He usually enjoyed it, and she paid well for the pleasure of it. Flying was one of her great joys, and there was nothing quite like a bright blue Colorado day at two thousand feet.

Happily she got dressed and went to make a call.

## Chapter 5

Robert and Crystal had lunch at a little Mexican spot he loved—one thing about living in "Tourist Central" was the wide variety of restaurants—then headed for the animal shelter. Crystal started out cheerful and happy, but she seemed to tire as the day ran on. Outside the shelter, he peered at her in concern. "You feeling all right, babe?"

"I'm fine," she said with annoyance, but she looked very pale to him. "Let's go find our cats."

Inside the pound, she perked up. The felines were housed in a room with humanely sized cages—tax money here extended even to the animal shelter—and there were not a great many of them. A skinny female who'd not long ago given birth, with a lone black kitten worrying her tail, a cage full of various sizes of kittens, and a battered-looking tom who gazed at them sorrowfully. Robert stuck his fingers through the bars with the mom and baby, and the rowdy black kitten rushed over, stood up on his back legs and gave Robert's index finger a sharp, one-two punch. Crystal, petting the mother, giggled. "He's cute."

On the other side of her, the tom stuck a paw through the bars, snagging her sleeve, and meowed with a low, plaintive sound. "Oh, he's so sad," she said. "What's wrong, guy? Somebody go off and leave you?"

He gave her the same sad sound, turning to put his body against the bar. His gray-striped fur was grease-stained, and one ear was nearly folded over with war wounds. Crystal bent her head close to the cage and murmured to him softly, words Robert couldn't hear.

Then she talked to the others. Touched every single one, talked to them, petted their heads or played with them through the bars. "I used to go to the pound to pet the cats when I could in Albuquerque," she told him. "Me and…this friend of mine. We rode the bus down there, all the way, and just hung around, petting the cats. It made them happy to get the attention, and after a while, they put us to work sometimes when we showed up."

"That's great. You could probably volunteer over here if you wanted."

She nodded without enthusiasm.

"Who was your friend?"

"Just this guy."

He let it go. Another tiny clue.

He wasn't surprised when she chose the battered tom as her own. He was slightly more amazed to find he personally could not leave that starved-looking mama cat and her rowdy baby. Being there had made him remember why he hated looking at the animals at the pound. He always wanted to take them all home, tend them and keep them safe. It was like the idea of war—you thought you could do it, maybe, to protect and keep the innocents safe.

Never really turned out that way. But maybe—the thought surprised him a little, sneaking in sideways—a man could make a difference one little life at a time.

When they got home, carting in dishes and kitty litter and cat food and cats, Crystal was so alarmingly pale that Robert made her go to bed, with orders to yell for him if she needed him. He called Ramona to report Crystal's symptoms, and she was concerned but not worried. "Keep an eye on her," she said. "If she's not better tonight, I might want to take a look at her. But this is the first warm day we've had, and maybe she just overdid it a little."

Relieved, he settled the cats and found himself completely besotted with the small black monster, who roared through the house, exploring every nook and cranny as if they were his for the conquering. Exuberance, Robert thought, amused by its attitude. Great quality.

Lying on the living room floor, the nearly weightless body of the mama cat on his belly, he fell asleep, thinking he liked having so much life around him.

Crystal did not feel good at all. She didn't want her uncle frowning over her like he did, all worried and stuff, so she curled up on her bed with her new cat, who stretched out the length of her, purring and purring. He made her think of Mario, which she tried to never, ever do, and she knew that it was thinking of him that had made her feel so bad.

She tried to sleep, but something at lunch must have been bad, because she had to keep getting up to run to the bathroom. Which was why they called them the runs,

she guessed. Gross, Crystal, she told her face in the mirror as she washed her hands for the third time. A face,
she had to admit, that didn't look all that good, and when
she was overcome with a wave of dizzy nausea, forcing
her to rest on the sink for a minute, she decided maybe
she needed to tell Robert she wasn't feeling good.

She didn't want to. Her mother used to get kind of
mad when Crystal was sick. Not mean mad, but annoyed, and it made Crystal feel bad. Robert wouldn't do
that, but when she made her way shakily into the living
room and saw him asleep on the floor with that ugly,
skinny cat on his tummy, she hesitated.

But her body decided to send its own message. Before
she could stop herself, Crystal threw up, like a little kid,
right on the clean floor. She burst into tears.

Ramona met them at the clinic. Robert's hands were
shaking with terror, and Ramona gently pushed him into
a chair. "I'm sure it's nothing serious. Relax, huh?"

But he knew he should have paid better attention to
Crystal earlier in the day. Should have seen that she was
really sick. He knew she hated to be vulnerable, to ask
for anything, and it was his job as the parent figure in
her life to be alert and aware of such things.

Ramona checked her over with calm, swift, efficiency,
asking Crystal questions that stabbed right at his worse
fears: had she had any lower back pain, loose bowels,
cramping? Had she done anything extraordinary today?

When Crystal denied doing anything unusual, Robert
spoke up. "She moved around some furniture when I
was gone."

Ramona smiled. "That would do it. Crystal, you're in
labor, honey, but we've got drugs to stop it." The nurse

brought a syringe and Ramona nodded. "I'm going to have to keep you overnight, keep an eye on you and then you can go home, but you have to stay in bed for a couple more days."

"Labor?" Crystal's eyes filled with tears. "Am I going to lose the baby?"

"No." Ramona took her hand. "This is not uncommon, and the drugs will halt the labor. But you have to stay completely off your feet for the next three days, do you understand?"

A woman came to the door. "Dr. Hardy? Phone. Urgent."

Ramona excused herself. "I'll be right back."

Crystal looked at Robert, shame on her cheekbones. It gave him a hard, thick lump in his throat, but he managed to wink. "We'll manage, babe. Trust me. I've had to take care of smelly soldiers on a battlefield. I think I can handle one tiny girl."

She closed her eyes, and tears leaked out from under her lids. "I was so stupid!"

"No, no." He jumped up and came around the bed, putting his hand on her hair. "It was just a little mistake, and everything's gonna be okay." He put his hand against her cheek, willing her to trust him to take care of her. "I'm so sorry, Crystal. I should have figured it out sooner. I'm not the greatest parent, but I hope you won't give up on me yet. I'm learning fast, eh?"

That only made her cry more, but he understood. At that moment, he wanted to strangle his sister with his bare hands, strangle his own mother for the failures that had caused all this to happen. "Why don't you try to get some sleep? I'll stay with you."

She opened her eyes. "You can't leave the cats alone all night."

"They'll be all right."

"No." Her voice was strong. "I'm the one who's going to be all right. Buster can't stay alone tonight, he'll be too sad. You can stay for a while, but you have to take care of them. They're our responsibility now."

He chuckled. "Okay. It's a deal." He settled down next to her, holding her hand. They kicked him out at ten, anyway, only an hour after he'd brought her in. Robert knew she was in good hands, knew Ramona meant well by sending him home to get some sleep. He went home, cleaned up the mess that had so upset Crystal— a hot thread of anger at his sister twisted through him again—checked on the cats, who were all in a heap on Crystal's bed, and fine as he'd known they would be.

He stepped outside, patting his shirt pocket, remembered he didn't smoke and took a long, deep breath of cold mountain air instead. At certain times in his life, he would have gone directly to the nearest bar and drowned his roiling emotions in serious quantities of bourbon, after which he'd have found either a fight or a woman, depending on the level of his rage.

He'd given all of that up when Jake went over the side of a mountain. He couldn't say, even now, why it had shaken him so, when his own brushes with death had done nothing, but it had. Jake had been in the middle of an epiphany about his life, and the ground just gave way beneath him. He'd nearly died.

And that was life, wasn't it? Sometimes the ground just crumbled beneath you. Robert couldn't get rid of the rage that had been his shadow all his life, but he'd learned how to cope with it without falling into self-destruction. Sometimes he took a run, blowing off steam that way, but it was too late now, too dark in the mountains, and he didn't like the idea of meeting a lynx or a bear.

He stood on the steps in the cold, his hands stuck in his pockets, and finally admitted to himself that there was only one person he really wanted to talk to. He thought of her standing on his porch—only this morning?—flustered and pretty and earnest, and it made him smile. She'd risked making a fool of herself. He guessed he could do the same.

As he pulled the keys out of his pocket, he felt the rage ebb.

Interesting.


Marissa was slightly giddy by the time she got home. Giddy with the wild pleasure she felt in flying low over the mountains in a little plane, with the champagne served at the reception; giddy with the unheralded power she'd commanded in her new dress. Laughing a little to herself, she put some water on to boil for a cup of tea, stripped off her shoes and stockings and turned on the stereo, programming a Celtic Bagpipes CD. The music rolled out, rhythmic and sad and joyful all at once. Dancing a little as she moved through the house, she relived the evening just past.

She was dying to call Victoria and tell her what a splash she'd made tonight, but that would require confessing her weight loss, and the moment of surprise would be so great she couldn't bear to ruin it, so she contented herself with reliving it in her mind.

Luck had just been with her. She walked into a department store in downtown Denver, waltzed over to the women's department, and plucked it off the rack. Size 12. Oh, yes, she loved that part. It was even a teeny bit too big in the shoulders, so she'd tried the ten but couldn't zip it.

Smoothing her hands down the skirt, swaying to the slightly exotic flutes and drums filling the air, she called up her most triumphant moments. Men *stared* at her. Flirted with her outrageously. Waiters rushed to fill her glass—which was how she'd ended up drinking more than her usual limit of champagne—and when she gave her little speech, every eye in the room had been on her and she hadn't thought of her body once.

The doorbell startled her. Very few of her friends ever just dropped by. Cautiously she looked through the peep-hole, then swung open the door. "Robert! Is everything okay?"

He blinked, slow as a cat, at her dress, then looked at her with a small frown. "It's really late. I'm sorry. I don't know what I was thinking."

"Is it your turn to play the oh, shucks game?"

He lifted his brows, a rueful smile turning up his mouth. "I guess it is. How about this instead? May I come in?"

"Please do." She backed up, swung her arm to let him in, bowing a little like a game show girl. "I was making a cup of tea. Want some?"

"That would be great." His gaze darted toward her body, flickered away, came back to the devastating neck-line. "Some dress," he said roughly. "Been to a party?"

"Thank you. It's brand-new and I spent a bloody fortune for it." She grinned, closing and locking the door out of habit, and led him into the living room. "A princess must have princess clothes to do princessly things, you know."

He smiled. "Are you a little tipsy, maybe?"

"Yes," she said firmly. "And enjoying it tremendously, so don't you dare wrinkle your nose. If you disapprove, you might as well just toodle on home.''

"Toodle?" This time it was a real grin, one that crinkled his eyes. "No way, babe. You in that dress, and tipsy to boot—I wouldn't miss this for the world." He seemed to notice the music for the first time. "I like the music, too."

"Hmm." She narrowed her eyes a little. "You don't strike me as a bagpipes kind of guy."

"I like music in general. I went to Scotland once, when I was overseas. There was this old guy with a red beard and a kilt playing the bagpipes on a very overcast, dark kind of day, and the sound just went right through me." He paused, listening. "Really moody stuff."

She inclined her head, delighted in spite of herself. She couldn't think of any guy she'd met in the past who wouldn't have given her that slightly pained glance over this CD. "Well, Mr. Martinez, you do delight and surprise."

A genuine grin broke the sober angles of his face. With one hand tucked over his belly, he gave a short, formal little bow. "My honor, ma'am."

The teakettle started whistling shrilly. Moving by him, she said, "Let's sit in the kitchen."

He followed. "This house is great, Marissa. Arts and Craft, right?"

"Yes. Thank you."

"Who did the restoration?"

"Tyler, of course. He's an expert on woodwork like this." She pointed out the elaborately carved molding over the door. "There was a big section of this that had completely rotted out, and you can't even tell where he fit it together."

He whistled appreciatively. "Excellent work."

"There's more. Hang on." Marissa dashed into the kitchen, pulled the kettle off the burner and dashed back out. Pushing the authentic push-button fixture for the overhead light, she moved to the stairway. "This earned him an article in *Old House Journal*." She knelt and touched the tiny, intricate carving of leaves and flowers. "Some kids lived here for a while at one point, and there were a lot of parties from what I gather. He had to re-carve about half of it."

He bent close to examine it. Marissa settled on the third step up, bracing her elbows on her knees, and admired him as he admired the wood. A lively dance began to play and she tapped her foot in time to it, wondering if he liked dancing.

She liked everything about the way he looked—the straightness of his limbs, the darkness of his glossy hair, the blade of his nose, which was almost too thin to be attractive. Idly she admired his mouth, thinking it would be lovely to kiss.

As if he felt her examination, he looked up. It was as it had been this morning, their faces close enough that it wouldn't take much to close the gap, and she blinked slowly, letting him see that she wouldn't mind if somehow they found themselves in a nice hot kiss. He wanted to. A little movement of his mouth, a slight shift in her direction told her he was thinking about it. His lids flickered downward, eyes touching her face, her neck, her décolletage. Lingered.

He stood up suddenly, backing away. "Your dress... uh..." He tapped his chest, pointed at her. "It's...uh... gaping a little."

Marissa looked down and realized he'd probably had quite a view from above her. "Oops. Sorry about that. I knew it was a little big."

"No apology necessary, trust me." He cleared his throat and stuck his hands in his pockets, looking anywhere but at her chest.

She hooted with laughter. "No wonder all those men were being so nice to me tonight!" She stood, pulling the shoulders up and back a little. "You were the only one gentlemanly enough to tell me about it."

His attention was snared by something across the room. "Holy sh-er-cow." He pointed. "Do you mind if I look at that?"

Even in her giddy state, Marissa suddenly felt wary. "Go ahead."

Reverently Robert moved to a stained-glass screen. Light from the living room and kitchen struck it from both sides, setting the wisteria ablaze, not a simple purple and blue, but touches of rose and yellow, and colors she couldn't even name.

She crossed her arms, eyes narrowing to see what he'd say. Everyone who came in the house admired it—thought it was beautiful, unusual. They admired it like a nice stand of roses, then went on.

But by the way Robert bent, by the way he kept his hands behind him like a museum visitor, by the wonder in his face when he turned to her he knew that it was not just beautiful, but priceless. The long dark eyes were alight. Quietly he said, "It's not a copy, is it?"

Marissa shook her head.

"Good God," he said in a hushed voice. "A Tiffany screen. I've read about them, but I've never seen one."

"Now you have."

He moved around it, mesmerized by the shifting colors. "No one has ever come close to his work with glass. Nowhere close. It's my hobby, you know, stained glass. I've seen it all over the world, all the cathedral windows, all the museum collections.'' He moved again, narrowed his eyes, inclined his head. ''Then you walk into the Metropolitan Museum in New York and there's that window, and you know.'' Very seriously he raised his eyes. ''Nobody will ever touch him.''

Marissa had gone from wary to amazed during this long speech. First that he'd spent so much time abroad— it shamed her, that this fact had stunned her. And second that he'd just strung more words together in a string than he usually put together in an hour. ''You like old glass?''

He nodded, still a little distracted by the screen. ''Stained glass is my big thing, and I'm not as well versed in some as others. Tiffany, I know. Chagall. A few others.'' He bent close, peering at a cluster of wisteria. ''The colors, the grace of it...'' He shook his head. ''This is unbelievable.''

She grinned. What were the chances that Red Dog, the wild soldier who'd had a taste for bourbon and wilder women, would be the one person she'd met in years who could identify an original Tiffany? ''If you think you can tear yourself away from the screen, I think you might like seeing some other things I have.''

''More?''

''Glass is my hobby, too,'' she said. ''Collecting, not doing.''

That bothered him, though Marissa wasn't sure why. His eyes narrowed slightly, and for a minute she thought he would make an excuse and leave. Instead, he followed her, his face serious.

She led him into the den, a room she loved, which she'd exquisitely restored. Cherry wood shelves lined three walls, and she'd had lights and glass doors installed, in order to display her treasures in safety and beauty. On the fourth wall was a bay window with a seat covered in chintz, where her three-year-old black cat, Damien, slept all the time—thus the safety precautions. He blinked when they came in the room, his eyes bright green.

"Hi, sweetie," she said, patting him distractedly, and clicked on a switch that turned on the lights in the cabinet.

"A black cat," Robert said. He sounded disturbed.

"Are you superstitious?"

"No." But he frowned as he moved to look at the cabinets. His expression softened, grew nearly as iridescent as some of the glass within. He pointed to the perfume stopper she'd shown him earlier, now displayed on a small round of black wax. "That's the piece you found today. Is it valuable?"

"Oh, yeah." She pulled open the doors to give them both access, and pulled it off the shelf. "Rene Lalique, who is by far my favorite. He did a series of perfume bottles for D'Orsay, Houbigant, Worth. I haven't looked this one up yet, but I gave the woman three thousand dollars for it, and it was probably a steal at that." Marissa drew one finger along the curve of it, smiling. "She was going to sell it to me for fifty cents."

"Amazing." He leaned forward to look at a bowl. "Now, this one I know," he said. "Quezal, right? About 1919, 1920?"

"I'm impressed," Marissa said honestly. "How did you learn so much about it?"

He raised a hand, put it down and Marissa said, "You can touch them. This isn't a museum. A lot of these pieces aren't even particularly rare or valuable. I just like them."

He picked up a glass-and-enameled metalwork dresser

box. "It's such a frivolous art form," he said quietly, touching the piece with gentle awe, as if he could imprint the beauty on his fingertips, "and that's one of the things I like best about it. There is no reason for a window to be colored or a bottle to be anything but a container. Only for beauty."

"Beauty matters," Marissa said. "It feeds our souls."

"Yeah." Carefully he replaced the piece, a shadow blotting out the wonder on his face. "I guess."

"You disagree?"

"Not exactly." There was anger in his eyes. "It's just so much more available to some people than it is to others."

"Is it?" she challenged. "Can we only find beauty in expensive things?"

With a faint scowl he backed up. "Look, thanks for sharing your treasures, princess, but this was a mistake. I gotta go."

She crossed her arms and lifted one eyebrow in imitation of him this afternoon. "Did I scare you, little boy?"

"Don't," he said in a dangerous voice. "Don't play with me."

"Is that what I'm doing?" Her voice, too, had dangerous registers.

"Sure looks like it from here. Slumming. Isn't that it? Isn't that what you've always done? Dated bikers and bad boys?"

How did he know that? And how did she answer it when it was essentially true? Instead she took the offensive. "You know, I thought you were different."

"Different?"

"Yeah, like maybe because you've been a victim of

labels all your life, you might be a person who might be able to look past them with someone else.''

"Am I supposed to feel sorry for you, princess? Brokenhearted that you didn't want for a damned thing your whole life?" Real anger sparked in his eyes. "The only walls you faced were the ones you put up yourself.''

That stung. Not because it was true, but because he was putting her in the same little box—a glass cage—that everyone else did, never seeing *her,* only what she represented. But she'd be damned if she let him know he had the power to wound her. Not tonight. Not ever again.

Lifting her chin, she said in a low, hard voice, "Do you wear war paint, Red Dog? Do you have a breechcloth at home? Can you teach me about the Great Spirit? I know you guys are so much more spiritual than we are.''

The flesh across his cheekbones went tight, and his nostrils flared. Good, she thought darkly. One good box deserved another. She didn't back away, didn't look down, just met his furious gaze with her own fury.

"I'm sorry," he said abruptly. "That wasn't fair.''

Now she did look away, afraid he would see the sudden brightness of tears. He took a step closer, but Marissa kept her arms crossed, her head down.

He said, "I'm standing here, thinking about my imitation leather belt, you know?" He stepped into the room. "I'm thinking about my ten-year-old truck and the hole in my sock, and it makes me feel like I did when I was a kid. I hate that, feeling small and unimportant because I don't have money.''

She looked up. "And I hate that people think they have to worry about ten-year-old cars in my presence." Her arms were still tightly crossed, and she felt one hand in a fist. What was at stake here, to put her in such a defensive posture? "I get tired of apologizing for where I was born. I didn't pick it, any more than you picked."

"Marissa," he began, taking another step.

"Let me finish. I love what money can do. I'm not going to lie and say I wish I were poor, because that would be stupid. I love having that Tiffany screen in my living room, and I loved seeing your face when you looked at it and knew what it was—that you should see something you wouldn't see anywhere else, and you appreciate it. And it makes me happy you know glass, and I don't have anyone to share that with, and I liked it, feeling that for ten seconds I had something in *common* with someone."

"Marissa," he said again, firmly. He put his hand out, his open palm landing half on the upper swell of her breasts, half on the fabric of the bodice itself. "It's really gaping."

Electric light, not that soft ghost of blue that it had been, but a bright, sharp, white-blue of lightning, shot between them, almost audible, when his flesh touched hers. A tumble of blistering emotions bolted through her at once—humiliation and terror and desire—and she knew all of them burned in her eyes as she looked at him. Before he could take his hand away, she put hers on top of it. Holding it there, she stepped close and stood on her toes.

He bent at the same moment she lifted up and their mouths met in a violent kiss. Not even a pretense of gentleness, only open mouths colliding, tongues thrusting deep. Marissa's head was bent backward under the force of it, and she heard herself make a little, hot noise when a tooth struck her lip.

Deep thrusts of tongues that wanted a lot more,

mouths wide open. No sweetness, no ease of greeting, just that fierce, pure expression of overwhelming sexual alignment.

It stunned her, and she put a hand out to push him away at the same moment he broke away. Shocked, they stared at each other, both panting. There was a painful sense of recognition in it, a chemical reaction neither had expected.

"We can't do this," Robert said hoarsely.

"No. I know. Crystal—"

"Oh." He backed up a step, covering his eyes. "That's why I came over here."

"Why?" Instantly sober.

"She's at the clinic tonight. She's okay now, I guess, but she went into labor early. They stopped it."

"Oh, no." She put a hand on his sleeve. "I'm sorry. I was so selfish tonight, and you had this worry."

He looked down at her. Closed his eyes. "Damn it, Marissa. You've got to do something about that dress." Suddenly he just turned on his heel. "I have to go."

Marissa didn't even see him to the door. It seemed wiser not to somehow.

# Chapter 6

He'd tried to be a gentleman. He really had. The dress was not just delectable, it was dangerously sexy. Made of some thin fabric that clung and moved around her body, the top was supposed to be fitted against her breasts. It was supposed to be sexy. It was low-cut in an elegant kind of way, designed to display generous swells of breasts, maybe a nice diamond necklace.

But Marissa had worn no jewelry. She didn't need it. Her skin was flawless, poreless, perfect, the twin rise of breasts all the adornment necessary.

He wasn't, strictly speaking, a breast man. He liked legs, hair, hands. He noticed lips, and had a thing for a pretty backside, which Marissa definitely had.

Breasts in general were all pretty nice, in his opinion, the most female of attributes in whatever size or shape they took. He'd never been particularly attracted to a woman's body because of the size or shape of her breasts—it had even seemed odd to him that men would rate them. It was like rating a woman because she was a woman.

Or something. He rubbed his face. Damn, she got to him.

But when she sat there on the stairs, he'd had a long, electrifying look down her dress, and he'd been astonished to discover that he'd just never got it before, why men went so nuts. Her breasts were beautiful, that white, white, supple skin rising in such plushness. The bra she wore beneath the bodice was one of those wispy, barely there deals, a kind of glittery transparent blue, and the edges of her nipples showed through, a very dark color. The colors—dark blue on the dress, transparent blue shimmer, milk-white skin and dark nipples—had gone straight to his sex and burned there.

Still, he managed to keep it together. Tell her it gaped, get himself under control. Once she straightened, with that surprisingly lusty hoot of laughter, he saw that the bodice wasn't all that bad. He could still see a lovely, rich valley that screamed for his tongue. He was sure it was that valley that those men had been eyeing at her party.

But he couldn't get the vision out of his mind. It wasn't so much now what he could see, but what he wanted to see. That tiny transparent thing embracing all that alluring flesh, the dark nipples. The vision burned right at the base of his groin, a hurried, steady pulse that pumped blood all too fast into his willing servant.

Out in the biting night, with a wind blowing down off the snow that was still piled in dark places at higher elevations, he shivered and hunched his shoulders. What was he running from here?

He turned the ignition key and let the truck warm for a few minutes. Through the windshield, he stared at the house. Light shone through the leaded glass that graced the top third of the arched front windows set into solid, sturdy brick. It promised stability, that house. Stability and protection and calm.

On the second floor, a light clicked on, and Robert imagined Marissa in her bedroom, unzipping that amazing dress and tossing it onto some massive, carved four-poster bed. He imagined her dark hair tumbling down in a glossy swath to her flawless white shoulders, thought of her, dressed in that elegantly transparent bra and a similarly elegant silk slip, padding on manicured feet into a bathroom with a claw-footed tub and original wood on the walls.

And with every cell in his body, he wanted to be in there with her, putting his hands on that flesh, climbing into that tub, that bed with her. He thought—no, he knew—that she would like it. That kiss had told him that much.

What would it hurt? He'd get up before dawn and Crystal would never know.

But he knew why he wasn't about to go back to her door. Not only because Crystal would scent the subterfuge. Not only because he sensed that Marissa was somehow dangerous even if he didn't care to examine in detail just why.

He wouldn't go back to that door because he thought of his scarred, tattooed hands on her smooth, perfect shoulders, and in reverse, her small, neat hands against the marks and scars of his chest.

Different worlds. Way too different.

He drove home.


Sunday morning, Marissa stopped by the grocery store bakery and picked up a selection of bagels, doughnuts and croissants, some hefty paper cups of latte and a quart of orange juice, then drove to the clinic to see Crystal. She'd dithered over her clothes the slightest bit, finally— rather to her amusement—choosing a crisp, no-nonsense pair of khaki slacks and a similarly crisp cotton blouse.

To her relief, Robert had not yet arrived. Crystal was ensconced in bed, flipping channels desultorily with a remote. "Want some company?" Marissa said, poking her head around the door. "I brought goodies."

"Hi, Ms. Pierce." She looked a little confused and surprised. Wary. She was always wary. "Come in."

Marissa grabbed a rolling table and started taking things from the grocery bag. "What's your pleasure? It would make me very happy if you'd eat that chocolate-covered doughnut so I can stop thinking about it."

A tentative smile. "I guess I can take it off your hands."

Arranging the pastries in an attractive way on the bag, Marissa said, "My mother used to hide doughnuts from me," she said, and picked up a cruller defiantly. She held it up, admiring the slanted grooves where glaze had caught, letting her mouth get truly ready for the completely nutritionless, absolutely magnificent flavor. She would eat half of it, and throw the rest away. It was one of the tricks she'd picked up—rather than abstaining from sinful foods, she indulged in them when she really wanted one, but only ate half. Now she bit into it, closing her eyes in pure pleasure. "Mmmm."

"Jeez, Ms. Pierce. You should be on a commercial." She gingerly ate a tidbit of her own. "Why'd your mother hide doughnuts?"

"Because I was fat and she wanted me thin."

"You were fat?"

Marissa grinned. "Oh, yes." She put down the cruller,

wiped her fingers carefully on a napkin and opened her purse. "This is me, two years ago." She gave Crystal the picture of herself and Lance Forrest, dressed up for a country club dance.

"Oh, man!" Crystal stared at the picture in disbelief. "I wouldn't even have known it was you." She scowled. "Why'd you cut your hair, though? It was so long!"

Marissa took the picture back and looked at herself. In the picture, her hair tumbled in thick, glossy waves past her waist. "I got tired of hiding behind it."

"What were you hiding from?" The dark eyes were intent.

Marissa thought of the windbreaker Crystal wore and the way her hair hid her face, and took a moment to consider her answer. It wasn't something she'd articulated before, but it was probably time. "The world, I guess," she said slowly. "My father told us from the day we were born that men would only want to marry us for our money."

"So you decided to be fat so they'd have to really love you," Crystal said. It wasn't a question.

"Very wise, my dear." She'd reached the halfway point in the cruller, took a teeny tiny little crumb more, then wrapped it up in a napkin and threw it away. "I think it was also a way of sort of controlling the world, you know what I mean? My sister and I had no freedom at all, but they couldn't control what we ate."

"So why don't you have to hide anymore?"

"You know—" she picked up her paper cup of latte "—I don't know. Maybe I just decided to take my chances with the world. Be happy anyway." She sipped her coffee. "Now you."

"Me?"

"Yeah. What are you hiding from?"

Crystal touched the rise of her belly, an almost protective gesture. "Bad people, I guess." Absently she stroked the round. "When I was little, my favorite movie was *The Invisible Man* because I thought that would be such a great thing, to just be able to be invisible."

"It's not so bad here, though, is it?"

Her face shuttered instantly. "Not at home."

"School is bad."

A shrug. Subject closed. Accepting it, Marissa leaned back comfortably, letting the quiet fall. Beyond the hospital window, aspens shimmered in an invisible wind, pale green against the blue backdrop of mountains.

"Do you like movies?" Crystal asked, eyeing the doughnuts.

"Have another. Please." She pushed the table a little closer. "I love movies. My sister and I watched them by the zillions."

"Yeah? Me, too. The video store was right around the corner and my mom used to rent big ole stacks for me even when I was really little. All the ninety-nine-cent ones, you know?"

"Sure! Keep 'em for five days."

Crystal actually smiled, and sat up a little. "She put the VCR in my room with this little TV that was kinda small, but had real good color, you know? It was like totally safe and quiet and nobody bugged me." She picked out another doughnut, sitting up completely straight now, more animated than Marissa had ever seen her. "Then this boyfriend of hers? He rigged up cable to the apartment and even found this little box to get the pay channels, so I could watch movies twenty-four hours a day." She took a bite of doughnut, gestured with her hands. "I watched all the big ones you know, the first day they came out on Pay-Per-View, and in between I saw everything else—even those ones with the little box with English in them, you know what I mean?''

Tickled at such an outpouring, Marissa nodded. ''Subtitles.''

''Right. The French ones are pretty boring most of the time, but I liked some of the Japanese ones. You ever see them?''

''Sometimes.'' She considered and decided to be honest. ''I actually like the French ones. They make a lot of historical romances.''

''Yeah, some of those are okay. There was this one? A queen and this poor guy in France during some disease? It was *so* sad. They fell in love and all that, and then he got killed at the end. I cried for a day.''

''*Queen Margot!* I love that movie!''

''Yeah, that's it! You like the sad ones?''

''Some of them.'' Marissa frowned. ''I don't like it when there's no reason for it to be sad, just bang, somebody dies. But I love it when there's some lesson in the sadness.''

''Exactly!'' Crystal tossed her hair back. ''Like in *Dangerous Liaisons,* he dies because he did something awful and that's part of the lesson, that if you treat people like that, you know, take advantage of real love, then you have to pay the price.'' She licked a little sugar from her finger. ''And in *Romeo and Juliet,* the parents are so stupid that their kids get killed over it.'' She paused a moment, narrowed her eyes. ''And sometimes it's a message—what's the word? Maybe like a metaphor?—to make something real to you that wouldn't be. Like in *Titanic,* if he had lived, it would have still been a good romantic story, but he stands for all those people who did die. You know? And so you *get* it. Your heart is just trashed because you want him and all those other good people to live.''

Marissa blinked, then grinned broadly. ''Wow—that's the best summation of the purpose of tragedy that I've ever heard, Crystal.''

Not even this seemed to deter her. ''I think about it a lot,'' she said, nodding. ''Tragedy kind of makes the bad stuff make sense sometimes, you know? Like this teacher said once that stories create order in our lives.''

''What order do you find in tragedy?''

She narrowed her eyes. ''Well,'' she said slowly, looking into the distance as if the answer were written there, ''there are lots of different kinds, you know? Like there's the ones when somebody gives something up for somebody else, and the ones when the tragedy is the reason the whole story happens, and the ones that the death or whatever seems really sad, but it really shows that the character grew somehow. Like in *Last of the Mohicans,* when the sister steps off the cliff?'' She put her hand to her chest. ''I cry and cry and cry over that one, every time, but it's really beautiful in a way, you know, because she showed how brave she was by doing it.''

A shiver of excitement and amazement crawled up Marissa's spine. She'd known Crystal was bright, but she obviously had a very literary bent of mind, a sense of structure and the meaning of literature, all gleaned from movies. It was tragic that Crystal hated school so much.

Marissa would have to figure out some way to gently illustrate all the possibilities awaiting such a mind, and she was doubly excited that her sister was coming to town. It seemed almost fated.

Now she said only, ''Do you like only the sad ones?''

"No way." She grinned. "I like *all* of them. Funny, sad, happy, silly. Scary. All of them."

"What's your number-one favorite?"

Her eyelids fell, and the shoulders almost imperceptibly hunched forward. "I have a lot."

"You don't want to tell me?"

She lifted one side of her mouth and rolled her eyes. "It's not that. It's just that everybody gets it wrong, why I like it, because they think it's my age, that I'm just stupid, that I don't know about good movies or that I have some crush."

"You don't have to tell me if you don't want to."

From the door came a raspy, low voice, laced with amusement. "I think you should tell her, babe."

They both turned to see Robert coming in, a paper bag from the bakery in his hands. Marissa had been lost in the conversation, enjoying it so much that she forgot to anticipate his arrival. The sight of him sent a thick, hot ripple over the surface of her skin. Dressed this morning in a simple, long-sleeved Henley and jeans, his hair gleaming in its braid, a quirky smile on that wide, mobile mouth, he looked like everything good in life.

His dark eyes tangled with Marissa's for a single second. Marissa flashed on the taste of his tongue against her own. She looked away.

"More doughnuts!" Crystal said, laughing. "I haven't seen so many doughnuts since I was little!"

"We want to fatten you up, little girl," Robert said. He pulled a second chair over and settled easily. "You guys talking movies?"

"She gets it," Crystal said. "Unlike some people here."

"You don't like movies?"

He shrugged. "Take 'em or leave 'em." He took out

an apple fritter and Marissa found her gaze lingering on the long, dark length of his beautiful fingers. He had such great hands.

"You gonna tell her, Crystal?"

"No," she said emphatically.

"It's all right. Another day." Marissa stood up. "I just came by to cheer you up a little. I'll let you two visit."

"Oh, don't go!" Crystal protested. Then she looked horrified. "I mean, I guess you have lots to do."

Robert raised his eyes to her. "I'm going to take her home as soon as Ramona gets here. I already rented a big pile of movies. If you wanted, you could come over and watch with us a little later."

There was something in his voice that made her want to put her hands on his face, on his neck. It struck her with a sense of surprise. He sounded vulnerable. As if it mattered. "I'd like that," she said. "I'll bring the popcorn."

She picked up her purse, trying not to look at the length of a jean-covered thigh, lean and hard looking, trying not to imagine what it looked like without the cloth. "See you later."

"Bye, Ms. Pierce," Crystal said. "Thanks."

Marissa couldn't remember how to walk normally. She was aware of his eyes on her back, maybe even on her rear end, and the perusal made it feel too big, too full of movement. She turned into the hall with a sense of relief, and relaxed into her normal stride. A little bubble of happiness rose in her and she swung her purse like a girl. He liked her a little. She could tell. He was trying hard not to, but—

"Marissa, wait up!"

She turned. He half jogged to catch her. "Look," he

said, "I wanted to apologize for last night. I said some pretty rude things and I'm sorry."

"So did I, Robert." She shook her head. "I'm sorry, too."

He stuck out his hand. "Friends, then?"

She accepted the offering. Put her small hand into the engulfing breadth of his strong palm, felt the heat of his fingers close around hers. And it was just as electric as each touch before now had been. She looked at his mouth, remembered the full thrust of his tongue against her own, and to her horror, her nipples pearled.

He noticed with a little exhalation, and he shook his head. "We're going to have to deal with this sooner or later," he said roughly, holding her hand tightly.

"Maybe it would be better if I didn't come over."

"Crystal likes you. It would hurt her." He looked at her mouth, closed his eyes. "We'll just…take it easy."

"All right." She pulled on her hand. He pulled back.

"Why do you think it happens like this?" he said, stepping closer. "Out of nowhere?"

It wasn't out of nowhere on her part. "I always saw you, Robert. You just never saw me before."

He moved even closer, until his hips and hers were nearly touching. "Yes, I did."

She rolled her eyes. "Right."

"You used to have this green dress," he said. "With gold on the hem. Your hair fell all over it, like a pelt. And you wore red lipstick in those days. Bright red, like something sinful." His eyes were intent. "You've always been beautiful, Marissa. You just didn't know it till now."

With a soft little cry, she pulled free. "I'll see you later," she said. It was her turn to bolt.

She rushed home like a demon was following her,

breathing on her neck, raising the little hairs on her body. There was a kind of roar in her ears, making it hard to think clearly.

She changed into bike shorts and an oversize T-shirt, and dug out her in-line skates and pads. There was an almost frenetic edge to her movements as she carried the stuff out to her car and drove to a little parkway with a network of good concrete. On a park bench, she put everything on—helmet, knee pads, elbow pads, wrist protectors—and struck out.

She skated hard in the bright day, skated around and around the network of walks. In a little while, her heart stopped racing and she could breathe more easily, and she could think again.

He had seen her before. In her favorite green dress, wearing red lipstick because it made her teeth look so white. With her hair swinging all around her like a cape she hoped hid the rest of her.

He'd seen her. She could just imagine it, him sitting in a booth with his buddies at the Wild Moose Inn, eyeing the beauties waiting for a dance. She could just imagine what had been in his mind when she danced, the jokes his buddies probably cracked about her exuberant dancing.

To her horror, she found she was very close to tears. Urgently she dashed off the path, tripped on a stick and went sailing. Her left elbow and knee crashed into the gravel, but the pads took the brunt of it. Her wrist twisted a little as she landed, and she yelped.

For a minute, she didn't move, catching her breath and waiting to see if any alert of pain went up from any part of her. Only the wrist. Rolling over to sit on her rear, she admired the thick gouges the heavy plastic pads had taken on the left elbow and knee.

A boy on a skateboard stopped. "You okay?" Surprise lit his face. "Ms. Pierce?"

She chuckled. "Yeah, it's me. Thanks for witnessing my big spill."

He grinned. "You okay?"

"Fine, thanks."

"Cool." He gave her a thumbs-up and skated off.

With a sigh, Marissa stayed where she was. A big something going on here. Was she grieving for the lonely girl she'd been? Or was she angry that Robert had noticed her now?

Maybe both. She zipped open the Velcro holding her knee pads on, wincing a little when her wrist protested, then followed with the elbow pads. Wrist was definitely pretty sore. Maybe even broken. With a frown, she took off the right wrist guard, and her socks, then laced everything together and slung them over her shoulder, leaving the left wrist guard on until she got home. It would keep it immobile until she could look at it properly. Barefoot, she made her way back to her car.

It was one of those airy spring days, threatening to be windy, but only just gusty at the moment. Overhead, the sky was as blue as…she eyed it and smiled, unable to think of anything just that color. Van Briggle pots, maybe. Very blue, anyway. The grass below her feet was tender and new, her skates a solid weight over her shoulder. She ambled easily, smiling softly at a toddler and her father, who smiled back appreciatively. A knot of young teens played Frisbee.

Marissa realized suddenly—once again—how much her life had altered the past eighteen months. Two years ago, she would have huffed and puffed across this lawn. She might even have had to rest. She would have been sweating profusely by now, and felt self-conscious over her arms. Her arms had always bothered her a lot—not the sight of them, because she never allowed them to show, but the slight way they angled out from her body, never truly relaxed.

And *she* had done it. All by herself. One step, one day at a time. Last night had been a triumph, but in a funny way, her annoyance and worry that Robert might be after her *body*—not her money or her influence—was even more of one. She laughed softly. He'd been lusting over her in a big way.

She wanted to tell Victoria all of this. Soon.

But an odd, soft pain lingered. He had seen her, even then. But what would have happened if they'd had a chance to get to know each other then? Would his eyes have filled with that heat she so enjoyed? Would he have been tempted to kiss her?

Marissa didn't think so. Why should it hurt? It was just reality.

At home, she gingerly slid the left wrist guard off her hand, keeping it straight. It was tender and beginning to swell, but she could move it without severe pain, so she filled a bag with ice and hunted down a stretchy bandage.

The phone rang and Marissa grabbed it happily. "When are you going to be here?"

"Thursday. Is that good?"

"Yes! The turret room?"

"I called. It's not open. I got the suite instead."

Victoria always stayed in the ski lodge where they'd spent so many happy weeks as children. Every winter, for three weeks in February, they came to Red Creek to ski. They'd both learned the sport here. It had been one of the few places they'd been given freedom to run like other children. "I can hardly wait!" Marissa said. "I'm dying to tell you about a million things.'' She turned her hand too fast and winced. ''I have to go wrap my wrist. I banged it up a bit. Talk to you.''

''Ought to have it X-rayed. I broke mine three months ago and didn't do anything with it.''

''It's just a sprain.'' No way she was going to miss the afternoon she had planned. ''That reminds me—I really want you to meet one of my students. She's almost sixteen, adorable and lost—pregnant—and absolutely has the best movie sensibility I've seen in a long time. Victoria, she's seen everything. You guys will love each other.''

''No kidding. What kind of movies?''

''Literally everything. She's very bright and hasn't had many breaks, and I bet she's going to get a real kick out of meeting you.''

''Has she seen any of mine?''

Marissa chuckled. ''I don't know. I'll be sure to find out.''

''Ah, this wretched ego. Don't tell me if she hates them. Don't tell her they're mine if she hates them.''

''It's a deal.''

''See you Thursday, gorgeous.''

''Ditto.''

## *Chapter 7*

Robert got Crystal settled on the couch with her movies, a remote and big bottle of water handy at her elbow. Her orders were to stay down completely for three days, only rising for long enough to go to the bathroom. She could sit up for short periods, but Ramona insisted it should mainly be a reclining position, so he'd shifted her to the couch to make it easy for her to look at the television, and propped her up with pillows.

Crystal was remarkably cheerful about it, but then she had a giant stack of movies to watch. "Do you think Ms. Pierce will really come over?"

"Yeah," he said. "She said she would, so she will." He retreated to the little alcove in the kitchen to work off some of his restlessness. His skin felt like it didn't fit right. Taking out his tools and some small pieces of leftover colored glass, he thought about the Tiffany screen, that gradation of color that was so extraordinary.

On a blank piece of heavy paper, he sketched a small design, abstract, and started cutting and fitting.

As he worked, he slid away from himself, into that other land where nothing existed except color, a place where color represented all the sounds and smells and sights that had ever existed in the world. In that place, he did not think in words at all, only images, this shade overlying this tone, this sliver changing that hue. Tension eased from his neck, from his chest.

The release in color had been with him as long as he could remember. As a small boy, he had loved the giant boxes of crayons and would spend endless hours layering stripes of one shade against others, trying the combinations to see how they worked. He saved any money he could earn by running errands or walking dogs in order to buy cheap watercolor sets and colored pencils and coloring books. He adored the ones with little dots that you painted with water to make color appear—they seemed like the ultimate magic, making color where there had been none.

And even then, he'd loved glass. At the St. Vincent de Paul's near his elementary school where his mother bought most of his clothes, he ambled along the junky aisles full of chipped dishes and stained silver, always looking for something beautiful. A blue vase, a little cracked, but of such an elemental blue he gladly paid the quarter for it; a red glass statuette of a dog. Hokey, but breathtaking when he put it in a window to catch the light.

When he was in the seventh grade, wandering far from his house to avoid his cocaine-frenzied mother at all costs, he discovered stained glass in a cathedral. He spied it from outside, dully glinting in the afternoon. A single shard of deepest ruby caught his attention, and he'd gone inside to see it.

The window had been enormous, covering most of one wall. It depicted the stations of the cross, though Robert had no idea what they were at the time. Stunned, he crept into the church and slid into a back pew to absorb it. Hours later, he had emerged feeling like he'd eaten a fantastically rich meal. His retinas were transformed.

And now, twenty years later, he could still lose himself in the pleasure of it. Glass held color in a way that nothing else could. Held it and reflected it and shimmered with it, the deepest hues, the most delicate.

When the doorbell rang, he had no idea if it had been twenty minutes or two hours. Blinking, he glanced at the clock and saw that it was three. No wonder his neck was tired. Stretching happily, he went to the door, seeing that Crystal had fallen fast asleep on the couch. Not even the doorbell had awakened her.

It was Louise on the other side of the door, not Marissa as he'd expected. He grinned at the casserole she was carrying. Putting a finger to his lips, he pointed at Crystal and gestured for Louise to follow him to the kitchen. Once there, he released the swinging door between the rooms and took the dish. "This is fantastic, Louise. Thanks."

"You know it's my pleasure." She tossed an unruly silvered curl from her forehead. "How is she doing?"

"Really well," he said. "Ramona said it's not unusual for young girls to go into labor early, and the drugs should take care of it. She moved something heavy yesterday."

Louise tsked. "It's tough for such a young thing to understand all there is to know about this. I had to stay in bed for most of the time with Tyler.'' She crossed her arms, and Robert found himself bracing for…something. ''I reckon she has to stay down for at least a few days, and I know you have to work, so why don't you let her come on up to the house during the day so I can make sure she's not doing more than she should?''

''I appreciate the offer,'' Robert said. ''But it's not necessary. I'll take off for a day or two.''

''Well, if you want to. But I happen to know you're working by the hour, sir, and it seems plain foolish to give up a few days' pay when there's somebody who can lighten your load.'' She gave him a little space by shifting a little, her attention caught by the tools and glass on the table. She pursed her lips and wandered over for a closer look. ''You'd really be doing me a favor, Red. In case you haven't noticed, all my sons and grandsons are male except that little tiny baby girl. I enjoy spending time with my own sex now and again.''

''Louise—''

She picked up a round of stained glass. ''This is your work?''

''Yeah. It's just a hobby.''

She put it back down again. ''Mmm. Listen, at least think about it. You're a good uncle and all, but a woman likes to have another woman around now and then when she's in this condition.''

He hadn't considered that. He grinned. ''Don't know why I'm arguing. You always get your way.''

''That I do.'' She poked him lightly in the arm. ''And don't you forget it.'' Tossing the long strap of her sturdy purse over her shoulder, she said, ''Put that dish in the oven at three hundred and fifty degrees for an hour and you'll have a nice hot supper.''

Looking down at her, at the bright blue eyes her sons

had inherited, and the comfortable kindliness that surrounded her, Robert felt suddenly very grateful. He'd not had many mother figures in his life, and neither had Crystal. Impulsively he bent a little and gave her an awkward little half hug. "Thanks, Louise. I'll ask Crystal how she feels about spending time at your place while I work."

"You do that, son."

He walked her out, finding Crystal sitting up again. He willed Louise not to say anything about spending time at the older woman's house, but she saw Crystal and turned abruptly. "There's the sleepyhead!" She settled on a footstool and brushed Crystal's hair out of her face, a gesture that Robert would have expected to make her cringe. "How you doing, sweetie? Scare you good enough?"

Oddly, Crystal didn't seem as defensive with Louise as she was with many adults. She nodded ruefully, touching her belly. "It still doesn't feel that good."

"I know. Tell the truth, this last stretch ain't all that much fun, no matter how strong and healthy you are." She folded her hands. "Is he kicking you good yet?"

"All the time."

Louise looked over her shoulder. "You mind giving us girls a little privacy here?"

Robert lifted his brows at Crystal, who gave him a vague nod. "No problem." He went out on the porch, inhaling the crisp day and patting his shirt pocket and smiling softly to himself. Beware the force of mothers, he thought. And Louise Forrest was the Queen of Mothering—nosy, meddling, stubbornly nurturing, reliably kind. Within weeks of knowing her, she'd known his favorite meal—a rare steak with a big potato and butter but no sour cream—and cooked it for him. Her sons had been very blessed indeed. What would his life have been like if he'd had a mother like Louise?

A car turned into the long drive, Marissa's surprisingly modest, dark blue sedan. A solid, fairly new car, but nothing extravagant or unusual. Millions of teachers across America must drive one just like it. He thought of her house—a perfectly, lovingly restored bungalow, and even though he knew renovation on such a place could cost well into hundreds of thousands, by Rich Girl standards it was pretty damned modest.

Like the car. Like the exquisitely tailored clothes, expensive but not designer. She'd chosen to live in Red Creek, in a bungalow, hiding her Tiffany screen in plain sight because not many people would ever dream it was the real thing, or even that there *was* a real thing.

With a pinch, he realized she wanted to fit in.

And how could she? Ever?

She got out of the car, wearing a plain oxford shirt, tucked neatly into the waistband of her jeans. Ordinary-girl clothes. Except there was nothing ordinary about those hot, hot curves or her heavy swing of hair or the eyes blue as pure glass. He grinned.

"What big teeth you have, Grandma!" she called, opening the back door and reaching inside. Belatedly he saw that her wrist was bandaged and he rushed to help her.

"All the better to eat you with," he said, wiggling his eyebrows. Smoothly he took the grocery bag out of her arms. "Let me take that. What did you do?"

"In-line skating accident. Just a minor sprain."

"You skate? Where do you go?"

"The park. There are zillions of concrete sidewalks. Do you skate?"

"Love it, man. Pure freedom. Call me the next time you go."

"I will." She halted, narrowing her eyes at the white Lincoln in the driveway. "Louise is here?"

"She brought over a casserole. Why?"

A bright flash of amusement crossed her face. "Oh, you'll see." Louise came out on the porch and Marissa smiled. "How's the patient?"

"Just fine. We had a nice little talk, and, Robert, she is going to be coming to my house in the morning. Just drop her off on your way to work."

"Louise, you really—"

"Shhh." She waved a hand. "Not a word. We have an understanding, me and my girl." She winked at Marissa and got in her car. "We on for walking tonight?"

"Always."

Louise waved as she drove off, and Marissa waved, too, then tucked her hands in her back pocket, or at least started to, and winced, taking the left back out. Still, it was a nice posture in Robert's opinion, showing the nice straight line of her shoulder, the neatness of elbow to hand. And well...yeah...putting her breasts in relief against the dark green pine tree behind her. For one hot, long second, he remembered that transparent blue bra, the darkness of nipples—

"You're staring, Wolf," she said without altering her posture.

He winced. "I am. Sorry." He lifted his eyes to her face, grinning ruefully. "That's...uh..." He shook his head. "I'm usually a leg man, I gotta say."

"Is that supposed to be a compliment?"

"I think so."

She looked at his face, as if trying to piece something together. "Maybe it's because I haven't been looked at in the past, but I think I kind of like it. How sick is that?''

He laughed. ''Babe, it's the rules that seem skewed to me. Haven't you ever eyed a guy's…jeans?''

''Not I.'' Her eyes glittered, that red mouth quirking up in a smile that admitted the truth.

''We're animals, no more, no less. Natural to look at those areas that are part of mating.''

''Really.'' She slid her gaze down his body, boldly letting it linger just below his belt.

Electrifying. He expected her to look up, maybe even to blush, but she took her time, and only after a long, long moment during which he forced himself to think about those beads of glass on his table, did she look up. ''I see what you mean.'' Her nostrils flared in amusement.

''Let's go inside,'' he said a little gruffly.

She laughed.

Marissa had brought popcorn and tortilla chips for the two skinnies, and for herself a huge pile of broccoli florets, zucchini and summer squash sticks, her beloved celery sticks, apples and a skim-milk-based dressing with no fat and lots of flavor. She could pig out on it all day and never feel a moment of guilt.

It had been a great surprise to her to discover that she loved veggies. As a child, she thought she hated them because Victoria did, and had simply made a habit of avoiding them. She'd adored the fruit sections of the market, all those piles of beautifully shaped apples and pears and bananas and melons, and splurged on whatever was in season, but the vegetable section bored her.

But the weight-loss plan she'd eventually settled on had insisted on up to five servings of vegetables and fruits per day, and to her amazement, most vegetables didn't count at all. She was a grazer, nibbling all day long, and had started trying various experiments with vegetable nibbles.

So far, she hadn't met a vegetable she *didn't* like. They were—unlike meats—infinitely varied and beautiful in color, texture, flavor.

They all kicked back, Crystal on the couch, obviously not feeling tip-top, but pleased to have company for the moviefest. Robert slumped in a much-used easy chair, and Marissa got a cozy little chair with a footstool.

"Okay," Crystal said. "What do you guys want to watch?"

Marissa said, "It's up to you, sweetie. You're the one stuck on the couch."

She rolled her eyes. "And you're the ones stuck here trying to pretend there's nothing you'd rather do than hang out with me."

Robert jumped up. "Wow, you mean I don't have to? Come on, Marissa, let's go find something better to do."

"Very funny," Crystal said, but Marissa could tell she was pleased. "Let's vote, then. *Braveheart, Cruel Intentions, Lonely Street* or—" she turned the movie sideways "—*Casablanca?*" She made a face. "Yuck, uncle."

He lifted a shoulder. "What?"

Crystal looked at Marissa. "Do you like it?"

Marissa pressed her lips together, trying not to smile. "Not really, to tell you the truth." She closed her mouth to keep from insisting they watch *Lonely Street,* a bittersweet tale of misfits, a movie that had done modestly well at the box office. It was one of Victoria's early works, the first that had illuminated the quick humor mixed with pathos that had become her trademark.

He flopped back in his chair in mock disgust. "Cretins."

"I've seen all of them except *Cruel Intentions*. Have either of you seen it?" Crystal asked. "I'd kinda like to see what they did with it. Remake and all, you know."

"Remake of what?" Robert tossed a piece of popcorn into the air and tried to catch it with his mouth. It bounced off his lip and fell on the floor.

"If you make a mess with that, I'm going to be very unhappy with you."

A kitten dashed out from under the chair and slapped the popcorn with a tiny black paw. "Not a mess. It's a toy."

Crystal shook her head. "It's a remake of *Dangerous Liaisons*."

"Hmmm. Never saw it."

Marissa grinned at Crystal and nodded. "Let's do it. Don't tell him the end."

"I don't think they'll do the end the same, do you? How can they?"

"I guess we'll find out." Marissa shifted, thinking vaguely that she needed to find out who Crystal's English teacher was.

But her pleasure in the movie—silly, in her opinion, and by the scowls on Crystal's face, she thought so, too—and the good company was slowly undermined by her aching wrist, an ache that grew from mildly throbbing to quite distracting in two hours' time. She needed ice, but waited until the credits rolled before standing up with a little smile. "Interesting," she said.

Robert scowled from his chair. "I hate that ending."

"You field this, Crystal," Marissa said. "I need to get some ice for this wrist."

He leapt to his feet. "Let me help."

"I think I can manage it," she insisted, but he followed her to the kitchen anyway, taking out a big plastic bag to put the ice in. Quietly she said, "I'm sure she's dying to talk about the movie. Go listen to her. I'll take care of this."

"I have a better idea." He grabbed the ice bucket and the bag, and her free hand. "Let's both go. You'll know more than me."

And for one instant, as he moved around her, to tug her gently into the living room, he was close enough to kiss. And to her amazement, he didn't duck away this time. He simply bent, touched his lips to hers lightly without even closing his eyes. A hint of a smile crinkled his eyes and he pulled her quickly into the other room before she had a chance to respond.

He pushed her gently into a chair, and then took a moment to touch Crystal's head. "Want anything, kiddo? Some limeade?"

"No, thanks." She frowned. "What's the ice for?"

Marissa said, "Sprain. No big deal." She started taking off the elastic bandage, swallowing to keep her face free of expression. She jumped up. "I'll take care of this, really. Just give me the ice and I'll do it in the kitchen."

Robert gave Crystal a glance. "I think that arm's hurtin' pretty good. What do you say?"

Crystal nodded. "Might as well let him just look at it, Ms. Pierce. You ain't getting out of here till he does. It's that soldier thing."

"Don't expect me to salute," Marissa said. Tears sprang to her eyes when he gently unwrapped it, and the sudden lack of support caused her to move the wrist the smallest bit before he managed to get his hand beneath it.

''That hurt,'' he said.

It really did. Blinking fiercely, she tried to focus on the sensation of that hard, flat palm beneath hers, but not even the glorious Robert could distract her just then. ''Ice,'' she said sharply.

He glanced up at her, a half smile on his mouth. ''Ice will help for a minute, but it's not a sprain. It's always hard to know for sure, but just guessing, I'd say this is broken.''

''I can still move my fingers and everything,'' she protested, and would have illustrated, but he caught them before she could.

''Don't.''

''I had my wrist pads on,'' she said, and hated the querulousness of her voice. ''Oh, I feel stupid. Maybe I'm too old for in-line skating.''

''No way, Ms. Pierce. You're cool.'' Crystal shifted a little. ''Mario, this good friend of mine, he loves anything on wheels—in-line skates, skateboards, bikes. He was always breaking something, and he's only eighteen.''

Marissa smiled. ''Thank you.''

''You can't drive with this,'' Robert said, ''and I can't leave Crystal, so who do you want me to call?''

She sighed. ''Louise of course.''

He chuckled. ''Of course.'' He put her hand down gently on her knee. ''Don't move a muscle for a sec. I'll get you fixed up and then call Louise.'' He jumped up.

Marissa was so disappointed she wanted to wail like a five-year-old. *Not fair, not fair, not fair.* She looked up and saw Crystal watching her very closely.

Too distracted herself, Marissa said, ''So, who is Mario?''

''Just a friend,'' she said without emotion, and turned

over on her back, clicking the television on. Her mouth was set in a resigned kind of line.

Marissa almost asked, "Is something wrong?" but bit the words back in time. She knew very well what was wrong, that Crystal had observed the subtle interplay between the two adults.

Robert returned with a sheaf of newspaper which he wrapped in a thick bundle around her wrist. "Louise is on the way."

Marissa managed a small smile. "To the rescue."

"Cheer up. They'll have you fixed up and home in no time."

# Chapter 8

Crystal did not feel all that great the next day. The pain in her back and belly had stopped, but now there was a jumpy irritation in her limbs, along the back of her neck. The doctor told her the drugs might make her feel this way. Walking cautiously to the truck, leaning on Robert, there was a part of her screaming, *Hurry up! Move it. Do something.*

"I don't want to go to some white lady's house," she said suddenly. "I don't know her. She probably thinks of me as a project." Even as she said it, she knew it wasn't true, wanted to take the words back.

Robert looked at her in surprise. He'd been about to put the keys in the ignition, but let them fall beside him. "Okay," he said easily. "Tyler won't mind if I miss a day or two of work." He smiled. "Gives me a good excuse to play hooky."

Even that friendly smile was kind of irritating. She slumped lower. "No, never mind. We need the money.

We're not rich like all these people.'' She gestured at the town in general. ''I know that.''

By now Crystal's mother would have been shouting at her, but Robert only said, ''What's going on, kiddo? Who are you mad at?''

''Nobody.'' Which wasn't exactly true. ''Everybody.''

''Me?'' He stretched out a hand and put it on her shoulder, steady and warm.

Yeah. Because he had that look in his eye when he looked at Ms. Pierce, and she had it back, and it wasn't fair. When adults wanted to have sex, that's when life for Crystal went downhill. She found herself chewing on her little fingernail and put her hand down. ''You like her, don't you?'' she said.

''Who? Mrs. Forrest?''

She rolled her eyes. ''No. My teacher.''

He narrowed his eyes a little, not looking away, which was good. But thinking how to answer her, which was bad. ''I do, a little.''

''I knew it.''

''Look, Crystal, I'm not gonna lie or hide things from you, okay? I'll be honest as I can be—and here is my promise. No matter what happens, I'm here for you. As long as you need me, nothing and nobody will ever come before you.'' He put his hand to his chest. ''Cross my heart and hope to die.''

Now that really made her cry. Big tears just welled up and fell down her face. She nodded.

''C'mon,'' he said. ''Let's go in and I'll fix you some eggs for breakfast. How's that? Scrambled with icky American cheese, just the way you like them.''

That wasn't what she wanted, either, for him to miss work. And she liked Mrs. Forrest, who had promised to watch movies with her and cook green chili, which Crystal had confessed was her absolute favorite. She craved it every single day—almost like those people she'd read about who ate clay because they didn't have enough iron in their bodies—and Crystal already knew from the smell that first night that the chili would be good.

"No, I'll go to Mrs. Forrest's house."

"Sure? It's really okay with me if you don't want to."

"I'm sure." Blinking back tears, she looked at Robert. "I don't know what's wrong with me. I feel all weird."

"Ah! It's the drug, honey. Remember? Ramona told you it might make you jumpy."

"Oh, yeah." Not that it helped, knowing why. "We better go. I don't want you to be late to work."

They were, she saw by the clock, already late, but Robert took a minute to squeeze her hand and give her that wink. "You and me, kiddo, all the way."

And in that minute, she loved him more than anybody in the whole world. Except Mario and the baby of course, but it was close. She nodded. "Thanks, Uncle."

Marissa's wrist had indeed suffered a hairline fracture, which she should have known since Victoria had warned her. Odd how even the warnings they gave each other ended up acting out the same way. Not the same day or the same week, but their lives mirrored each other's so often that it would only make sense to listen. Marissa hadn't asked, but she knew instinctively that Victoria had broken the right wrist instead of the left, just as Marissa was right-handed, leftbrained, math-and-logic oriented, while Victoria was left-handed, rightbrained and one living creative nerve.

Hairline fracture made it sound tiny and harmless, but

Marissa spent a miserable night. In spite of the painkillers they gave her, she had wild dreams and awakened several times to the idea that her arm was being bitten through by a tiger's teeth, or caught in a door. She woke up cranky, groggy, slightly hung over from the painkillers. She flirted with the idea of calling a sub, but needed to get to school to pick up assignments for Crystal anyway and decided to just get through it the best she could.

The phone rang when she was on her second cup of coffee. She could always sense her sister, and it wasn't her this time. "Hello?"

"How's the arm?" Robert asked.

She closed her eyes, shutting out everything so she could just listen to that lilting tenor. "I have a bright blue cast to my elbow."

A hint of laughter as he said, "Mmm. Sexy. You can wear it with that dress."

Sexy. The word, low and edged with amusement, made her think of his hair. She cleared her throat. "How's Crystal?"

"Safely under Louise's wing. She's done double duty on the mother front lately."

"Good. Do you want me to collect her assignments for the next few days so she doesn't get behind?"

"That would be excellent. She'll be at Louise's until five or so. Might be a good idea to take them there."

Marissa thought of Crystal's measuring expression yesterday, the disappointment she'd sensed in the girl. "Okay."

He was silent for a long time, and Marissa wasn't sure what was supposed to come next. She twirled the phone cord around her finger, waiting, thinking of his hair. "Well, I just wanted to make sure you were all right. See ya around."

Ouch. "Okay. Thank you for calling, Robert," she said formally, and replaced the receiver gently, a thick taste of missed opportunity in her mouth.

But things happened the way they were meant to—Robert was right to put Crystal's well-being above everything else. As her teacher, Marissa had the same responsibility.

She just wished it didn't have to be a choice. Still, her sister would be here on Thursday, only three days away, and Marissa would have something to distract herself. In a few weeks, she'd forget about ever kissing the devastating Red Dog, count it as a sweet little something along her path.

Right after school, Marissa got a copy of Crystal's schedule and went to the teachers one by one to explain what was going on and to pick up her assignments. Most of them were harried—the seniors were as restless as wild mustangs, and the rest of them had spring fever—and simply scribbled out assignments. The science teacher was more interested. "Poor kid," George Dugan said. "She's had a pretty rough time, hasn't she?"

"I think so. But she has someone in her corner now and that can make all the difference."

"She's smart as a whip, but has no self-confidence." He flipped open his grade book, ran his finger down a column of names. "Is she keeping the baby, do you know?"

"I haven't asked."

He scowled at the line of red marks behind Crystal's name. "You know, it's going to take a miracle for her to pass this class. She hasn't turned in homework, and refuses to participate in the group experiments." He tapped the line with his finger. "Not sure what we should do."

"What if she created and carried out an experiment on her own? Is it possible she could at least pass?"

"I'm open to that." He closed the book and put his hands on his hips. "Tell you what. I'll give her till the end of the week to come up with a hypothesis and experiment, anything to do with the earth sciences."

Marissa beamed. "Terrific. Thanks."

"It's nice you took an interest." He smiled. "I wasn't sure about you when you started, but you're a good teacher, Marissa. Whatever your reasons for coming to slum with us here, I'm glad you did."

She tried not to mind the taint to the compliment. "Thank you. I love it."

The last stop was the English teacher's room. Marissa tapped lightly. Marianne Wollinski was intimidating. Tall and bosomy, with a wealth of silvery blond hair she wore in a French twist, she had the commanding presence of a general, and the same standards. She insisted upon calling all the teachers by their titles, and expected the same in return. "Good afternoon, Ms. Pierce. Is there something I can do for you?"

The room was as neat as a diagrammed sentence. "Yes. I'm collecting assignments for one of our students who is going to miss most of the week, thanks to a problem with her pregnancy."

"Crystal Avila." A tight, hard smile. Mrs. Wollinski did not approve of pregnant girls being allowed in school.

"Yes." Marissa squared her shoulders. "Do you have assignments for her?"

"I don't know what the point would be, since she never completes them." A heavy silver cuff fell forward as she adjusted a blotter on her desk. "I have a good many students who are hungry for what I offer and I don't know why I should waste my time with one who is so obviously uninterested."

"She is hardly uninterested." Marissa crossed her arms. "Yesterday we watched *Cruel Intentions,* and she dissected the entire underlying structure of tragedy, comparing and contrasting the modern, watered-down version with the original *Dangerous Liaisons.*"

She waved a hand. "Movies. Yes, I know all about her passion for movies. I am not a film instructor. I am engaged in teaching literature."

"I see." A thick burn heated her throat and chest. "Where, exactly, was she going to find books?"

"Oh, please, Ms. Pierce, even poor children can go to the library."

"Not if the library is across town, and in order to get to it you have to get on a bus because your mother doesn't have a car, but getting on that bus means you have to cross through the gang territory of three rival gangs."

Marissa made it up, but only a little. The fund-raiser she had attended earlier this week had been to raise funds for a desperately poor area of Denver. She knew the generalities of Crystal's situation, if not the specifics.

"She couldn't go to the store without crossing those paths. The school she attended was riddled with the fights and violence that was part of her daily life, so she didn't go." Furious now, she took a step closer. "She locked herself in her room and watched movies because she was desperate for the transportation of story, and she found those stories where she could—on a stolen cable box one of her mother's boyfriends rigged up. That room, with those movies, was the only place she was safe. And if you'd give her ten minutes of opportunity, you would be amazed what she knows about structure. You would be astonished at her command of literary concepts. She might not know what to call them, but she might gain the vocabulary from someone like you, *if you don't dismiss her.*"

The discreetly penciled brows rose. "What would you like me to do?"

"Give her a chance. That's all."

"Very well." She crossed her arms. "Have her write me a paper, fifteen pages, with footnotes and sources, on that subject you mentioned. Let her analyze the tragedy in *Dangerous Liaisons.*" The lips pursed. "I'll give her twenty points free on grammar mistakes, and allow some informality in writing style. But make it plain that I do not want a single word of reference to that awful melodrama *Titanic.*"

A soft, clear bell of recognition rang in Marissa's head. *They always think I like it for the wrong reasons.* Delighted to have this new puzzle piece, she smiled beneficently at Mrs. Wollinski. "Thank you." She moved forward, shook her hand. "You won't be sorry."

"We'll see."

At the restoration site of the old mansion, Robert stepped back and admired the new plasterwork on the receiving room ceiling with pleasure. He held up a black-and-white photograph of the original ceiling, and the new one matched perfectly, in every tiny swirl. "Great work," he said to the plastering crew.

"Thanks, boss."

He glanced at his watch. It was almost four—no point to starting anything new so late in the day. "Go ahead and knock off if you want."

"Robert," Tyler Forrest said, stepping carefully around a scaffold. "Can I talk to you for a minute?" He held a clean manila folder in his hand, and Robert figured it was more original photographs. Tyler's wife, Anna, ran a museum in town, and had been ceaselessly working to come up with photos of the original mansion.

"Sure. Find some more pictures?"

"Yeah." His grin was infectious. Whatever it was was good. They stepped out on the porch where the light was better, and Tyler handed over a picture of the stairway, terrifically well detailed. It was beautifully worked wood, amazingly detailed. "She found them in some file in the basement of the Tacker House."

"Fantastic." Robert ignored the giant stained-glass window, though he found himself intrigued once again by the mythological aspects of it. "You've got your work cut out for you, I'd say."

"Yeah, well." He took out another photo. "I'm hoping you do, too. Here's a close-up of the original window."

Robert took the photo, already formulating objections. He whistled softly. "It's a beauty."

"Anna said it's Demeter."

"Such a loss," he said quietly, thinking of the scores of windows he'd seen in Europe, many of them hundreds of years old.

"Can you do it?"

Robert raised his head and grinned. "I keep telling you no way. Not this big, man."

"You've done church windows. This can't be any bigger than that. Jake said there's one you did in some little New Mexico town that's bigger."

"Indian churches. A different thing. They wanted an Indian artist, didn't matter how good or not."

Tyler inclined his head. He wasn't a man given to grinning, but the amusement shone in his eyes. "Give me a break."

Robert shook his head. "I'm flattered, man, but I'm not the artist for this job."

"Will you at least think about it? We've made inquiries, and no one can do the work for at least seven or eight months."

A car pulled in, and Marissa jumped out, waving her blue-casted hand. She wore a simple white dress today, a completely ordinary, straight, sleeveless sheath with a demure neckline, and yet he felt a sizzle straight through his body.

"Maybe," he said to Tyler, forgetting him as he stepped down to meet her. She looked radiant, her cheeks rosy, her hair mussed a little by the wind, but quickly smoothed down. "Hi," he said, and heard the warmth in his tone. "What are you doing here?"

"It's *Titanic,* isn't it?" she asked. "Crystal's movie of movies."

He grinned, putting his hands on his hips. "And I thought that big smile was for me."

A flicker of uncertainty dimmed the vividness of her eyes. "I wish you'd get your signals straight. Or is that part of your game, to keep a woman off balance?"

"No game, Marissa." Dangerous territory, that. He switched direction. "*Titanic* is right. She's almost sixteen. What else could have hit her that hard?"

She frowned a little. "I don't think that's it with Crystal. It's not the teenager thing with her."

"Maybe not." One part of his mind kept up the conversation while another, earthier part was imagining her small neat hands on his body, imagining all that enthusiasm focused on him.

And he realized this was exactly what Crystal was afraid of. That his interest in Marissa would end up leaving Crystal out. He crossed his arms. "When she showed up on my doorstep, she had a backpack with her. Three pairs of socks, four pairs of underwear, all the makeup she owns and a copy of that movie. She watches it over and over."

Marissa grinned. "Thanks." She turned back to her car. "I'm going to take her homework over to her now. See you."

He nodded.

She popped back up. "Robert, one of the teachers asked me today if she's going to keep the baby. Has she said?"

"We haven't talked about it, but I'm guessing she will. Not a word."

"I just wondered." She got back in the car and, with a little wave, drove off. Robert watched her for a minute, then went back inside. "I'm knocking off for the day," he said. "I'm going to go rescue your mother, take Crystal home."

"Is that where Marissa's going?"

"Got a reason for asking that, bro?" Robert unbuckled the tool belt around his waist.

Tyler smiled enigmatically. "No reason."

But even though Robert only stopped long enough to wash his face and hands, he wasn't quick enough to catch Marissa at Louise's. It was almost embarrassing how disappointed he was. Covering, he winked at Louise. "How's my girl this afternoon?"

Louise frowned. "She's sleeping right now. Why don't you come on in and have something cool to drink?"

But before they moved from the door, Marissa pulled

up and got out of the car with a big bouquet of flowers and a bag in her hands. When she got to the door, she said, "We have to stop meeting like this." A glitter in her eye said she knew he'd come to try and catch her, and she liked it.

"Oh, aren't you a doll," Louise said. "Such a pretty arrangement!"

Marissa brushed by Robert and he was enveloped suddenly in her scent, that expensive, exclusive cosmetic smell. It clung to her hair and her neck; he would smell it on her belly, on her legs. He found himself admiring the curve of her ear, and shook himself. "Is something wrong with Crystal?" he asked, more harshly than he intended.

Louise waved them to the kitchen, and repressing his impatience, he followed, along with Marissa, who was really much smaller than he. How was it possible he hadn't noticed before? Her head only came to his shoulder.

"It's not the physical thing I'm worried about," Louise said. "There's something else going on with her." She frowned. "Do you know anything at all about the boy involved?"

"Nothing," he said. "She won't say a word."

Louise sighed. "Can't say for sure, but that's where the big pain is, with the boy."

"Maybe," Robert said slowly.

"Is there any chance she was abused? Raped or something?"

A lump formed in his gut. "Of course there is. I like to think she'd say so, but the chance is she wouldn't." It made him sick to even consider it.

"I don't think that's it," Marissa said. "I think it's her friend. Somehow she lost him."

"How do you know that?"

She lifted her shoulders. "If he ran away from the pregnancy, she wouldn't have that softness in her voice when she says his name."

"Right," Louise said. "She'd be grief stricken or full of hate."

"I don't know what that changes," Robert said gruffly. "He's gone, one way or another."

"I don't know, either. But maybe you need to find out."


Crystal heard their voices very plainly. The guest room was on the other side of the kitchen wall. She heard them talking, worrying about her, and in a way it made her feel pretty good. That anyone would spend that much time trying to figure her out. It made her want to tell them.

But lying there in the dark, cocooned with pillows and the lemon-scented coverlet, she thought of Mario, testing the possibility of talking about him, and she suddenly couldn't breathe. The thick tears that had threatened all day rolled down her cheeks, silent and hot, as she closed her eyes and thought of him.

Mario. Her best friend since she was six years old. The only one she could ever trust completely. His bedroom was across the vacant lot where a house had burned down three years before, and they'd learned Morse code to talk to each other in the middle of the night. At ten, they made a pact to stay away from the gangs and somehow get out of the neighborhood together. They watched each other's backs. He kept her fed when her mother spent all the food stamps on trades with her friends for cigarettes and booze. He hid her when the sicko from around the corner started eyeing her. In return, Crystal helped him with his math, kept an eye out for Johnny Penasco who wanted to beat him up.

They had never intended to have sex. The kissing started a long time ago, when they were thirteen and fifteen. Just a natural thing, one day, obvious. They would get married someday, and keep taking care of each other—it was understood. They loved each other. And really, she'd thought about it so many times before he did it, finally, in the back stairway of her building. They'd run there to hide one night, because word on the street was that the 50s, the worst gang in the neighborhood, had a beef and had their guns.

Sitting in the dark, looking through the window to the moon, it was almost possible to believe they lived somewhere normal. Crystal put her head on his shoulder, natural as breathing, and finally he just bent down and pressed his lips to hers. They didn't really know how to do it, but they learned.

They didn't let anybody know. And they were careful to stop before they got too hot. At least for a long, long time. A long time.

But one night, Crystal's mother and boyfriend had a fight, a very loud fight, with broken glass and furniture turned over, and both of them were arrested. Crystal hid in her room, way back in the back of the closet, so they wouldn't put her in juvie for the night. And when everything was calm, Mario showed up.

She was shaking and scared and he settled her in her bed, then lay down beside her, the way they'd done a hundred times before. He smelled so good. He was thin, but strong, from lifting boxes at the grocery where he worked, and he smelled like oranges. He didn't want anything from her. He touched her, the way he often did. But it was the first time they'd ever been alone anywhere warm, and it was awfully hard to resist the temptation of finally just taking off their shirts to lie side by side.

Crystal squeezed her eyes shut with a little cry. It was her fault. All of it was her fault. Because she was the one who'd kept going. Who wanted to feel all of him. They hadn't been much better at all of that than they had at the kissing at first, but they did practice. A lot. Over and over.

And it was like every boy in the whole neighborhood knew it, because they were on her like they never had been before. Mario had to fight sometimes. His mother started cursing the gangbangers, right in public, and everybody knew that was dangerous. Crazy.

*Oh, Mario,* she thought, wrapping her hands around her belly. *I'm so sorry.*

She buried her face in the covers, in the quilts, and never wanted to move. Louise would let her stay, Crystal knew she would. And somehow this was safer. Safer because she wouldn't gently lean down and say to her, like her uncle would, "I'll be here for you."

How could he be? He wanted to. She knew that. But life didn't work that way. Even when you wanted to be there for someone, you couldn't always do it. She knew that better than anyone.

# Chapter 9

By the time she got home, Marissa was in no mood for a walk. Her arm hurt, more than she wanted to admit, and when Ramona called to cancel, citing an emergency, she was relieved. Restlessly she roamed the house, feeling as if her mind was filled with noise—the teacher who'd made her angry, and Crystal's sorrow, and…everything. She found herself in the kitchen, peering into the fridge for something delectable to eat.

It was a startling moment. She only became aware of it after a long minute, maybe two, when she'd been bent, staring restlessly at the contents long enough that her neck got cold.

She closed the door and took a deep breath, closed her eyes. Was it really food she wanted? She tested her stomach—yes, it was hungry. That interesting hollow feeling. She hadn't been feeling that well this morning and had gone light on breakfast. Lunch had been in the cafeteria since it was a duty day—wilted iceberg lettuce drowned in dressing and a truly disgusting rigatoni.

What sounded excellent, then? She was tempted to turn around and look through the cupboards for ideas, but resisted, turning into her hungers instead. Avocados. Mmm, yeah. Cheese—a nice musky goat cheese, maybe. Yes. Wine. Oh, yes. A valpolicella, dense and red. And—oh, siren—focaccia dipped in olive oil.

She opened her eyes and grinned, then turned around to look at the calendar, checking off the days in her cycle. Bingo. In the middle of her menstrual cycle, she wanted this kind of food, dense with fat and nutrients. Resisting only caused a binge, but she also knew it would be a bad idea to go to the grocery store in this state. She'd come home with all kinds of weird things that would look strange tomorrow. Instead, she called the upscale grocer who catered to the ski-lodge set, put in her order and went upstairs to take a shower.

But the phone rang before she made it to the stairs. Raising her cast, with a smile, she picked up the phone and said, "You were right. It's broken."

"I don't know why you don't listen to me."

"I know." With a pinch in her chest, she curled close, holding the phone next to her shoulder. "I guess it's because I haven't seen you in so long, and now you're really going to be here, but I miss you terribly all of a sudden."

"Me, too. I have so much to tell you." She laughed wickedly. "Show you."

"So do I." The doorbell rang and Marissa said, "That's my groceries."

"Save some for me."

"Will do." She hung up and dashed to the front door, swinging it open and grabbing for her purse in one smooth motion. "That was fast!" she said, and then registered who it was standing there.

His hair was down, a thick, glossy curtain falling across one shoulder and down his back, framing that intensely Native American face. He'd showered since she'd seen him last, and put on a clean white shirt, plain as bread, but somehow all the more compelling for that. A twist of silver twined around one wrist, making his skin seem very dark, his hand all the more elegant.

"Hi," he said, as if he weren't sure of his welcome.

Marissa realized she was gaping at him. "Hi. Anything wrong?"

"Not really." He tucked his hands in his front pockets, kicked out a booted foot. "Crystal wanted to stay with Louise. Thought I'd see if you wanted to get some supper or something."

Or something. Yes, that definitely. "Truth is, I just ordered my dinner. It's sort of a strange collection, but I'd be glad to share. We can take it out in the backyard."

He shifted, looked out toward the street. "I'd rather go out," he said, and swung his gaze around to hers. A lift of one shoulder, acknowledging the chemistry between them.

Go out. In public. With the most heavily-lusted-over male in Red Creek. She grinned, and he gave her a puzzled expression. "What?"

"Don't suppose I could talk you into going to the country club?"

He got it. A quick twinkle in the dark eyes. "Thinking of a little revenge, eh?"

She raised her eyebrows. "One does hate to waste such a splendid opportunity."

"Honored as I am to be a trophy guy for an evening, I'll have to pass on the country club."

"Oooh, sorry. I didn't mean like that." Marissa realized they were still standing on either side of the threshold. "I only... It was just—" She widened her eyes, sighing. "I'm only making it worse."

He grinned. "I knew what you meant. I'm flattered."

"Good." She pushed open the door. "Come in and let me change."

She opened the screen door and he took it. He came close, took a breath, shook his head, a faint grin on his wide, mobile mouth. "I come within five feet of you, princess," he said ruefully, "and my heart starts pounding. That doesn't happen to me."

It gave her a quick rush of emotion, that sudden, plain, honesty. All the details that electrified her came together—the blurry breadth of his shoulders at the periphery of her vision, that long, healthy, gleaming hair, his dark throat and sharply cut jaw, his long, dark eyes and high cheekbones. "Me, too," she confessed quietly, lifting a hand to touch the tiny scars down the side of his face. She realized with a start what they were. "They were tears, weren't they? Tattoos?"

He flinched away. "Good guess."

A car door slammed outside and the delivery boy from the grocer came up the walk, carrying the bags. She paid him, tipped him well enough that he grinned happily and turned back. Robert watched her intently. "What is it?" she asked.

"Nothing," he said gruffly, and took the bags from her. "Go change. I'll put these away for you."


Robert took her to a small Mexican restaurant, run by a family—the mother and father and kids all taking part. Marissa walked in, breathed in deeply and groaned. "Oh, this is a dangerous place, I can tell."

"Dangerous?" He gave her a perplexed little smile. "How so?"

She closed her eyes. "I ordered groceries to be delivered because I am in one of those hungry moods and I was afraid to go to the grocery store. This is even worse." She closed her eyes. "I smell enchiladas, smothered in cheese, and tortilla chips begging for salsa. And margaritas. Oh, I do love margaritas!"

Robert laughed. "I love a hungry woman. I was afraid you wouldn't like it."

A young girl, maybe seven, under the tutelage of an older sister or cousin, led them to a booth by a window that overlooked the grassy center of town. Marissa settled. "There are not many foods I dislike," she said wryly.

"You know, I didn't stop to think that you've been dieting for ages. Would you rather go somewhere else?"

"No," she said firmly. "I can be sensible." She opened the menu. "But I really must have one of those margaritas I smell. Do you like them?"

"Took the oath," he said.

"Ah. Should I abstain then?"

"Nope." He grinned at her over the big menu. "I can be sensible."

"Good." Marissa read the menu, her mouth watering—and stomach growling. Avocado had been on her mind already, so she decided on the guacamole tostadas. Beans for the fiber and nutrition, but no rice, which had very little of either. "And please hold the cheese," she told the waitress. The chips were, dietarily speaking, expensive, as was the margarita, but she was pleased with herself for her order, and didn't even feel a twinge of envy when Robert ordered a monster burrito with the works. Sheepishly he said, "I worked hard today."

"You work hard every day." She picked three large tortilla chips from the basket, freshly fried, still hot, and put them on her napkin. "Put that basket on your side of the table, please, sir."

"Gotcha." He pulled the basket to his side of the booth. "Is it rude to ask you about that weight loss thing?"

"Not at all. What do you want to know?" She broke the chips into three pieces each and dipped one into the chunky salsa. "Oh, that's great salsa! I can't believe I've never been here."

"I'm curious mainly why you started dieting. You always seemed to be really comfortable before. Had a long string of boyfriends, plenty of money—I mean, why bother?"

It wasn't the kind of question she was expecting. "I guess," she said slowly, "I just got tired of myself. It wasn't healthy. I was twenty-four years old and couldn't walk up a flight of stairs without gasping for breath." She found his gaze a little too attentive, and she plucked one of her chips from the napkin and looked at it, considering.

Then, thinking of his simple honesty at her house, made a decision to do the same. Just be herself. "I got sick of waiting for someone to ask me to dance. Waiting for that really gorgeous guy across the room to notice me. Waiting for someone to see beyond…the externals to the real me."

"And did everything change?"

She looked over her shoulder to the room full of locals. "When we walked in, Robert, every woman in this restaurant took one look at you and wished she was me." She raised her eyebrows. "That's a fat girl's dream."

A frown flickered between his brows. "Doesn't really seem fair, does it?"

"No," she said. "But it's real. You had tears tattooed on your face once," she said, changing the subject to him. "Isn't that a symbol of grief or fallen comrades?"

"How do you know something like that?"

"Don't try to wiggle out of the question, Mr. Martinez. I just know. And you had them removed at some point. Why?"

"I was in the army," he said slowly. "It was a great world to me at first—so orderly and disciplined. I loved the hell out of it. And an officer took me aside one day and told me I could probably advance in rank a lot faster if I got rid of the facial tattoos." He lifted a shoulder. "So I did."

"Reality," she said, smiling. "People judge us by how we look."

"So they do." He leaned back lazily. "And I gotta say, babe, the new look is pretty hot."

Marissa laughed. "Thank you."

He inclined his head, speculatively, and his hair swished in a heavy, glossy spill over his arm. Unbelievably extravagant, that hair. She had visions of burying her face in it, of the way it might feel on *her* shoulders. Her bare shoulders. He said something, but Marissa was so lost in her little fantasies that she only caught the end. "...like a dieter."

"What?" she said. "I'm sorry, my mind was wandering. I missed the first part."

The long dark eyes tilted the slightest bit, that almost-smile she'd come to recognize, as if he knew where she'd let her imagination go. "I said, 'You don't eat like a dieter.'"

She shook her head. "Diets don't work—and believe

me, I've been on every single one ever invented. Low
fat, low carb, high protein, grapefruit twelve times a day,
shakes—everything. The only things that work are the
simple things. Move your body, figure out what the bad
habits are and think up new ones. I changed one thing
every week. Just one.''

"Like what?''

"Robert, this can't possibly be interesting to you.''

"Sure it is. *You're* interesting.''

She looked away for a moment, then back to him.
"There are much more interesting things about me than
my path to weight loss.''

His gaze was straight, direct. "You know, most people never make a really big change in their lives. They
just stick with the program, like it's a big game of seven-
card stud, never realizing they can get rid of a couple
cards and try some others.''

She laughed. "Gambler metaphors! I love it.''

"A man goes with what he knows.'' He winked, then
polished off the chips and gestured to the waiter for
more. "You tossed back a card you didn't like and took
a chance on a new one. That's pretty brave.''

"Thank you.'' She toasted him with her margarita.

"So, what kind of changes did you make every week?
You never know, Crystal's probably right. My family
runs to fat big-time along about forty.''

She picked up her heavy goblet, admiring the green
color of the drink, and the look of the kosher salt around
the rim. "One of the first things I did was to *look* at my
food. Look at every bite, and think about it.'' She lifted
it to her lips, then paused. "This is going to look seductive, but I'm not trying to turn you on or anything.''
She licked a little salt off the glass to get the salt in her
mouth and then took a measured sip of margarita and

closed her eyes. "Salt and sweet and sour and that bite of tequila." She opened her eyes and looked at him. "Perfect. But in the old days, I would have gulped it, feeling guilty that I even wanted it."

He licked his bottom lip, slowly, and grinned. "Made my mouth water."

"Me or the margarita?"

He laughed—that rough, unfamiliar, thrilling sound. "Both."

In that instant, Marissa felt a stab of something hot and terrifying. She really *liked* him. There was a good helping of lust, she wouldn't deny that. She was dying to dive into his hair, kiss him until her knees would no longer hold her, but in that instant, when he laughed his rusty laugh, she felt a vivid shift. She liked *him*. Liked who she became in his company, liked the easy way he was himself without apology, liked even the slight vulnerability she glimpsed now and then.

He must have seen some of that in her eyes. "What?"

She shook her head, smiling lightly. "Nothing."

They lingered a long time after their plates were cleared away. Robert told stories of his army days, making her laugh with all the absurd, strange, alarming things that went on in the service. He discovered that he enjoyed her amusement so much that he scoured his mind for more, finding himself grinning along as he watched the flash of her white teeth, admired the line of her jaw.

The margarita loosened her, made her cheeks rosy, her eyes as vivid as a blue jay's tail, and she grew more confident, more expansive. Not quite as expansive as the night he'd gone to her house the first time, but a man could hope. "Want another one?"

She laughed. "No, thank you. I'm quite chatty enough already, don't you think?"

That was one word for it, but he thought a better one was *charismatic*. The waiter kept finding excuses to stop by the table and flirt in a demure and admiring way. A man in a booth across the room hadn't taken his eyes off her for more than three seconds the entire time they sat here. When she laughed, there was such exuberance in it that even women looked up and smiled, too.

He lifted a brow. "Can't blame a guy for trying."

A woman abruptly showed up at the edge of the table. "Marissa? Oh, my God! It *is* you!"

Robert repressed a scowl. The woman was a country club gal—that ever-so-perfectly-frosted hair, gelled into perfect messiness; even a sweater tied around her neck. But Marissa shot him a mischievous little glance and he couldn't rob her of a moment. "Julie! It's been ages. How are you?"

"I'm fine." She put a hand on her hip. "You know I kept thinking you looked familiar, but I didn't figure it out until a minute ago. How much weight have you lost? A hundred pounds?"

The grin slipped a little. "Close," she said.

"I can't believe it." She smiled again at Robert, and he caught a strange little tail of something in it. "At least your choice of company has improved."

"Robert Martinez, this is Julie Allen," Marissa said.

"Pleased to meet you." Brightly the woman turned back. "Well, you should stop by. I'm off to Switzerland at the end of May, but come by and we'll have a drink."

"I'll look forward to it," Marissa said.

"You're welcome to come along," Julie said with bright falsity to Robert.

He only nodded, aware of an odd shutting down in

Marissa, a dimming of the light that had been radiating from her only a moment before.

"Nice to see you," Julie said, waving her fingers. Robert watched her return to her table and bend over urgently to her companion, a hale fellow in a ski sweater, then looked back at Marissa. Her smile was gone, and the light, and everything else he'd spent the whole evening reveling in.

"Why do you let her do that?"

"I don't know what you mean," Marissa said. She ran a finger along the line of her cast.

"Steal away all that—" he sought a word that captured it "—joy. That's why she did it, you know. Couldn't stand to have you over here enjoying yourself when she's clearly miserable."

"Oh, please," she said. "You sound just like my mother. 'Oh, honey, they're just jealous.'"

He grabbed her hand before she retreated entirely, grabbed it and pulled it over to him, raising the palm to his mouth. "I don't know about the others, but, babe, she was jealous." The feeling of her soft, clean palm against his mouth was so rich, so right, he kissed it again.

"You're awfully good for my ego." She sighed, and he saw a little of the cheer come back.

"You're pretty good for mine." He let her go. "Let's get out of here."

She smiled. "Great idea."

He helped her with her sweater and took her hand, inclining his head at the blonde at the booth. Outside, in the brisk night, he halted in front of the window. "Let's give her something to talk about, huh?" he said, catching Marissa close.

"What do you—"

He kissed her. Slid his hand around the back of her neck, his other against her face, and bent to capture her mouth. He told himself to make it look good, to make it hot and tender at once, because that woman in there had never had tender.

But he didn't have to pretend. This wasn't like the last time, when the touch of their lips had caused an explosion. This was sweet. The taste of salt and chili and tequila on her lips, the softness of her breath sighing out of her mouth. Gently he tasted that full mouth, easily their tongues tangled, exploring, wondering.

He'd intended just to make it look good. But he found himself lingering, shifting a little to draw her into a loose embrace, close enough that her breasts pushed a little into his chest, that she had to put her arms around his waist, that he could touch her neck beneath her hair. All the while kissing her slowly, so slowly, so deeply. A kind of brilliance seemed to seep through him, like a submarine's spotlights cutting the gloom in the depths of the ocean in Crystal's movie.

When the first jagged threads of red spiked through him—sexual hunger—he lifted his head a little, touching his thumb to her jaw. Her eyes opened slowly, and she only gazed up at him, her expression serious. "Was that for her?"

"No," he said quietly. "I don't think it was."

"Neither do I." She lifted a hand and touched his hair, just let a swath of it pour over the outside of her hand. "Did you wear your hair down on purpose to tempt me?"

He grinned. "Guilty."

"It's working."

But sex tonight, right now, was too much. Dangerous

for reasons he didn't care to examine too closely. "I'll wear it down again."

"Promise?"

"Cross my heart and hope to die." He pulled away, took her hand and went back to his truck. They were quiet, not in awkwardness, but a strange, deep kind of calmness as he drove back to her place. A deep, soft Van Morrison tune was on the radio, and when he pulled up, Marissa held up her hand. "Do you mind if I listen to the rest of this? It's not much longer."

"Not at all." So they sat there, in the cozy dark, listening to Van sing a soft, bluesy love song.

"My sister has met him," Marissa said. "He's friends with some musician who did the score for her last movie, and she sat with him at a cast party."

"Is your sister an actress?"

"Writer," she said. "I think Crystal will like meeting her."

"Do you think Crystal could write?"

"I don't know. I haven't seen anything she's actually written." A scowl crossed her face. "I didn't tell Crystal, but I will tell you. You need to be careful with that English teacher. She's old school and I think Crystal has had a rough time with her."

He nodded, trying not to bend close and put his mouth against Marissa's neck, right at the spot above her collar where moonlight shone down on it. Some of the same light must have fallen on his wrist, because she raised a finger and traced a line around it. "You have interesting tattoos," she said.

If only she knew. "A lot of them, anyway." He lifted a shoulder.

"Really? More?"

"Yeah," he said gruffly. A lot more, but he didn't

say that. Didn't like to think about it, think about the
fact that if he reached across the cab now and put his
hands on her the way he wanted to do, he would almost
certainly have to reveal them. And maybe that was more
than he wanted this particular woman to see about him
just now.

"Robert," she said quietly, her hand on his. "I'd like
to just kiss you good-night."

It was said almost wistfully, and any resistance he'd
been mustering abruptly collapsed. He turned and bent
his head, keeping his hands firmly on the wheel. At least
for a minute. It was like giving up drink, he thought a
little wildly, feeling himself fall. One taste was too
much, and a thousand would never be enough. The jagged red spike shot through him—sex and something
more than that, something that ached to feel her soft
body against his. She slid free of the seat belt and put
her hands in his hair, stroking her fingers through it, and
made a soft little sound of pleasure.

And suddenly it didn't seem all that important to keep
his hands on the wheel. So much better to put them
against her shoulders, narrow against the heart of his
palms. So much better to let one of his hands slide downward, slowly enough that she could stop him, and cup
one heavy, full breast, the nipple rigid against the last
joint of his middle finger. A nipple that begged to be
stroked, stroked the way he stroked her tongue with his
own, the way his organ longed to be stroked by the hand
combing through his hair.

He rubbed his index finger over that rigid flesh, feeling his sex grow more rigid still, filled with blood rush-
ing to his aid, and her kiss suddenly grew more urgent,
her teeth catching lightly at his lower lip before she
opened, taking his tongue deeper into her mouth.

He heard a rattling groan and realized he'd made the noise himself, made it as he urgently pulled up her shirt, his palm stinging with pleasure as he skimmed it over incredibly soft skin, upward to that heavy breast clasped in some silky something, the nipple easily freed with a small tug on the skimpy cup. He rubbed the edges, thinking of that very dark areola and the contrast with her very white skin, and his organ started to pulse more urgently, the blood thumping with his heartbeat as he touched just the top with one finger, just one—

A knock sounded on the cab, and they broke apart hastily. Marissa jumped so violently she smacked Robert in the nose with her cast, sending scalding pain across the bridge and into his teeth. He yelped, but Marissa was urgently pulling away, straightening her clothes. She rolled down the window. "Mr. Peterson? Is something wrong?"

An older man stood there, scowling. "Your lights are shining right in my window. A person needs sleep, ya know." He stalked away.

"Sorry!" Marissa called. She looked at Robert. "Are you okay? That had to hurt."

"I'll be all right," he said. But it hurt like the devil. Black eyes—hell, he hoped not. "But you'd better get that hot little body inside before we end up having sex in the truck."

"Let's just go have sex inside."

He heard a noise, the sound of his will to resist crumbling. He looked at her for a long moment, trying to summon just one of the many reasons he had come up with not to do this. But she reached out and slid a hand up his leg. "Just for us," she said. "Just for tonight. No one has to know."

A dozen images whirled in his head, all splashed with

vivid color—her glass-blue eyes, the white of her teeth when she laughed, the darkness of her hair, falling in that elegant swathe to her shoulders, the green of the margarita tonight—and the fragments coalesced some-how, rearranged themselves, morphed into that Tiffany screen in her house.

Too much. Too rich. Too dangerous. Gently he kissed her and moved her hand from his raging organ. ''Not tonight, princess.''

She didn't seem to mind. A twinkle lit her eye and she tossed her head. ''Well, if you change your mind, you know where to find me.'' Laughing easily, she opened the door and jumped out, a jaunty little spring in her walk as she went up the sidewalk. From the porch, she turned around and gave him a little wave.

Damn.

## Chapter 10

Louise waited through the first whispers of twilight settling on the mountains, through the first solid nightfall, till the silence of the mountains spread like a warm fur blanket through the house and town, till most of the lights in the valley had winked out.

Only at midnight did she act. She came out of her bath wrapped in a thick chenille robe, noticing that the light was still on beneath the guest room door, just as she'd known it would be. Quietly she made big mugs of cocoa from scratch, sliced some nut bread and carried it all to the room, balancing it on one arm as she knocked gently.

A muffled "Come in" came through the door.

Crystal leaned against the headboard, her eyes red from crying and watching movies for hours and hours back to back. Her hair fell like wrinkled satin ribbons over her arms and shoulders. "Hi," Louise said, closing the door behind her. "I can't sleep, either. Want some cocoa?"

The girl wiped her nose with a tissue. "Okay. If I won't keep you up."

"Heck, no." She settled the tray on a table and gave Crystal the heavy mug. "Older I get, the more I seem to wander, like a ghost, all through the late hours."

A wan smile.

"How 'bout you?" Louise asked. "What's keeping you up?"

Crystal shook her head. "Probably the medicine." She rubbed a place between her eyebrows. "Every time I lie down, I think about—"

Louise sipped her chocolate, waiting. It took a long time, so long she thought maybe she needed to do some prompting, though her usual tack was just to let folk talk. Children, especially, got talked *to* a lot. Giving them room to talk themselves was often all they needed.

But finally Crystal said, "I want to keep my baby."

"I can understand that."

"My boyfriend was the only good thing in my life, ever, till I came here," she said. "Ever, you know? If I give up the baby, it feels like I'm betraying him."

"Mmm." Louise sipped her chocolate. "Betraying him?"

"Yeah," she said heavily. "He lost everything because of me."

"Like what, sugar?"

But Crystal put down her cup and let her head fall on her knees, and began to weep in earnest. Deep, heartfelt, heartbreaking sobs. "I miss him so much!" she cried.

Louise knew that sound. She put her own cup down, climbed up on the bed and put her arms around the girl. "Go ahead and cry, sweetie." She stroked her hair, rocked her back and forth, and Crystal did cry. Not just the leaking tears she had been indulging so easily, but the kind of recognition weep that brought out the truth of a thing.

"He was so good to me," she choked out. "And the gangs got him. I know they did. Nobody knew where he was the next day. Only that the 50s got him. When I went in the alley, I found all this blood. All over. On the walls and the pavement and even some on a trash can." A rigidness in her body, a stiffening at the horror of the memory and a soft, mournful howl. "The police said nobody got killed, but I went to all the hospitals and he wasn't at none of them. I asked and asked.

"And then—" a falling cadence, resignation. "I went to his mom's house and it was empty."

"Oh, darlin'," Louise said, "I'm so sorry."

"I just wish I could find him," she said.

Louise just rocked her. And in a little while, the sad little girl, the brokenhearted woman, the mother-to-be, fell into a hard, slack-mouthed sleep against Louise's grandmotherly bosom, like an exhausted five-year-old. And Louise didn't go anywhere. She held the child in her arms and thought.

And it was good, so good, when her own man came to the door with concern on his brow, his hair ruffled and standing up, to see if everything was okay. When he saw the way of it, his mustache twitched and he nodded, waving a hand.

Marissa was humming as she went inside, literally and not so literally. She put her purse and keys down, locked the door and heard herself singing a lighthearted piece of music that must have been playing at the restaurant. Feeling light as air, she floated upstairs to take off her makeup, her mind flashing little pieces of the evening back to her.

The bathroom was one of her favorite rooms in the house. She'd knocked out one wall to include two dormer windows. An enormous claw-footed tub sat between the windows, and there were ferns hanging from hooks by each one. The walls and floor were finished oak—simple and elegant.

She shed her clothes in the same airy pleasure, pinning up her hair and riffling through the various bottles and boxes of bath scents she kept for one that suited her mood. Green Goddess—oh, yes. She started the water running and poured in a generous handful, inhaling the soft green scent happily.

Robert, Robert, Robert. His name sung over her nerves, down her spine and the backs of her thighs.

She turned and caught sight of herself in the long mirror over the sink.

And just that fast, her mood plummeted, so fast and so far that it felt as if she were falling off a cliff. Because the body she saw in the mirror was not one she wanted him to see. The arms were still too big. The breasts were not as high as she wished. But the worst was her belly—too soft, still too much *of* it.

She thought of him sitting across the table tonight in his white shirt, his body hard and lean and muscular. She could only imagine how perfect he looked without his clothes. How could she bear the mortification of having to be naked with him?

Idiotic thoughts. She closed her eyes. She'd been naked in the past with men who were in much better shape than she. But in those days, it had been a what-you-see-is-what-you-get proposition—her last boyfriend had definitely liked her extra weight. A lot of men did.

But now she looked a lot better with her clothes on than she did with them off. He might be expecting something completely different. He might not—

The doorbell rang.

Victoria! Marissa laughed. Grabbing her robe from the hook, she turned off the water and scrambled down the stairs. It was just like her sister to show up early as a surprise, and with a broad smile, she yanked open the door.

For a moment, she only stared. In all of her life, she had never been wrong on this. She knew when Victoria was on the phone. She could feel her when she was close by.

But it was not Victoria on her porch. It was Robert.

An almost visible aura of tense heat surrounded him, taut and orange, and just the sight of him made the little hairs on her body stand up, every single one, at solid attention. She had one second to remember a flash of his hand on her breast, his mouth on her neck, the thick heat of his sex below her hand.

Then he pulled open the screen, stepped in, turned, closed the door behind him and pushed her against it. "I could have been a murderer," he said roughly, and then bent and kissed her.

And it was like the first time they kissed—a pure, wild, deep explosion of sexual connection. She opened to him completely, taking fistfuls of that hair into her hands and pulling it around her. His hands cupped her buttocks hard, hauling her close. Marissa arched into him in a blistering swell of lust, pressing her breasts against his chest, her belly against his rigid sex. There was nothing in her mind but a sense of utter starvation, of pointed, clear need.

Robert.

In her.

Now.

There was nothing elegant about it. "Condom?" she whispered against his mouth, reaching for his belt buckle.

"Front...left...pocket," he said, pulling open the top of her robe. Air struck her breasts a millisecond before the heat of his hands covered them, and it was so intensely exactly what she wanted that she squeezed her eyes tight for a moment, then stuck her hand in his pocket, closed it on the slippery packets and pulled one out. Safe.

She went back to the belt and zipper, fumbling with it as she kissed him, sucked at his mouth. His hand slid between them and Marissa shifted a little to give him access, biting a little on his lip when his fingers slid home. She let go of a small, tight cry at the sensation of it, hurrying to free him, to touch him, the silky, rigid flesh of his sex leaping into her palm. For a blind space of moments, their hands and bodies collided, breath and skin brushing. Marissa struggled with the condom, tearing at the package with her teeth, and covered him.

With a groan, he suddenly lifted her, and Marissa felt a shock of pleasure at this evidence of his strength, the power of his body. She met his urgency with her own, bracing herself on his shoulders, wrapping her legs around his waist, a faint thought in her mind that she'd done it many times, many ways, but no man had been able to lift her like this against a wall before. But then he grasped her hips in those wide hands, and he plunged.

They both let go of a guttural, amazed cry at the power of it, and halted for one instant, looking in shock at each other, but it was too late to change anything now, and there was so much force of need in Marissa that she wouldn't have let him go anyway. She kissed him, feeling a wild pulse of reaction to the thrust of his tongue and his organ, all together in a violence of need that thrilled and terrified and aroused her. She found herself coming apart too quickly, shattering in completion. A low, deep moan of pleasure escaped her, and she bent forward, biting at his long throat as the waves shook her, then him, his body going still and rigid as he pressed her hard against the door.

"Marissa," he whispered, panting, and pressed his forehead against her neck.

"Don't think," she murmured fiercely, her hands and arms trembling in reaction. "This is now, this is us, that's all."

His body, too, was trembling, and she eased away, put her feet down. He was far more dressed than she, and she pulled her robe together a little, but he caught her hand, and pushed it away. "That night I was here before," he said softly, his hand raising to clasp her breast in one palm, "you were wearing a little blue bra. I've been dying ever since to see—" he looked down "—this." His thumb grazed her nipple, and then he bent and kissed it. Lightly.

His loose hair fell around his shoulders like a cape, so dark and silky and thick, and she put her palm flat on it, a shivery kind of wonder echoing through her. "Robert," she whispered, just to say it aloud.

He straightened, looking down at her gravely, putting his hands on her face, then shook his head and pressed his brow against hers. "I keep wanting to say I'm sorry. I don't know what got into me. But that would sound like I want to leave, and I don't, unless you want me to."

"No," she whispered.

"Take me upstairs."

And Marissa thought again of her body, revealing it to him. "Robert, I'm not...I..."

A quizzical expression. "What?"

"I don't look that great without my clothes on."

His smile was so tender it pierced her. "Neither do I," he said. "It's not about what anything looks like, is it?" He curled his hand around her neck, touched his lips to hers lightly. "It's about how it feels."

"I have candles," she offered.

"Candles are good." He reached behind her, turned the dead bolt and tugged her hand. "Show me."

He should have been less anxious after that wild scene at the door—what got into him?—but a tangled sense of nervous anticipation moved in him as they went up the stairs. This was insane. He should never have come back.

And every step convinced him that much more. The elegance of details in her house. The richly padded carpet under his feet, the delicate lace curtains, even the sight of her pink-and-white feet—all of it made him feel like an imposter, an interloper. The peasant with the princess.

But the other part of him—the part that had insisted he had to come back—wanted her too badly to even consider leaving. A pool of anticipation stirred in his belly as she led him into her bedroom and let his hand go. It was a big room, with five or six windows, and a four-poster bed, just as he'd imagined. She moved, picking up a book of matches to light candles on the mantle and windowsills and dresser. He waited, watching her self-conscious movements—the quick tightening tug she gave the tie to her robe, the restless brush of her hands through her hair.

And he suddenly realized that everything about her would be revealed when she took off that robe. He knew a lot more about her than she knew about him.

He settled on a tiny, chintz-covered chair and bent to untie his boots. "My mother," he said, "had me when she was fifteen. She was lost, even then."

He let the left boot fall, started on the other. "She had drug problems, man problems, problems that got worse and worse and worse." The right boot. "When I was fourteen, one of her boyfriends kicked my ass for talking back to her, and I'd just had enough. I ran away from home, lived in the streets for two years."

She listened through all this, her hands tight on the ties of her robe. Standing, he unbuttoned the front of his shirt. "In those days," he said gruffly, feeling the tension even in the confession, "we marked ourselves." He took off his shirt and let it drop, watching her face carefully. "I marked myself."

Whatever she was thinking didn't show, not right away. She moved closer, her face unreadable, and touched his wrist first, the bracelet of Celtic knots she touched before. Then her finger tips moved to his left biceps, where a gangland tattoo sprawled in ugly blue ink. "So many," she said softly. She trailed her fingers over his arms, his chest, his belly, brushing each one, the violent marks and the sorrowful ones, the declarations and the wounds.

At last, she bent close, and pressed a kiss to his chest, to the stylized cross there. When she raised her eyes, there were tears in them, and he shook his head.

"It was a long time ago." He reached for her. "Come lie down with me, Marissa."

"Fair is fair," she said, and stepped back, still so desperately reluctant that it broke his heart. She reached for the ties of her robe and, with a quick intake of breath, let it fall.

A jolt of purest, deepest lust burned through him, but he forced himself to be still, let her see him looking, seeing, liking. "Do you know how erotic your coloring is?" he said, and urgently skimmed out of his jeans, so they were both standing naked in the candlelight, revealed. She had touched his tattoos, and in return, he knelt and pressed his mouth against her full, soft lower belly, put his hands on the love handles that still lingered, that did not show when she was dressed. He spread open his palms and traveled over thighs that would never be slender, then stood up. "Come to bed, princess," he said.

They tumbled together, tangling naked limbs that slid and explored along with hands and mouths and eyes. He closed his eyes to feel the press of her belly against his own, the plush, incredible softness of breasts against his ribs. "Oh," he breathed, "that's good, that's good." He curled his hands around her buttocks, traced the length of her spine.

And she, too, explored, careful not to hit him with her cast, learning the shape of his body, the taste of his skin. The low roar of desire in him grew higher, hotter, and he pushed her gently onto her back and started at her mouth, kissing her lips, her chin, her throat. She made a low sound, and moved restlessly as he moved lower. "I need—oh!" His hair fell in a rush, all at once, over her chest, and she reached up to touch the hair, her own flesh, and a bolt of something unbelievable went through him, a flash point of electricity. He touched his tongue to her lips, to her breasts, and her uncasted hand moved to his organ, urgently but lightly touching him, guiding him, urging him.

And this time they went slowly. Rolling easily into a thick, deep rhythm that pulsed through his entire body, through hers, and he knew it was corny even as he thought it—that it was almost musical. Such a long, easy, slow movement, one that let them touch and kiss and more than he would have expected—look. Candlelight flickered over her face, across the vividness of those blue eyes, across her red lips that he couldn't resist dipping to taste, again and again.

He was lost and he knew it, lost in a sweetness and warmth he had not ever been able to hold on to and had learned to stop wanting. So much easier, so much safer to make do with what was than to want so much. Even as he supped at the wonder of her, he knew he shouldn't have come back, but as she reached for him, urgently, gasping his name as she kissed him, hard, and climaxed, he couldn't be sorry.

Marissa felt her body, every single part of her body— her toes and her mouth and her knees—sailing back from wherever it had gone. She grew conscious of the intimacy of their bellies and chests, sweaty and slick, pressed together, heard again the sound of his breath in her ear. How many ears had he breathed in this way?

A sense of shyness, strangeness, came over her, an almost panicked sense of realization—she was naked, with a man she really didn't know well, and what had she done? Why had she done it?

As if he felt her stiffening, his arms tightened on either side of her and he lifted his head. "Just us, remember," he said. But Marissa closed her eyes, avoiding his gaze, mortification rising into her cheeks, tipping the edges of her ears. The flesh pressed against him felt prickly all of a sudden, uncomfortable. She could not move, could barely breathe.

"Marissa," he said, that raspy voice, too familiar in contexts that had nothing to do with this—

She squeezed her eyes tighter, acutely, painfully aware that they were naked—totally naked—that she could feel intimate parts of him still tight against her, could feel her naked breasts against his chest—

Oh, what had she done?

She could feel him looking at her, felt the faint drawing away, and wanted to both hold him tighter and shove him away at once. She wasn't sure if she was crushed or relieved when he rolled away, falling on his back beside her.

Marissa reached for the sheet and pulled it over her body, over his, still not looking at him. In the gulf of silence, she could hear a faint drip of water in the bathtub, the faint sizzle of a candle. She wanted to say something, but not a word rose to her aid, and still the quiet—unbreakable, a huge breach—lay between them, vast as a desert. She curled into the pillow, stared hard at the carved wooden post at the foot of the bed. The room smelled of vanilla.

Abruptly he moved. Sat up. "Well, I guess this was a big mistake." With a jerk, he reached for his jeans. "I'll get out of your hair."

And still the horror of so completely revealing herself was on her. Wild sex at the door, and he had now seen her completely naked, head to toe—

She risked a glance at him, at his rigid, long back, sienna- and smooth-skinned and tense. His hair hid most of a tattoo on his shoulder blade, but not all of the scars. A thin, almost invisible one, low on his ribs—a knife wound. So close to his lung—she thought of that thin, brutal blade finding a target and his blood spilling out before he got here, to this night, with her.

Without realizing she meant to do it, Marissa put out a hand, pressed her palm to the edges of the howling coyote tattooed on his shoulder blade. "You didn't get this one in the streets."

His body was rigid, flinching when she touched him. "No. Texas. In the army."

In one fluid movement, she left behind the protection of the sheet and pressed her body against his back, her arms around his shoulders. "I'm sorry," she whispered into his hair. "I panicked."

A very slight softening went through him, but he didn't move. Marissa knew a moment of sharp regret. She moved her hands, touched his jaw, felt the strong, sharp angle of his cheekbones. She pressed her forehead against the back of his head, breathing in the scent of some faintly peachy shampoo, and realized he'd probably let Crystal pick it out.

He caught her hands, pulled them down like a scarf around his chest. A quiet sigh, then he lifted her hands and pressed them to his mouth. "I've gotta go. This is— ah. It's not what I thought."

Hollow, Marissa pulled away, shamed and burning and wanting—what? For him to leave, now. For him to turn and kiss her again, make her forget, lose herself in that blazing lust that made it easy. She had no idea which she wanted more, and only fell back, pulling the heavy comfort of the quilt over herself, watching him in the candlelit room.

When he stood to dress, she saw the lean, long ropiness of his body. He kept his back to her, but moving, liquid shadows revealed more than they hid—the small bones of his spine, a row of tiny mountains; the hollow of his hip joint against high flanks; male flesh, dark and soft, at the base of his flat belly. He moved quickly, and the flesh was covered by shorts, hidden by jeans.

In her body was a rhythm of silent protest and relief in alternating beats—a pulse between her legs, a pound in her chest, a swell in her breasts, a cringe in her mind. She could not look at him while he buttoned his shirt, pulling the sleeve down over the long scar that ran along his inner arm, and put the covers over her face. All was silent, still, where moments ago, it had been roaring, loud, the air feverish with passion and satisfaction and discovery.

She felt him sink onto the bed at her side, felt his hand on the top of her head. He pulled down the thick quilt. Marissa didn't move, just waited for him to say whatever kind, parting words he'd decided to utter.

But she waited and waited and he said nothing, only sat there next to her, clothed when she was not. And he proved more steadfast than she. In the end, she turned, almost in defiance, without worrying how much of her showed. "I thought you were leaving."

"Me, too," he said gruffly, and pulled the cover over the top half of her breasts, moved his hand over her shoulder, a gentle movement she nearly could not bear. "This was a big mistake, princess, but we can't let Crystal know anything."

"I know that." To forestall anything else, she sighed. "Robert, you already said it, okay? This was a mistake. Let's just leave it at that."

He took his hand away and stood up. "When are you going to realize that life's going to be a lot easier for you when you just find yourself some senator's son and accept who you are?"

With a swift, furious gesture, she tore a pillow from beneath her and flung it at him. "When are you going to realize this is not about that?"

He caught the pillow easily, and tossed it gently back. "Isn't it?"

He left her.

Robert had forgotten to leave a light on when he left, and his house was dark when he returned to it. The porch lay in deep, flickering shadows cast by the streetlight shining on pine trees. No lamp burned in the living room window. No music made the walls breathe, no movie flickered blue against the curtains.

He sat in the truck for a long moment, dreading those empty rooms. He missed Crystal. He hadn't wanted her to stay at Louise's, didn't really know why she had insisted that was what she needed, but he also hadn't known how to protest. Didn't even know if it would have been the right thing to do. Maybe Louise was just better at taking care of her than he was. Maybe Crystal needed a mother figure.

And that was okay. He didn't need to be the only person in her life. He hadn't had much experience with kids, especially one as vulnerable as this.

His wish to have her here now was entirely selfish. The simple fact of her sleeping in another room would have eased this ache he felt now. He wouldn't have shared any of what happened, wouldn't have to tell her all the things he was feeling—that wasn't it. She was just…a comfort somehow. A bright light in his dull life.

With a little shock, he realized he loved her. It was simple and plain. He'd never had anything like a real family, had never even had the sense to long for it, until his desperate niece had shown up on his doorstep, fragile and strong, sensible and terrified. She'd never had it either, but she knew exactly what it ought to look like, and given the smallest possible chance, she'd set about creating it for both of them.

And for the baby she was carrying. Of course she was keeping it. Marissa had asked and he'd told her he didn't know, but the evidence was right in front of him. No way, nohow was she making this home just for herself.

Ah, Crystal. It would make things so much harder for her. Harder for her to finish high school, to even think about college, to find a man who loved and cared for her properly. Like her grandmother, like her mother, she was going to be a mother way too young.

He bent his head in the cold dark and rested his forehead on the steering wheel, wishing he could get over the feeling that he'd let her down. Not by seeing Marissa, necessarily. In the stillness, he could see that Crystal was not a naive child and would not expect him to live womanless for the rest of his life. She was afraid of being replaced, and given her life, he could certainly understand that, but only time could show her that he'd never, ever do that.

No, he'd let her down somehow in the past couple of days by not seeing whatever it was she needed, whatever it was that Louise sensed. He would have to take time to figure it out, help her feel safe enough and strong enough to share her problems with him. Show her that he could be trusted with her bruised and delicate soul.

Words that also described Marissa, God help him. He squeezed his eyes closed, cursing himself for going back up to her door, knowing what would happen, knowing it was wrong.

Don't.

No point. He got out of the truck and walked up to

the dark door, let himself into the house and flipped on
the lamp. A cat meowed at him, almost scolding, from
the back of the couch—Crystal's battered tom. The cat
stretched, yawning, and croaked out another meow.
Maybe it was just hello. Smiling, he reached out to scrub
the cat's tattered ears. He purred happily. As he stood
there, the kitten pounced on his foot, smacked paws
against his legs exuberantly and took off. Robert laughed
and scooped him up, turning the little monster into the
crook of his arm so he could waggle his fingers and be
attacked some more.

Such a little thing, animals there waiting, but it made
a difference. How had Crystal become so wise? But he
thought he knew—she'd dreamed this life a million
times, alone in her room watching movies while her
mother partied. She had stretched across her bed and told
herself the things she would have if she could—a tidy
kitchen and sweet-smelling bathrooms and cats to sleep
with her at night.

What a good mother she would be. And she did have
him to help her, someone to lean on, help watch the baby
while she finished school and saw the shape of the rest
of her life. That was something good he could give the
world. He wondered, with a soft sense of wonder, if she
would have a girl or a boy.

A baby. Wow.

He fed and watered the cats, then wearily went to take
a shower, aware again of the depth of silence. No Crystal
in there breathing in the other room. He shook his head
at his sentimentality. Odd that he, master of the foot-
loose-and-fancy-free life-style, was so smitten with the
family thing and hadn't even noticed.

He turned on the shower and started pulling off his
clothes, fighting the sense of loss that came with remem-

bering putting the shirt on in that awful quiet, remembering the last time he'd stripped it off, revealing himself, remembered—

The smell of her was on him, freed when he took off his clothes, drifting up from his skin like a quiet song, and the scent tore through his paper-thin guard against the memories of the evening. Her laughing eyes at the restaurant, the intense tenderness of the kiss in front of the window, the throaty sound of her voice when she asked him to come in.

Closing his eyes, he raised his hands to his face and inhaled, aroused again by a flash of that hot, hot, hot coupling against her front door. He'd expected it to be good between them, but he hadn't anticipated quite that intensity.

Grimly he stepped under the hot spray and picked up the soap, working up a lather on his hands first and rinsing them, over and over, so not even the smallest hint of her remained. But somehow the pain stayed with him, even when all he could smell was soap.

# Chapter 11

Marissa awakened very early to the sound of a black-bird singing in the trees outside. A soft, cool light poured in the windows, edging the white curtains she'd loved in combination with the dark wood moldings. She was naked beneath the heavy quilt, and it was strange to move her limbs beneath the cloth, feel it against her skin, all of her skin.

She stretched out a hand beneath the covers and put it where Robert had lain last night, thinking of his hair falling around her and candlelight edging that sharp nose. She thought of his kiss, so deep and involving, skilled and artless at once. It made her want to cry.

Instead, she got up and urgently dressed in her workout clothes, taking only time enough to splash water on her face and pull the mess of her hair out of her face. She was on the sidewalk before six, striding into the still mountain morning. A path from one end of the street led into a meadow, and deciding abruptly, she took it, walking hard. The air was cold and light. Her breath left her lungs in small, misty puffs, and the tip of her nose grew cold.

But her legs warmed quickly, then her arms, and then sweat was trickling beneath her sport bra. The need to weep left her as the sun began to rise, tipping the conical tops of pine trees and dancing through the flat, glittery leaves of aspens in their new spring attire. She walked and walked, walked away resentment. Walked away shock. Walked away the illusions she'd carefully constructed last night to protect herself as she slept.

On the fourth mile, she let the thought of Robert in. With it came a thud of desire, remembered lust and wistful yearning and surprised connection. It had been too intense last night. Too much to absorb at once. She had known she was very attracted to him, had known there was a powerful chemistry between them.

She had not anticipated the way being with him would blow her wide open the way it had, ripping away every vestige of protection she'd ever assembled, revealing her like a half-formed butterfly torn from its cocoon.

Rounding the last hill, headed down toward the top of her street, she flipped a loose lock of hair from her face. How would they handle the next meeting? Should she avoid him? Confront him? Wait for him to come to her?

No. At least on the last one, she knew the answer. His feelings had been gravely injured and she didn't blame him. He wouldn't come to her. And maybe that was good. She had not liked that feeling of such a loss of control last night, not one bit. It felt dangerous. It made her too vulnerable, too exposed.

A twining thread of heat slid through her breasts, touched her mouth, as if in denial of her thoughts. But that was sex. She hadn't said she didn't like the sex— that *would* be a big fat lie. That was the chemistry that was pulling them together, pheromones or hormones or pictures they saw in books as children. She had not really experienced quite that level of intensity before, but she had felt chemistry in that class.

What she had not liked was the *intimacy*. Laughing with him so much over dinner, and connecting on all those internal levels, discovering she liked them, then that wild and tender joining.

She pressed cold fingers to her temple. How could she even look him in the eye?

When she came around the hundred-year-old pine that stood sentry to her driveway and saw his truck, she came very close to bolting—her mind urged her to do it, to protect herself, to run, now, while she still could. He had not seen her. He sat on the top step, right in the middle, his long legs cocked at the knee, his hands clasped loosely. His hair was braided.

She didn't bolt because her body betrayed her, going hot and tight and soft at once, renewing the war she'd felt last night over him leaving. Rejection and passion and terror and something bright and soft she couldn't really name. She stayed where she was, beneath the long sheltering arms of the tree, frozen.

A squirrel skittered across the porch, catching his attention, and he watched it, sitting motionless as it crept up to him, a smile forming on that stern mouth. The rodent crept up very, very slowly, whiskers quivering, tail twitching, and still Robert remained utterly still. All at once, it seemed to sense human blood, because it stood up straight, like a cartoon character, every hair on end, and bolted. Robert chuckled, and without thinking, so did Marissa.

Startled, he looked around, and for one moment they were back in her bed, staring deep into each other's eyes as they kissed, made love. Everything but his eyes, long and dark and still, disappeared from her world. Even her sense of herself. It scared her, made hard knots of pressure come back. She took a breath, her smile gone. The laughter faded from the air as if it had never been.

Gravely he stood. Marissa unfroze and approached, halting at the bottom of the steps. "Hi."

"I don't want what happened to hurt Crystal," he said without preamble. "You're good for her, and she likes you and she needs anybody she can get in her corner."

Marissa swallowed.

He looked toward the mountains, spread one hand. "If you want to make sure I'm not around when you visit or whatever, I understand. We'll figure it out."

That feeling of wanting to cry came back. "No, I don't want you to leave." She bowed her head, and realized she still smelled of him, of them, along with the sweat of her walk. Her stomach twisted and she couldn't think of what to say. "Does it have to be so...final?" she said at last.

He took a step down. "I kinda thought that was what you wanted."

"No!" She looked up, felt that flash, the longing in her throat. She didn't have any words for this. Looking up at his grave face, she only wanted to lean into him, put her cheek against his chest, start over. "I made such a mess of things," she said quietly. "I don't know how to take it back. But I would if I could."

She saw his throat move. He took another step down. "It just wasn't right, Marissa. We knew better."

"Did we?" She moved this time, conscious of her wild hair and the makeup left from last night and the fact that she looked more than a little dumpy in her sweats, but it suddenly seemed like a lot rested on this very moment, that she'd remember it for the rest of her life if it went wrong. "I think it was so right that it scared us both."

Recognition flashed over his face, unmistakable, then a long cord of jaw went hard. He shook his head. In those conflicting expressions, Marissa saw her own struggle.

Her hands were trembling a little, but she braced herself and took that last step, the one that took her to stand right in front of him, and she swayed forward and put her forehead against his chest. "What if it was and we're too scared to do anything with it, Robert?" she asked. "Sometimes you don't get a second chance."

His hands flew up around her head, paused and then one landed across the back of her neck. "I gotta think of Crystal first. You and me, we've made it this far, we'll be okay. She might not. She needs us both." He used his other hand to cup her cheek, lift her face. "This is really volatile, this thing between us, and she doesn't need that." A quirk on his wide mouth. "You don't need it. You just found this new life, worked hard for it."

"And what about you?"

"I really don't need it." He let go of a humorless little laugh. "I'm sober. Got a job I'm crazy about. A home." That twitch in his throat. "Even a family. Might not seem like a lot to somebody else, but it's precious to me. Can't risk it."

An arrow went through her. Marissa stepped back, frowning, feeling suddenly sure that was the wrong answer, but unable to figure out just then what the right one might be. She wet her lips, about to speak, but a car pulled in the driveway behind her, honking, and Marissa screeched before she was all the way around. "Victoria!"

The woman stepped out of the car, tall and skinny, with reddish streaks in her dark, gel-mussed hair. Robert blinked. It was like seeing Marissa in a fun house mirror. She wore an orange tie-dyed dress, showing off a deep tan that seemed almost a sacrilege in comparison to Marissa's porcelain complexion.

The woman halted, her mouth dropping open as Marissa laughed and spun in a circle, evidently showing off her weight loss, and then they both started talking at once, hugging and screeching and standing back, talking all the while. The words were fragmented, spilling out in some shorthand or something. No, even more than that—they had words in there he didn't even recognize.

Feeling awkward, he pulled his keys from his pocket and headed for the truck.

Marissa turned abruptly. "Wait! Robert, this is my twin sister, Victoria."

Their faces were almost exactly the same—that vivid blue in the eyes, the same mouth—but oddly, Marissa looked about five years younger than Victoria, and where Marissa was probably still carrying about twenty extra pounds, Victoria was about that much underweight. Her cheekbones and collarbones and joints were sharp.

And where Marissa's face was always open, friendly, Victoria looked distinctly aloof. He disliked her instantly. "How you doing?" he said gruffly, and headed for the truck. "See ya," he said to Marissa, raising his chin. Unsettled, unsatisfied, he drove away.

By previous arrangement, Robert went by Louise's on the way home from work. He was tired, bone tired, but determined to get things off on the right foot with his niece today. He was pleased to see that Crystal was sitting in the living room, dressed, when he showed up, as if she were eager to get home.

"Hey, Uncle," she said. "Ramona says I can get up tomorrow, walk around, but no school till next week. Did you get my homework from today?"

"Not yet," he said, wincing inwardly. Hadn't even crossed his mind, actually. "I bet Ma—Ms. Pierce took care of it."

Crystal rolled her eyes with a little smile. "You can call her Marissa. I know you like her."

He let down his guard just a little, lifting one eyebrow in acknowledgment.

"Did you go out with her last night?" Crystal asked.

"Why?" A little ripple of guilt touched him.

A lift of one shoulder. "Just wondered."

Louise had been on the phone and she came out of the kitchen. "Hey there, handsome. Your girl's in great shape today. See that?"

"I do. You must have the magic mom touch."

Crystal sobered when she looked at Louise. "She's had lots of practice, Uncle. That's all."

He touched her shoulder, a mute thanks for her consideration of his ego.

"Let me talk to you a minute," Louise said, cocking her head toward the kitchen.

"You all right, kid?" Robert asked, catching the glance between the two females.

Crystal nodded, again very soberly, and Robert followed Louise with some concern. "Did something happen?" he asked when they got to the kitchen.

But Louise only shook her head, pulling open the long sliding door that led to the deck and pointing for him to go out. His concern deepened as she followed him out and slid the door closed. "You're scaring me, Louise."

She patted his arm, shaking her head. "She's fine, honey. But I've got a job for you to do."

"A job?"

She nodded, and took a breath. "Her boyfriend was beaten by the gangs and taken out of the city. She has no idea where he went. I betcha his mama spirited him out of there, just like any mother with any sense. But if that's so, why hasn't he tried to contact Crystal?" Her blue eyes, sharp and clear, met his. "See what I'm saying?"

"Yeah." He leaned on the railing. "You know his name?"

"Mario. That's all she'll tell me."

He scowled. "You know how many Marios live in Albuquerque, Louise?"

"Your sister's still there, isn't she? Call her."

He nodded.

"She wants to keep the baby, darlin'."

He closed his eyes. "I know." But somehow, stating it aloud brought a heaviness to his spirits. Any sense of possibility or joy he'd taken from this new, strange, disturbing connection to Marissa evaporated completely. He had not realized, until that second, that he'd been harboring hope that there might be a way for them, a way to work things out.

But he saw now how absurd it was. Not because of Crystal or her baby. He'd probably known all along that she wouldn't be able to give it up.

No, the mood evaporated simply because there was so much *reality* to his life, while Marissa's was full of unreality. It had been crazy to think there was any possibility of a solution to their attraction to each other. He should never have gone back there last night. Should never have—

*Her skin, so pure and poreless, gliding against his mouth; her soft, hungry cries, panted into his ear; the eager yet shy way she reached for him—*

He'd known better, and now he straightened, clearing his throat and putting out his hand. "Thanks, Louise. I owe you a lot."

She winked. "More than you know, son."

"What's that supposed to mean?"

An airy smile. "Nothing at all."

Robert got Crystal settled and started dinner under her supervision—grinning at her bossiness. "Not that pan, Uncle, the big frying pan." And when the girl was safely absorbed in watching a movie in the living room, he dialed his sister's Albuquerque number and carried the cordless phone outside to the backyard.

Alicia greeted him with a litany of false sweetness laden with guilt, the language of their own mother, and to avoid the anger it sent through him, Robert got right to the point. "Do you know Crystal's friend Mario?"

"Duh. He lived across the alley since he was born."

"Where did he go, Alicia?"

"Nobody knows. Just him and his mom took off one night. Crystal went crazy, calling the hospitals and stuff, but she didn't find him."

"What's his last name?"

A sudden suspiciousness. "What're you asking all these questions for? Why not ask Crystal?"

"I'm asking you," he said. Just this side of harsh.

"Eee, you don't have to get all mad. It's Trujillo."

Robert tsked. Not quite the Spanish version of Smith or Jones, but close enough. "And his mother's name?"

She told him, and Robert went back inside to scribble down the little details that might help. The mother was in her late thirties, very heavy, the boy her only family. She'd come from somewhere else with a man from the neighborhood who deserted her when Mario was born. She did telephone work, mostly. "Telephone work, like solicitations?" Robert asked.

"No, you know, like the big places where you answer phones and take orders from all over? She had a good voice, real proper. It's a good job."

Robert scribbled down a few more particulars, then hung up and stared for a long moment at the phone. It was obvious Alicia didn't even miss her daughter. How could she not? And how could she bear the guilt of kicking her out of the house over a man?

He scowled and shook his head. By now, Alicia had manufactured a scenario that would make her feel good about this arrangement, one that excused her entirely. Crystal, she rationalized, was happier, so Alicia had done the right thing.

Violence rose in him, hot and dark, and he wanted to smash a fist into the phone, kick the door. He did neither, only took a long breath and blew it out, let it go.

Looking at the notes, he recognized the monumental nature of the task that awaited him. Find Mario, Louise had ordered, and he shook his head, grinning ruefully. Mario Trujillo in the southwest. Sure, sure.

He peeked around the corner and saw that Crystal had fallen into a deep, slack-mouthed sleep. He turned dinner down to a low simmer and wandered into the alcove she'd created for his tools. Idly he sat down and picked up a drawing pad—thinking came easier to him when he had something in his hands.

Beside his knife was the photograph Tyler's wife had

found of the stained-glass window in the restoration project. Robert tugged it over and started outlining in colored pencil, letting his hand and eye take over as his mind puzzled over the problem of how to locate Mario. He'd hoped to simply make phone calls, but he saw now the best, fastest way would be to go down there, talk to neighbors. Someone knew something.

He could get down there and back in a day. Louise would certainly take care of Crystal, as she had last night, so he wouldn't worry about her. But Robert did not want to tell Crystal that he was going to look for her missing boyfriend. What if the kid had died? Or couldn't be found? Or worst of all, couldn't care less he had a baby on the way?

Crystal was very fragile right now—and this boy had obviously meant a lot to her. Robert wanted to discover the truth behind things before involving her. As it stood right now, she had illusions to hold on to, and as he'd learned all too often, there was a lot to be said for a good illusion.

As he mulled it over, he sketched out a section of glass in blue—that clean, wisteria blue of a Tiffany shadow. The color of Marissa's eyes. He scowled, skittered away from that and went back to the problem at hand. Mario, not Marissa. Crystal, not that snotty sister.

Mario and Crystal. He focused on the emerging sketch and the photo, and thought of the Indian church window he'd done a couple of years ago. In New Mexico. He'd tell Crystal that Tyler wanted him to do a new window for the restoration, and he wanted to get a look at the window at the church before he began. It wasn't a lie. He could make the rest of it true by actually stopping at the church, without obligating himself to do such an enormous project.

Abruptly Marissa flooded into his mind, a flood of sensation and color that bled through some chink in his armor. He worked his shoulders, shaking her away. It would be good to put a little distance there, too. Let the shattering power of last night fade a bit more.

Marissa felt snappish and wilted by the time she got home. Victoria was waiting for her, a glass of wine at the ready. She pressed the crisp white into Marissa's hand. "I've got dinner going. Chicken breasts and wild rice. Is that okay?"

"Wonderful!" Marissa hugged her. Victoria's spidery arms went around her neck, and for an instant, they were three and seven and ten, clinging to each other in the wilderness. Marissa breathed in her sister's smell, a bright, hot note, unique and dear, the color of lemons. She felt Victoria doing the same. "I am so glad you're here."

Victoria let her go. "Me, too."

Marissa showered and put on jeans, and she and Victoria ate the meal in the backyard, contentedly silent as the sun set over the mountains. Lazily stretched out, Marissa said, "This is two days in a row that I haven't walked. I need to take some homework assignments to Crystal—the little lost teen I told you about. Feel like walking with me?"

"Sure."

They set out just at dusk, their feet falling into an easy rhythm. "What started your health regime?" Victoria asked, and Marissa told her. Victoria's story was much the same. "I woke up one morning and saw there was no flesh on my body at all. Just bones. I found a counselor that very day, who sent me to a nutritionist and a support group for anorexics and bulimics. Here I am, thirty pounds later, almost a size eight.'' She smiled. ''I'm aiming for size ten.''

''Me, too,'' Marissa said with a grin. ''One more size to go. Maybe one and a half.'' She narrowed her eyes, thinking of that thirty pounds her sister had gained. ''You had to be wearing a one or something.''

''A zero,'' she said, horror in her tone. ''There are probably women who naturally wear that size, but I'm not one of them.'' She looped her arm through Marissa's. ''But here we are, childhood traumas healed at last. If we keep this up—and I certainly intend to—we can dress exactly alike and live each other's lives.'' She laughed.

''Ick!'' Marissa cried.

''Ick, indeed. I'd have to kiss your boyfriends.''

''And I'd have to endure your Goody Two-shoes types. Yuck.''

''We have certainly never agreed on men.''

''Not at all,'' Marissa said. They'd never agreed on colors, either. Victoria liked the fire shades—orange, yellow, red—while Marissa preferred cool greens and blues.

''So,'' Victoria said gingerly, ''how long have you been dating Mr. Brooding Intensity?''

Marissa looked at her. ''He's not like that.'' Seeing the little purse on her sister's mouth, she grinned. ''You didn't like him!''

''It was mutual, trust me.''

It wasn't uncommon. Victoria was often protective, maybe even a little jealous of any man Marissa dated. And although they didn't discuss these things as a rule, Marissa thought of Robert now, a taste in her mouth that had lingered all day. Chocolate. No, denser than that, more substantial. Beef burgundy. Fortifying, substantial, delicious. "I really like him," Marissa said.

"I know." They walked in silence for a minute, then Victoria said, "We're always looking for the other one, you know it?"

"The other one?"

"Yeah." She smiled. "I'm looking for you—someone neat and responsible and orderly. You're always looking for me—someone wild and creative."

Marissa laughed at the insight, thinking of Robert's stained glass. "Well, that seems natural for twins, don't you think?"

"In a way."

"Here we are," Marissa said. Tossing a loose lock of hair out of her eyes, she knocked on the door. The air smelled of supper, and she heard the television playing inside. Robert opened the door, and she grinned. "Hi."

There was a faint, bothersome hesitation as he looked from her to Victoria, then he opened the door. "Come in."

"I brought Crystal's homework," Marissa said, faltering under the soberness of his face. She frowned and asked quietly, "Is everything all right?"

For a moment they were close, bodies only inches apart, and the veil of whatever had been there last night shimmered, separating them from the rest of the world. A gilded sense of light moved through her, then shattered when he looked away. Almost dismissively.

Marissa didn't dare look at Victoria, who would see all too clearly what was in her heart. "Hi, Crystal," she said instead. "How are you doing tonight?"

"A lot better. Ramona said I only have to stay down one more day." She looked curiously at Victoria. "Wow. Twins."

Marissa grinned. "This is Victoria. I've been dying for the two of you to meet—because guess what she does for a living?"

Crystal shook her head. "No idea."

"She's a screenwriter. With what?" She looked at Victoria. "Seven movies produced now?"

"Eight," Victoria said with a grin.

It was good to watch that flickering of emotions on Crystal's transparent face. "Oh, my God," she said. "What movies did you write?"

Victoria settled easily on the ottoman near the couch, her limbs so long and ropy as she perched like a bird. She grinned and started rattling off the list. Happily, Crystal had seen several of them.

Marissa glanced over at Robert, who stood silently through this exchange, his presence exerting a thick pull on her attention, on her very skin. He did not look happy. Grimness marked his mouth, and she saw weariness around his eyes. And for one brief second, he met her eyes and there was yearning in them, very specific and focused.

She inclined her head toward the porch and he nodded. "We'll be back in a second," Robert said.

Neither Victoria nor Crystal even acknowledged them. Crystal spilled out questions a mile a minute, displaying her prodigious well of knowledge.

Outside, Robert closed the door and went to lean on the post, patting his shirt in an automatic gesture for cigarettes that were no longer there. The streetlight shone through the pines in front of the house, dappling his face with shadows. He made no move toward her, and Marissa said, finally, "What gives?"

He didn't speak immediately. Then with a breath, he

said, "I have to go to Albuquerque, see if I can find the father of Crystal's baby."

"I see." She folded her arms. "When?"

"In the morning, I think. I talked to my sister and she gave me a little information." Gruffly he added, "I don't want to tell Crystal what I'm really doing until I get back, so she thinks I'm going down to take care of some work things."

"I see," she said again. A sense of pressure made her lungs feel airless. "And…last night? Is that it? We're done?"

He bowed his head, and the light shone over the part in his hair, tied back neatly. She didn't help him, just let him work up whatever it was he had to say. Finally he did raise his head. "It was crazy to think it could be anything, Marissa. There's no place in my world for you. And none in yours for me."

She wanted to hit him. Hard. "Whatever," she said, and turned on her heel to go back inside.

He grabbed her arm. "Marissa, wait, it's not—"

She pulled free. In a low, fierce voice she said, "It wasn't a one-night stand? It wasn't something big? It's not me? It's not you? I guess it's just plain stupidity on your part, then."

Unexpectedly he grinned. "That's possible."

But the grin just made her remember a thousand things. "Don't try and charm me, Red Dog. I *saw* you last night. You showed yourself to me." Her voice was low, nearly inaudible even a foot away. "And that's what's scaring you, not any stupid class difference that doesn't mean anything in this world."

"You don't think it matters? You just don't know."

She drew herself up. "Prove it."

A frown. "What does that mean?"

She shrugged. "Prove it. Show me something I've never seen. Show me what I don't know. Show me how impossible it is that I could ever fit in your world."

"Marissa—"

"Never mind," she said, and pulled open the door before he could say another word. "Ready to go?" she said to Victoria.

Her sister stood up, patted Crystal's shoulder. "See you tomorrow. We can talk some more then."

Crystal looked from Marissa to Robert, her eyes narrowing a little, and said, "Sure. Thanks, Ms. Pierce."

Without another glance at Robert, Marissa left, stomping up the road in mute fury. Victoria was wise enough not to say a single word.

Marissa awoke before dawn, restless and depressed. She dressed in jeans and an oversize sweatshirt, made some coffee and carried it onto the front porch, where she had a view of the valley spilling down toward Lake Rosalie. It was cloudy and cold, threatening a storm before the day was over. This time of year, it could be rain or snow, probably both.

For the past couple of weeks, life had taken on a subtle, brilliant sheen. Every morning, she awakened with a sense of slight to middling excitement—and she recognized now that it had all been attributable to Robert. She had told her sister that she liked him, but the truth was, it was more than that. She'd acknowledged lust to herself, but it was more than that, too.

Something happened when they were together. Something good and rich and clean and real. It was almost as if she recognized him, or some part of him, his soul or heart or something, and in spite of that moment of strange alienation when in her bed, that connection only reinforced her sense that this was important.

What did he fear so much?

The whisper of tires on the driveway made her raise her head. It was not really a surprise to see that it was Robert's truck. He parked and simply looked at her through the windshield for a minute, then got out and came around, wearing jeans and boots and a warm lumberman's jacket, blue and green. It made him look foreign, very Indian and distant, with that thick braid going down his back. She found herself looking at his long-fingered brown hands.

He stopped on the steps, and Marissa waited. "I'm taking your dare," he said.

"What dare?"

"You want me to prove why this is crazy, I'm going to prove it. Leave your money and your credit cards and come as you are, and you can see what I mean."

"Right now?"

A sober nod.

There was a dare of his own in that expression. He didn't think she'd do it—drop everything to go on a doomed quest into a dark world. A ripple of fear touched her. What if she found out he was right, that the world he came from was too dark to be borne? What if it shocked her?

But beads of moisture clung to his hair, and even as he stood there, hands loose at his sides, she felt a powerful emotion riding in her. He was worth fighting for.

She stood up. "I'd like to wash my face and call my sister and the school. Five minutes, tops. When will we be back?"

"Seven hours to Albuquerque, seven back. Tomorrow evening at the earliest."

"Okay. Come in and I'll make the arrangements."

"I'll wait here."

She smiled. "Whatever you like."

## Chapter 12

He insisted upon driving his truck. They drove down out of the mountains, drinking coffee from paper cups that he'd bought for them when they stopped on the outskirts of Red Creek to gas up. The morning held spring and winter in a damp cold mix, the skies dark. As they drove down U.S. 6 along Bear Creek, Marissa sat quietly and admired the views of clouds dropping into little valleys and hovering above the river. "Mornings like this," she said quietly once, "are the reason I live in Colorado."

He only nodded. There was a taut air of grim anticipation about him this morning that had nothing to do with Marissa, and she didn't push into it much, just let him drive and think.

They were early enough that they didn't hit much traffic in Denver. He grabbed I-25 south and they kept driving, only the radio between them. Finally, outside Colorado Springs, three hours after they started, they hit the traffic jam they both had been anticipating—no one ever drove this highway with any regularity without having to face traffic jams—in a construction zone right below Pikes Peak. Or Pikes Peak if they could see it. All that was visible below a muffling of clouds was the blue lower skirt of the mountain.

With an annoyed huff, Robert slowed to a crawl and narrowed his eyes at the sky. "Rain or snow?"

"Smells like snow, I'm afraid."

"Yeah, that's what I thought, too. Damn."

"We might get ahead of it yet, and the traffic will thin out once we get through Colorado Springs."

"It's Raton I'm worried about."

Raton Pass, at the border between Colorado and New Mexico, had good, wide roads, but the grade and its position as a weather center made it hazardous in bad weather. Marissa looked at the sky to the south and saw the same low dark clouds stretching as far as she could see. Lifting one shoulder, she said, "If it's bad, we stop. If not, we go on."

He glared at her. "I don't want to be at this forever."

Marissa smiled sweetly at him. "Did you check the weather report?"

He adjusted his hands on the wheel. Cleared his throat. "No." A reluctant half smile touched the side of his mouth.

Marissa laughed. "Lighten up already!"

"I hate this trip. I've made it a million times, between Denver and Albuquerque."

She was relieved that he was finally talking. Stuck in the traffic, inching along, there wasn't much else to do, after all. "Why? Do you have family in Denver?"

That betraying pat of the pocket, looking for a cigarette that wasn't there. "No. I used to hitchhike, back and forth. Denver has better summers. Albuquerque winters are better.''

"This has to be better than hitchhiking.''

"Yeah, a bit.'' A faint grin. "I went back to Albuquerque when I got out of the army, and Jake ended up in Red Creek. When he fell off that cliff, I spent a lot of time going back and forth, driving to get my head together, you know?''

Marissa nodded.

"And one day, I just woke up in Albuquerque and wished I was in Red Creek and wondered why the hell I wasn't there. Moved there that very afternoon.''

"You must have been making the trip since then, or Crystal wouldn't have thought to come to you. Or did her mother send her?''

He sighed. "It wasn't that she had so much feeling for me, exactly, as the fact that she had nowhere else to go when her mom kicked her out.''

"Kicked her out?''

"Yeah. She's pretty useless, my sister.'' Traffic suddenly began to move, traveled seven feet down the road and halted again. "But it's not like she had any kind of example. She's turned out better than my mother.''

"Where is your mother?''

"Dead. She OD'd on crack when I was nineteen.'' A weariness on his face suddenly, and he swore. "I just realized she was younger than I am now when she died—she was thirty-four years old.'' A pause, and a slight shake of his head. "Man.''

Marissa wanted to say she was sorry, but something in the rigidness of his face made her halt her tongue and just wait.

"I was in the barracks, in the army, and my sister went into a foster home. It probably saved her life in the long run, but I always felt bad about it. That maybe I should have done more, but I was so damned glad to get out of there that I—'' He broke off, shook his head.

"That you what? Couldn't stand to go back?"

"Pretty much." He shifted gears, inched forward. "It was selfish."

"Maybe," Marissa said, a knot in her chest as she thought of Victoria starving herself. "Or maybe it just took all the energy you had to save yourself."

He looked at her. "That sounds like the voice of personal experience."

"Not really. Not like that."

"Like what, then?"

Marissa shook her head with a smile. "My life is so mild in comparison to yours that my traumas will sound totally stupid. Please don't make me share them after you told me your mother died of an overdose."

He raised a brow. "Your choice, princess." The traffic started moving suddenly. "Finally."

Marissa thought she'd escaped, but as they got to the southern end of the city and the traffic thinned again, he said, "Why is your sister so skinny?"

"Actually, she's gained a lot of weight since the last time I saw her." She wiped a mark of condensation from the window. "She's borderline anorexic."

A quickening of his attention. "And nothing happened, right, to make one of you gain a hundred pounds and the other starve herself."

A rush of images poured into her mind—images and colors and scenes jumbled together in a confusing and emotionally charged mass. "Not one thing, nothing you can point to, exactly, and say, 'It started right here.'"

"How about a good guess?"

Marissa felt pressure in her chest. "The summer we

were ten, my parents swooped out of their world and dragged us out on a world cruise.''

He chuckled. ''Poor dears.''

''I know. It's a rough life. First-class passage on a cruise ship—a room for us and a room for them. We were so excited—to be with them for months on end was the best thing we could think of.''

''You didn't live with them?''

''Well, we didn't *not* live with them. We had nannies and servants, and we lived in the house they called home. They just weren't there very often.''

''That's weird.''

''Not really. My father was terrified someone would kidnap us, so he kept us safe on this gated estate all the time. We didn't even go out to school.'' She straightened. ''So, there we were, ten years old, and have seen nothing of the world, and our parents swoop down and carry us off to see everything at once.'' She scowled.

''You didn't like it?''

''I loved a lot of it,'' she said. ''The world is beautiful.'' She took a breath. ''It's also very sad. I had no idea that poverty existed at all—and then we were in these places like India and the Caribbean and Africa, and it was just overwhelming. I was very angry with my father, and Victoria fell apart.''

''I can see that.'' Snow was beginning to skitter over the windshield, melting as soon as it touched.

''That was part of it,'' she said. ''But while we were on the trip, my parents freaked over how close Victoria and I were. We slept in the same bed. We finished each other's sentences. We even had our own language. It was natural, considering, but it scared them, and when we got home they sent us to boarding school. Different boarding schools, in different *countries.*''

He looked at her. "Different countries?"

"It was decided that we needed balance. Because I was so exacting, they chose Barcelona for me, to loosen up my anal attitudes. They sent Victoria to Switzerland so she might learn discipline." The memory still burned, even after nearly twenty years. "We had no control over any part of our lives, and we both felt like we'd been cut in half. It was awful." She attempted a grin. "And here's the pop psychology part. She starved, hoping my parents would come get us. I just fed myself constantly, trying to fill up that emptiness."

To her surprise, he reached over the seat and put his hand on hers, just for a second, a brief, comforting touch, then away. "It's sad." Then a puzzled little frown. "So, when you went on your diet, did you call your sister and tell her to start eating?"

Marissa laughed. "No. We were both planning a surprise—this is so classic—and must have started at the same time. She went for counseling and I started walking the very same day."

"That's weird." He stuck a wooden match in the corner of his mouth. "I don't get why I like you and don't like her at all. No offense, but she rubbed me the wrong way."

"The feeling is mutual."

"Yeah? She didn't like me, huh?"

"Nope." She shifted, huddling into her sweater a little as the temperature dropped. "But don't feel bad. She never likes any guy I like, and vice versa."

On the horizon, another city appeared. "That's Pueblo ahead," he said. "We can stop for some lunch and check the weather reports."

The weather reports only said "light snow" for Raton Pass, so after a simple lunch, they got back on the road.

Traffic was much milder as they headed into the sparsely populated southern end of the state, and there were only periodic bursts of spitting snow, so Robert relaxed a little. He didn't think about what was ahead or what lay behind—the act of driving had always cleared his head in important ways.

And just as it always was, he found it impossible to keep himself aloof from Marissa. She disarmed him completely, always, and he couldn't figure out how she did it. Just now, she was leafing through a magazine she'd picked up at the gas station, something thick and glossy and upscale, for which he'd given her a wry smile. Standing in the aisle of the store, she had protested that the celebrity magazines had extremely intelligent writing. "Sure," he'd told her. "That's why guys read porn, too."

She'd rolled up her magazine and smacked him with it, and at that moment, Robert had caught sight of a youth, maybe sixteen or seventeen, eyeing Marissa with appreciation—and looking at Robert with a little envy. Knowing how much it would please her, Robert had leaned close and said, "Don't look immediately, but you have an admirer at two o'clock."

A moment later, Marissa had looked up and caught the youth in the act. She'd smiled, and the youth had blushed happily. On the way out, Marissa had flashed a wicked grin and winked at Robert.

It had slain him. They'd walked outside, and snow had caught in her dark hair, sparkling like diamonds. He'd wanted to just go somewhere quiet and lie down with her. An urge that scared the hell out of him.

And he'd put up his walls right there in Pueblo, retreating back into silence. He didn't want to hear any more sad stories from her—and though he'd tried not to show it, that twin thing got to him. He didn't want to like her. Didn't want to tilt his head, listening to that liquid money voice, or thinking about her pearly skin.

But as if she were on to him, she simply opened her magazine and started reading, munching on some julienned carrots she'd charmed out of the waitress at the restaurant. Sometimes she hummed along with the radio.

In the distance loomed a tall, strange hump in the landscape, an abrupt mesa that rose out of the prairie like a fist. "Huerfano," he said, pointing. "The orphan. In the old days, it was a landmark, a place for people to meet. You can see it forever."

"Is that the old days as in the West, or the old, old days, as in before?"

"Both, probably. Can't speak to the latter."

Tongue in cheek, she said, "You don't have stories from the elders about this area? What fun is it to have an Indian guide who doesn't know anything?"

"I do know something. I just told you."

She waved a hand, flipped another page in her magazine. "I could have heard that from anyone."

He laughed, and realized even as he did it that she'd done it again—vaporized his walls like they'd never existed. "First of all, my people aren't from around here."

"Who are they?" She looked at him and pursed her lips. "No, let me guess. Apache?"

"Some. And a little Cheyenne and Ute and Shoshone."

"Oooh," she said lightly. "Exotic. I've never met anyone who was Shoshone before."

He looked at her. "Are you making fun of me, Ms. Wasp?"

That rich, almost bawdy laughter. "I am not a WASP, sir. I'm a Scot, thank you very much."

"Ah, you guys all look alike to me."

"That's what you all say." She lingered over a picture in the magazine, a young woman in a devastating dress.

"Wouldn't mind seeing you in that, princess."

"Me, either," she said. "Maybe I'll just fly out to Italy next week and buy it."

"Really?" He was taken aback.

"No." She rolled her eyes. "I'm not that spoiled, you know."

He lifted a shoulder. "You flew into Denver and bought a new dress for some fancy party last week. Why not Italy?"

"Last week, I was the guest of honor at a fund-raiser. I had to have a new dress." She flipped a page. "But there's a lot to be said for quick plane trips, you know. If we'd flown out of Red Creek, we'd be in Albuquerque by now. No traffic jams, no worry about nasty passes."

The snow was beginning to pick up and he eyed the sky with some concern. To distract himself, he said, "What does your dad do, anyway? Is he from old money or something?"

"Nope. He made every penny himself." She closed the magazine and crossed her arms over her chest. A position, he couldn't help noticing, that pushed her breasts up very nicely into the demure sweater.

"Stock market?"

"Everything. He's just a whiz with business. He has incredible instincts—knew when to buy, when to sell, what failing company could be turned around, which foreign investments would pay off." She shook her head. "And yes, the stock market. He's uncanny with the stock market."

"And you don't like him much, do you?"

"I don't know him well enough to like him or dislike him," she said. "I mean, we talk cordially once in a while. But he's just not part of my life. We were at odds so much about morality when I was younger that it's very hard to have a civil conversation now."

"Morality?" It made him think of sex, of bellies slick with sweat, and he shifted a little. "Were you a loose woman?" he asked with a grin.

"Not that kind of morality," she said, and he wondered if it was sidestepping the question. "The morality of having that much money and not doing more with it."

"That's a do-gooder mentality, sister. Doesn't do anyone any good."

She lifted one shoulder. "That's what he's always said."

"And you don't agree with him."

"No." The word was distinct. "I don't."

"What would you have him do? Build homes for the poor?"

"It's not up to me to tell him. Once my trust passed into my hands, I started doing it my way, and it seriously annoyed him."

A stab of something bothersome hit him—a vision of officer's wives doing a fund-raiser for the local hospital or library or whatever, their hair coiffed and their perfume expensive as they passed out pencils in a bad neighborhood. "Philanthropy?"

She didn't look at him, only smiled. "Something like that."

"I've gotta tell you, princess, you're not doing a damned bit of good." He thought of the coats the church used to give away every fall, thought of his humiliation as his mother dragged him over there to try on corduroy smelling of cigars and down vests leaking feathers, and the lipsticked mothers from other places, other neighborhoods giving him that pained and pitying look. "All they do is laugh at you."

"I'm a big girl," she said. Serenely. As if she already knew about the laughter.

Darkly he clenched the steering wheel. That summed it all up, didn't it? He'd been the kid getting the jacket, and she'd been the one giving it away. Not exactly level ground. "How rich are you, anyway? A millionaire?"

Dancing eyes met his. "You really don't want to know, Robert."

He slanted her a look. "How much?"

"That's a very rude question, Mr. Martinez. What if I asked you how much you're worth?"

"I'd tell you. I have mutual funds and assets myself, you know. Jake taught me a lot about investing when we were in the army."

"That's excellent. Most people don't bother."

He wanted to straighten, preen a little under her praise, then scowled at how neatly she'd changed the direction of the conversation, reflecting it back to him. "You gonna tell me or not?"

"No," she said. "I'm not. You'll just use it against me."

He probably would. "Ten million," he guessed.

"Robert, do you know who my father is?"

He frowned. "No." He ran through lists of millionaires in his head and didn't come up with one named Pierce. "Should I?"

"A lot of people do. Especially if they're in the stock market world. He's one of the richest men in America. He is a billionaire."

He choked on that. Maybe she was right. He didn't want to know what she was worth. Closing his mouth, he focused on the road and tried to ignore Marissa Pierce, heiress and siren, and just drove.

## Chapter 13

They made it over Raton Pass without incident and hit Albuquerque in the late afternoon. The snow that had been spitting around them all day had just begun to fall in earnest—big thick flakes drifting down from a windless sky—and Marissa expected Robert to find a room before he dealt with the problem of Mario. He did not.

As they hit the city limits, winding through traffic that was moving thick and sluggishly along the highway, Marissa watched a change come over him. A lightless mask come down over his features, thinning his mouth, narrowing his eyes. His hands were tight on the steering wheel as the truck left the interstate and headed into a world that did not appear, at least to her eyes, that threatening. It certainly didn't look like the "barrio" of her imagination—and staring out the window, she had to wonder what exactly she'd imagined it to look like. High-rise tenements, she supposed, the images of old, Midwestern and eastern cities.

This was the West. This barrio was filled with blocks
of single-dwelling houses, with front porches and small
yards that were often fenced in chain link. On garages,
she spied graffiti in a dozen styles, puffy letters and stylized gang marks, but she also saw colorful murals of
Southwest scenes, a Native American woman with a basket, a mariachi guitar player in black and silver, a mountain scene.

As they drove deeper into the blocks, she saw more
evidence of hopelessness—yards gone to dirt and weeds,
porches piled with old mattresses and other detritus, lots
littered with dead cars. Graffiti marred even the murals
that were painted—she realized suddenly—in a defensive move.

Even here, though, there were holdouts—a house with
freshly painted window casings, a garden of bright tu-
lips, a yard neat as a pin. A perfectly maintained car,
housed neatly under a carport.

There were a lot of dogs, behind fences and tied with
ropes to the front post. A trio of them trotted athletically
down one side street, their fur wet as if they'd been in
a ditch or river.

Robert pulled up in front of a shabby adobe house.
The stucco was cracking along the side wall, and there
was not a single blade of anything alive in the yard. A
giant tumbleweed had blown into a corner and shivered
in the wind, its prongs collecting shards of paper. "This
is my sister's house," Robert said. "I won't be long, so
you can come in or stay out here."

"Do you have a preference?"

Flat eyes met hers. "It's up to you."

She went in with him because she wanted to meet
Crystal's mother, see where the girl had come from. As
they slammed shut the doors to the pickup, a woman

came out on the porch, her arms crossed, her face un-welcoming. Her beauty was startling—here was a female version of Robert, an older version of Crystal. She was sensual and hard-looking at once, with heavy eyeliner and clothes that clung to her aging but dramatic figure.

Seeing Robert, she didn't smile, only raised her chin in greeting, and had not even that for Marissa. "Who's with you?" she said.

"A friend of mine."

Obviously reluctant, she led them inside to a room faded in every sense of the word. Faded carpet, faded furniture, faded paint on the walls. It smelled heavily of cigarettes and dust. A television played in one corner, showing a game show. Marissa felt cold.

They settled uneasily and Robert asked questions, then told Marissa to stay here while he went out to talk to some neighbors. Alarmed, she gave him a beseeching look, one he ignored. Her words came back to her—*Show me what I don't know. Show me how impossible it is that I could ever fit in your world.*

But maybe he thought people wouldn't talk about things if Marissa was with him.

Alicia, the sister, leaned back when Robert left, reached for a pack of cigarettes and lit a long white one, eyeing Marissa through a defensive cloud of smoke. "Are you some social worker or something?"

Marissa laughed shortly. "No. I'm a teacher."

"Hmm." A grunt that said nothing Marissa could de-cipher. "So you know my daughter?"

"Yes. She's very bright."

"Stupid, too." Bitterly she exhaled. "I told her and told her not to get pregnant. It ruined my life. Now she gets a taste of it."

Marissa nodded. "It doesn't have to ruin her life. It's just a mistake. Things happen."

The woman snorted, pulled on her blouse. "What do you think, she'll give it up for adoption? That mixed-blood baby? Who would take it? It's just gonna be another brown kid nobody cares about."

"I don't think she wants to give it up," Marissa said mildly.

A grunt. The woman looked at the television, evidently absorbed in some game show question, and Marissa settled back, thinking maybe that was the easiest way through this. Just watch television until he came back.

Rigidness lay on Robert's spine, making him stiff as he walked down the block to the house his sister had pointed out to him, where Mario had lived. Three little girls, none over five, played in the cold afternoon without shoes. As he passed, they stopped what they were doing to watch him, little tummies hanging out beneath shirts that were too short, and he had a pained image of a C.A.R.E. ad.

He knew there'd be no help there, and went instead to the house next door, one that had a handful of weary daffodils coming up in one corner. From across the street, a pack of boys in black clothes and ducktails slick with gel watched him, smoking expertly, blowing clouds of smoke from unsmiling mouths. He ignored them and knocked on the door of the little house.

The woman who answered was short and stout, maybe in her late fifties or early sixties, and she greeted him in Spanish. He started to talk, but she waved a hand holding a dish towel, dismissing him. She didn't speak English, she said, and closed the door.

It felt like a fool's errand, but he knocked on the doors at every house along the block, those boys watching flat-eyed and hard. No luck. The one or two willing to talk to a stranger remembered Mario and his mother, but no one knew where they'd gone. Disappeared. Maybe, they said, ask the lady next door.

Trudging through the cold, entering the bleak yards, seeing the defensive faces poking out of doors opened only a crack, depressed him. Each step took him a little deeper into his old world, reminded him all too clearly of another time. From within the walls of one house came the sound of a violent argument, a woman scream-ing epithets shrilly, and he winced involuntarily. An empty tequila bottle lay in the gutter. A pit bull, tied with a rope to a fence post, tried to take his leg off as he passed, and he heard music spilling out from within, the slightly doomed laughter of a drunken party at five in the afternoon of a weekday.

A car drove down the street slowly, an ordinary Pon-tiac, the radio booming out a rap song. Two men, in their early twenties, looked at him as they passed. Indian, these two, not that it mattered. Everybody here was as doomed as everyone else.

Out of luck, he paused, then approached the boys. "D'you know Mario Trujillo?" he asked.

A snicker from one. "Who wants to know?" asked another, the leader, with burly shoulders.

"Me," he said. They were trying to be tough, but there was an advantage to growing up in a place like this. He was as tough or tougher.

"He moved away, man. Months ago."

"Anybody know where?"

"I'd like to know," said the one sitting. Sharply handsome, a face like a coyote. Fresh, dark tattoo on his neck. "You find out, you let me know, eh?"

Robert had been about to ask if any of them spoke Spanish, since the old woman was his only lead. Now he met that hard-edged gaze, saw the hopelessness, the rage in that boy's eyes, and thought of Crystal, living here, facing this boy every day, and he felt sick to his stomach.

For a long moment he met those murderous eyes, letting the boy see he wasn't afraid, then he raised a chin and left them, walking across the street to his sister's house. "Come on," he said to Marissa. "I struck out."

She jumped up, eager to escape. "Later," he said to Alicia.

She waved.

Outside, Marissa said, "You struck out?"

"Yeah." He waved at the street. "Nobody knows or none of them are talking. Only one who might know only speaks Spanish."

"I speak Spanish."

Startled, he looked down. "You do?"

A wry grin across her pretty red mouth. "That boarding school my parents sent me to? Barcelona, remember?"

He couldn't help it; he grinned.

"You want to go back there?"

"Why not?" He shrugged. "But let's drive over there. It's only down the street, but those little bad dudes are just looking for trouble and you might be just the morsel they'd jump on."

The old woman frowned when she opened the door to Robert again, and started rattling off something in Spanish. Marissa smiled and said something in a soft voice, respectful and calming. The woman smiled, waved them inside, to rooms as brightly colored as the external house was dull. Bright pictures adorned the walls, and a smell of something delicious filled the air. She chattered to Marissa, ignoring Robert completely, and Marissa translated when she thought it was important. "She doesn't like to talk with those boys looking on," she said. "They're the ones who beat up Mario, beat him bad..." She listened a little longer. "His mother was scared and left in the middle of the night, but she sent a note the next day so our friend wouldn't worry that Mario died."

Robert said, "Where did they go?"

Marissa repeated the question, and Robert understood the answer. "Denver."

By the time they emerged from the woman's house, the snow was falling in earnest, a very heavy wet snow that melted as soon as it touched the ground, at least here. Robert eyed it darkly. If it had been clear, he would have headed back to Denver tonight. Everything about this city depressed him. He'd never been happy here, not for even an hour.

"I bet Red Creek is socked in by now," Marissa said, zipping her jacket while they waited for the truck's heater to kick in. "One of those springtime blizzards that make everything green."

He nodded, an ache in his chest. "Wish we were there instead of here."

There was nothing to do but find a room and hope the snow let up by morning. He drove into a better part of town, down a road with a strip of decent motels, and pulled into one of them, a faceless chain. "This all right?"

"Sure."

He turned off the engine and took his wallet out of the glove box, suddenly aware of the long night that stretched ahead of them, of the warmth of her body next to him, the silence that seemed to give him space. Two rooms would be better. Nothing he'd said in Red Creek was any different—whatever was between them was too intense, too much. He felt it licking the base of his spine now, winding around his belly. He wanted, so badly, to just escape his thoughts, and Marissa would make it easy.

And he knew it was a big mistake, second round, but he suddenly turned and found her mouth, kissed her deep and found her not only accepting, but encouraging it, her hands coming up around his face, her fingers cold against his temple. It was just what he'd thought—a place of refuge, of peace, of escape. Sliding his hand around beneath her hair, to the warmth of her neck, he pressed his forehead against hers. "You don't have a lot of sense sometimes, you know it?"

"Go get a room, Robert. We'll think about being sensible tomorrow."

He was a lot of things, but no one had ever called him stupid. "Be right back."

But by the time he carried both of their bags up to the second floor, letting Marissa go in ahead of him, all he felt was numb.

"At least it's good and warm," she said, and he had a bad moment, thinking of what she must be used to. There was nothing fancy about this place. It was comfortably clean and utilitarian, with a generic oil painting of the desert.

He dropped the bags and settled hard on the edge of the bed, suddenly winded. His head felt too heavy for his neck, and he rested his elbows on his thighs, rubbed his face. It had been a long drive, and the end had been discouraging.

She put a hand on his shoulder. "Why don't you lie down for a little while? I'll call for some food of some kind."

"There's no room service, Marissa," he said. Wearily he reached for his boots and pulled them off, falling sideways on the bed.

She chuckled, pulling open a drawer to get the phone book, which she pulled out and showed him. "Chinese? Pizza?" It was fat and heavy, and she had to put it on the desk to flip it open, ruffling through pages to find the restaurant section. "Here we go. Just about anything you could want. Hmmm. What are you in the mood for?"

"I don't care." Putting a hand over his eyes, he felt sleep lapping at his consciousness, and told himself to at least get under the covers so he wouldn't be cold and wake up stiff, but couldn't seem to get that far. Behind his eyelids, flashes of hard boy eyes and a tequila bottle in a gutter came and went, interspersed with the smell of onions and a bit of a song in Spanish. Distantly he heard her moving around, felt the give of the bed when she settled next to him, and the cradle of the blanket falling over both of them. He managed to shift enough to pull her close, her head on his shoulder, before he fell all the way asleep.

She awakened by degrees. Her toes were cold and she drew them up, only then becoming aware of Robert's shoulder beneath her cheek. His arm must surely have fallen asleep, she thought, and started to move, but he stopped her. "Don't go."

A ripple of heat moved through her body at the sound

of his voice, husky and a little raw, the wounds from his youth showing more clearly than he probably would have liked. His hands moved on her, sliding down her arms, her back, his other hand covering a breast, cupping it tenderly as if it held some magic power. And maybe it did.

She rose up a little to kiss him, lightly touching her lips to his, and then again, slowly, tasting bitter memories and deep regret and a child's sorrow there on the man's wide, mobile mouth. As they kissed, he unbuttoned her shirt, hands urgent and tender at once, and opened his mouth to her tongue, drawing her in, as he slid his palms beneath her shirt and stroked her skin, her back and sides, over and over, restlessly.

She moved over him, straddling his hips and straightening so that she could unbutton his shirt. His face was grave, his eyes unreadable and dark, but he let her reveal him, his hands resting on her thighs as she finished, pulled his shirttails from his jeans and exposed his dark chest with its record of brutality. She skimmed her fingers over the arch of his ribs, traced the stylized cross with its sad message, touched his scars and the little tattoos across his shoulder. There was a looping pattern around his belly button, and she smiled. ''This,'' she said, ''is really sexy.'' And she bent to kiss it, tracing it with the tip of her tongue, dipping lightly into that small dark hollow until his hands were on her shoulders, hauling her upward to his mouth. He held her head as she sprawled over him, their bellies pressed together naked, and kissed her with that fierce hunger she'd tasted once before, kindled it in her. Their bodies slid and moved and pressed, heat to heat, as their tongues and mouths and teeth expressed what was to come.

Marissa pulled up, sitting on him, and shed her shirt,

then her bra, and was gratified by the sharp fire in his
eyes, his urgent move to touch her. He flipped them over
and captured her wrists, pulling them over her head with
one hand as he came down to kiss her breasts, kiss and
lick and sup, the dark circle of nipple and the sides and
the valley between, settling at last on the pointed tip, his
teeth scraping lightly, his tongue swirling, the sweet, ex-
plosive pressure. Urgently he turned his head, still holding her wrists in one big hand, and looked down to the
fastening of her jeans so he could get them off, and for
once, Marissa was not self-conscious as he managed the
trick. She lifted her hips to help him and he skimmed
everything down her legs, to her ankles where she could
kick them off. So she was naked. And he was not, and
it didn't matter how she looked in her own eyes or in
the eyes of the world, or if this body was not the best
he'd ever seen, because right now she only saw him,
saw the fall of his braid as he turned back, saw the
graveness of his face as he touched her thighs, slid his
fingers between and touched her.

Just right. She made a guttural cry and broke out of
his grip, reaching for that long rope of hair so she could
pull him to her, and he came, his mouth sealing hers,
his fingers working their magic. "You have to get un-
dressed," she gasped, shivering now with the heat in her.

He raised his head, looked her in the eye. "It's going
to be worse this time," he said in a husky voice. "You
ready?"

She knew what he meant. That as intimate, as terrifying as it had been in her room that night, this was a
lot deeper. She nodded.

Without hurry, he straightened, first taking off the unbuttoned shirt and tossing it off the bed, then working
on his jeans and shorts and socks, which all went over

the side in a heap. A hitch caught in her throat at the sight of all of him, kneeling in ropy strength beside her, and he raised his hands, his eyes on hers, and pulled the rubber band off his braid, deftly working his hands through it to let the slippery, heavy mass of it free.

Marissa could barely breathe. There were no flickering candles now, only the plain light of a basic-issue lamp. He stood on his knees beside her, looking down, and she was as vulnerable as she'd ever been. She opened her arms and whispered, "Come inside, Robert."

He moved, gathering her, their limbs entwining, and still he poised, staring hard at her. "It's me here, Marissa. Me."

"And it's me, Robert," she said. "Do you see me?"

"Yes." He slid into her, his eyes as intense and blazing as anything she'd ever seen. "I see you."

She arched and pulled him down, wrapping her limbs around him. "I see you," she whispered over his mouth. "I see you."

And they started to move, falling into that other world, and Marissa felt tears on her face as he took the refuge she offered, as she breathed his nearness, reached for the shattering intimacy that grew and grew, sober and beautiful and humbling. Each move, each kiss, each exchange of breath took them deeper into it, until Marissa felt that light between them burning from blue to white, brilliant and enveloping, and far more than she could ever have anticipated.

When they finished and lay tangled, she put her arms around his neck and held him close, letting the hot tears run down her face unashamed, because she had been transformed and she knew it, and there was no turning back now. And he did not turn away, as she had half feared he would, only lifted his head and saw her tears and kissed them, took them into his mouth as if they were some sacred fluid, then kissed her mouth gently, returning them to her, a salty sweetness.

It didn't matter, Marissa thought, weak and depleted and pierced clear through, that she hadn't known him very long, that they were from wildly different worlds, that he was never going to be able to let her in and take what she offered. She'd found him, her man, the one she'd been looking for. Not because the sex was good or because she loved that slippery hair falling over her, or because he needed her. Because she knew this soul, because there was a right alignment in the world with them.

Or maybe it was simpler than that. There was no reason. It just was.

## Chapter 14

Robert was the one who insisted they had to have food several hours later. They'd been insatiable, touching, kissing, joining, until both of them were wrung out and trembling. Even as he pulled away from her, he felt little sparks of longing, a wish to fall to it again, just in case there was never another chance. But it had been a very, very long time since lunch, and he was bone empty and dying of thirst, and she had to be, too.

On knees that were just slightly unstable, he stood up and pulled the phone book back to the bed. "What do you want?" he asked, flipping through the listings.

"Chinese," she said, her head resting on her upper arm. "Japanese. Italian, Mexican and American. All of it. Right now."

He chuckled. "Pizza's pretty hearty and fast. The works?"

"Yes. And some of those little breadsticks. And

something to drink. I'm dying.'' She scowled. ''I don't like soda, though.''

''You like wine.''

''I don't think the pizza joint will be delivering a bottle of wine.''

''Yeah, but somebody else might.'' He dialed the pizza number and ordered, then flipped back through the Yellow Pages for an upscale liquor store and picked up the phone and dialed the cab company. ''What kind of wine?'' he asked.

''Something deep and red and Italian,'' she said, stretching luxuriously. Her shoulder, smooth and white, gave him lustful visions. ''Valpolicella.''

He gave directions to the dispatcher, named the liquor store closest to the motel according to the Yellow Pages and hung up. Putting the phone aside, he said, ''You are not to get dressed, understand? I'll keep the deliveries at the door.''

''Greedy, greedy,'' she said. ''I was going to take a shower.''

''Wouldn't you rather wait and share it with me?''

She gave him that sensual, knowing grin that was so at odds with her daily teacher look. ''I could be convinced.''

''Yeah?'' He lifted an eyebrow. ''How?''

''I'll think of something.'' With a sigh she asked, ''What time is it?''

He could just see the digital clock they'd knocked on the floor. ''Almost eleven.''

She laughed. ''Really? My, how time flies.'' She touched his knee. ''Don't you want to call Crystal?''

''Nah. I told her I wouldn't. She'll hear the lies in my voice.''

''Ah. What does she think you're doing?''

He put on his shorts and jeans in preparation for the deliveries, and tugged a wad of bills out of his front pocket and started counting them. "Tyler wants me to do the stained glass in the house restoration, and I told Crystal I was coming to check out this church window down here, at a pueblo." He settled a pile of rumpled bills on the desk. "She knows it's a story, but I'm hoping she thinks it's so I can get off and be alone with you, check things out without hurting her feelings."

"Is she okay with that?"

He nodded.

Marissa sobered, lifting up on one elbow. "And is that why you asked me to come along?"

"No." He picked up her hand, grinning ruefully, his blood light in his veins. "Believe it or not, I thought we'd have separate rooms. I just didn't really want to be alone in this."

"That was the right answer," she said, her eyelids falling to cover the brilliance in them. Her gaze must have touched on his inner arm, because she lifted a finger and dragged it down the uneven, raised scar on the inside of his forearm. "What happened here?"

"Wrecked a car," he said regretfully. "Wasn't even drunk. Just stupid." He frowned, remembering that night. "For a while, when I came out of the army, I didn't much care if I lived or died. The world just seemed like a really bad place and nothing I could do would ever change it."

She stroked the scar with one finger. "I'm glad you lived, Robert." She raised her eyes and he saw the earnestness in her eyes. It was an expression he'd seen dozens of times in a woman's eyes. That soft yearning and admiration, that misty romantic glaze. Usually he ran like hell. This time he felt grateful. And with a wry sense of the world shifting, he wondered if she saw it in his eyes, too. Because he sure as hell felt it when he looked at her.

"Me, too," he said roughly, and kissed her.

They ate ravenously, Robert drinking soda from plastic glasses filled with ice, Marissa sipping her bloodred wine from the same. "Real elegant, huh?" he said, wondering if she minded.

"It's like a picnic."

She ate heartily, leaving only the crust behind. "Don't you like crusts, baby girl?" he teased. "Were you one of those kids who had to have your sandwiches trimmed?"

"Heck, no. I inhaled everything. I'm so hungry right now, though, that I want the nutritious parts." She examined the slice in her hand and looked at him. "It's moments like this, when I'm so hungry that I don't care if I'm ever thin, that I worry I'll be fat again someday."

He lifted a shoulder. "Well, maybe you will. Maybe you won't. I'd guess your walking addiction will keep it down some." He picked up another slice. "In the end, it's really inside that matters."

She huffed. "That is a big fat lie and you know it."

He chuckled. "Is it? Are you really any different from the woman you were?"

"If I were the woman I used to be," she said distinctly, "I would not be lolling half-naked with you eating pizza, now would I?"

He raised his eyes, hearing real pain behind that, and because of that pain, he didn't answer immediately, trying to sort through his answer as honestly as he could. "I don't know," he said finally. "You were pretty prickly before. I always had a big thing about your hair and that—'' he waved his hand in a circle, trying to describe the light that had always been there ''—an exuberance or whatever. But you used to give me that haughty eye, like I was some bug.''

"I did not!"

"Yes, you did." He plucked off a mushroom and tossed it on the box. "Miss Hoity Toity rich girl, with her biker boyfriends. You were too scary to talk to."

She started to laugh. "I was scared to death of you!"

"Sure, sure." He raised a brow. "The point is, Ms. Rich Girl, it was you who came on to me this time, not the other way around. I would never have had the guts."

"I did not!"

"Did, too. What was that bit about the dresses?"

"I didn't follow me out to the deck at Louise's house."

"Oh, yeah." He nodded. "Forgot about that. Wanted to kiss you, too, but you were too scary."

She rolled her eyes. "Well, it's nice of you to say so, but I don't buy it for one second."

He lifted a shoulder. "Believe it or not, princess. Up to you."

"Stop calling me that!"

He laughed, and, finally full, rolled over onto his back, staring up at the ceiling. Outside, the wind howled at the windows, a sad and lonely sound that took him back. "So tell me, princess, what's it like to be so rich, anyway?"

She made a noise of disbelief. "What do you think?"

"I don't know." He looked at her. "Serious question."

"Fair enough." She closed the pizza box and moved it to the dresser, then came back, carrying her wine. Sitting cross-legged, dressed only in his shirt, she said,

"It's pretty much what you think it is. I mean, what's not to like? Money can do almost anything. Save a condemned house, put a kid through college, build a shelter for runaways." She grinned, impishly. "Not to mention it's not that bad to fly off to Venice if you're in the mood."

He put his hand around her foot. "Are those things you've done? Saved a house and built a shelter?"

"Yeah, my house. It was trashed, ready for the wrecking ball."

She didn't affirm the runaway shelter, but it gave him a sense of how much money she really did have. "You have more money than you'll ever be able to spend, don't you?"

She nodded sadly. "'Fraid so. I can't even seem to give it away significantly. Foundations here and there and everywhere. But the thing is, seed money seems to just grow, so pretty soon they don't need me as much anymore."

He laughed. "Hell of a problem to have." He wondered why it didn't seem to matter so much tonight, that she was from that rare, strange world. But he knew: it was just the two of them. No outside influences. Idly rubbing her toes, he asked, "And what's bad about it? The way you grew up?"

A shrug. "Not that so much. It was a drag, but it was survivable, always. No," she said, frowning a little. "The hard part is that old saying, you know, 'To him much is given, much is required.' I'm always worried that when it comes time to give an accounting for what I did, I'll be judged shallow and silly and not earnest enough."

"Tiffany screens?"

She toasted him. "*Exactement.* What earthly use is that?"

"I don't know, but it sure is pretty." In the soft yellow light, her breasts showed a deep cleft, and he thought lazily about putting his hand, or maybe his mouth, there. "Maybe not everything has to be sensible, not every single bit. If there was no one to buy great art, what would artists do?"

"That's true." Her gaze wandered a little, too, touching his chest, his mouth, and he quirked his lips in a smile. "Are you going to do the window?"

"No. It's too big a project for me. I've never done anything close."

"I think you should try anyway. There's plenty of time. If it doesn't work out, they can get someone else to do it."

"Yeah, and waste all those materials."

"But they won't pay you if it doesn't work out, so how much will they really be out?"

He lifted his hand and unbuttoned the top button of her shirt, then the next. "I don't know."

"I somehow suspect you don't really care," she said with an earthy little laugh as he pushed apart the loose fabric and exposed her breasts.

"Nope," he said, bending close. "Not a bit."

Morning dawned cold but clear, and the road reports said that I-25 was clear to the Wyoming state line, so they headed out early. Before they could get out of town, Robert said he needed to go to the pueblo church and look at the window he admired, so his lie to Crystal wouldn't be a lie.

They stopped at a gold-colored pueblo, old and somehow exhausted looking, even with a dusting of sparkling snow. "It'll only take me a minute," he said, and, sensing that he wanted to look at it alone, Marissa waited in the truck with the engine running for heat. She waited, but when he didn't come back for a little while, she turned the engine off and went looking for him.

She found him inside, standing with his hands loose at his sides, his head tilted up to look at a stained-glass window. Sunlight set it ablaze, and bits of red and yellow and blue light fell on his figure. Marissa took an involuntary breath and came to stand beside him in awe.

It was a Madonna image, a Native American Madonna with a Native American baby Christ. The colors were pure and perfect, the shape and form of the principles perfectly, artistically rendered, Mary's face so alight with motherly love that it brought an involuntary rush of tears to Marissa's eyes. "Oh!" she said softly. "It's beautiful!"

"It's not Tiffany," Robert said.

"No," Marissa agreed, her throat tight. The colors were much bolder, more primary—almost medieval. "It's different." Embarrassed at her easy emotions, she wiped a tear away. "Who's the artist?"

He stuck his hands in his pockets. "Me." He looked at her, his mouth cocked in a rueful expression. His eyes were puzzled. "I'm kind of surprised. I didn't think it was very good."

Marissa looked up at it, and that same deep wash of emotion came through her, a function of the work itself. "To whom much is given, much is required," she said.

Only when the sun moved off the window did he move, tugging her hand lightly. They nodded to a youthful priest, so handsome, the local girls must be in a swoon at every Mass, and got back in the truck. Robert didn't say a word.

It was one of the best days of Marissa's life, riding with Robert in his truck, sometimes laughing, sometimes sober. Sometimes they talked about themselves, sometimes about world events, sometimes about Red Creek and the people there.

And they talked glass. Endlessly. Marissa had never known anyone who knew as much about glass as she did. Colors, glazes, styles, artists. He knew everything. He'd spent six years in Europe with the army, and spent any free time wandering through the museums and cathedrals in the great capitals. It amazed her.

But as they neared Castle Rock, a small town outside of Denver, the buoyant nature of the conversation changed. "Do you have any idea of what you're going to do?" Marissa asked.

"None. Call every Trujillo in the phone book?"

"That could take a century or two." Hesitantly she said, "I have some contacts who might be able to help."

"I'm listening," he said. But Marissa felt a clutch in her belly. It was one thing to hear that she had established foundations. If she used these contacts, he'd learn a lot more. But Crystal was the most important consideration here, and she told him where to go.

Marissa directed Robert to a downtown Denver office building, spanking new, in a central location. When he would have parked on the street, she said, "No, go around to the back. There's a ramp with parking below. I have my own spot."

That was his first warning. The second was the deference of the security guard when Marissa popped her head into view. "Hi, George," she said sweetly. "It's me."

The old black man bent into the window. "How you doing, sweetheart?"

"Just fine. How's your wife's chemo going?"

"Some days are better than others, but she's holding her own."

"Tell her I said hello."

"Will do." He straightened and hit the car on the hood, like Robert was a chauffeur. It rankled.

Inside, things went steadily downhill. The building was a warren of offices, most of them referral services, Marissa told him, for various kinds of problems in the community. One floor was devoted to teens and their troubles, and Robert was slightly startled to see a room full of hoodlum-looking kids taking a martial arts class of some sort. "What is this place?" he said with a scowl.

"It's all kinds of things," Marissa said. "Mainly resources of various sorts, a place people can come outside the government structure to get help for whatever it is they need help with."

"Whatever they need."

"Yeah." She gave him a puzzled smile. "Why is that so hard to imagine?"

"Everything seems a pretty big palette."

"It is sometimes. But that class for example, has really been a godsend. It keeps a bunch of kids off the street after school during that work period before parents get home, and it's free." A thin black woman spotted Marissa and rushed over to hug her. Marissa, startled but pleased, hugged her back.

"I am so glad to see you!" the woman cried. "I missed your big night, and wanted to be there so bad. Did you get my present?"

"The bowl! Yes, I did. It was wonderful." Marissa introduced her as Ruth Idamiller, head of counseling services, and Robert nodded politely, but the woman simply wanted to adore Marissa.

It happened over and over as they made their way through the halls, up the stairs, down another hallway. Over and over people stopped, hugged her, kissed, asked after her health. It wasn't the obsequious bowing and scraping Robert had sometimes seen in the army when a four-star general showed up out of the blue, either. It was something else. They loved her. Young and old, the people who ran the programs and the people who presented them. They felt free to approach her, not awed, as he would have expected.

She secured the use of an empty office to make phone calls, and gestured for Robert to make himself comfortable while she rounded the desk, tossed down her purse and picked up the phone. "It might take me a little while," she said. "Feel free to wander around or whatever. We can get some supper when we're finished."

Oddly unsettled, Robert paced the office, peering at the books stacked in a tumble on the shelves—this must be a fund-raising office, since there were dozens of materials on how to write and apply for grants and special services. Degrees on the wall confirmed his guess. Idly he moved toward a series of framed newspaper articles, hearing behind him Marissa make small talk with various officials. No one was busy when Marissa Pierce was on line one, he noticed. They all took her calls, pronto.

Amazing. He felt a stab of admiration and another of something else—maybe discomfort?—at the easy mantle of power that lay on her shoulders. He'd never have guessed it.

The framed newspaper articles were matted nicely and showed the progression of the center, starting with one on the upper left, a photo of a group of people in hard hats breaking ground. Foundation Center Begun it read. The photo was blurry and showed a smear of smiling faces. Other articles, most without photos, chronicled the progress.

It was the last one that stopped him cold. It showed a picture of a beaming Marissa—in that devastating blue dress she'd been wearing the first time he kissed her— with a giant pair of scissors in her hand and a symbolic ribbon between the blades. Benefactress Blesses Building it read. Nice bit of alliteration, he thought with a grin, leaning closer to read the article.

And his heart sunk.

He turned around to look at her hard. She'd put the phone down, scribbled a note to herself and seemed to feel his attention. "What?" she asked, obviously picking up something from his expression, because the word was defensive.

"This whole place is your doing?"

"Not at all," she said with a frown. "You see all these people in here."

"Yeah, but none of them had the money to make it happen, did they? The seed money, you called it, I think."

She frowned, pressing her lips together, smoothing a lock of hair from her face. "Right."

He didn't know why he felt betrayed, but the emotion was unmistakable. "Twenty-five million dollars isn't *seed* money, Marissa." He swore. "How rich *are* you? Tell me the truth."

She folded those clean white hands neatly on the desk blotter and met his eyes without a single hint of expression on her face. "One hundred and seventy-five million," she said calmly. "Feel better now?"

If a knife had cut him from neck to belly, he could

not have felt it more deeply. He closed his eyes, a little dizzy, and sat down in the chair. "God."

"I told you you didn't want to know," she said, and stood briskly. "The good news is, I've got a lead. Let's go."

Crystal was cranky and restless on Thursday morning. Her back was achy, but not in the labor-pain way, but from lying around so much. She wanted to get out, do something, see real people instead of movies on the screen. And she was a little depressed, too, thinking of her uncle off with her teacher, maybe falling in love. Would there be room for her after that?

She was slumped in the kitchen, working on her homework when Louise called to her. "Crystal, darlin', can you come here for a minute?"

Crystal winced, threw down her pencil and lumbered into the room, holding her belly where the baby was sliding a foot in one long, slow kick all the way down her left side. She rubbed it hard, trying to make him stop. "Quit, baby, that hurts!"

Louise stood at the window, her arms crossed, a funny expression on her face. "There's someone here," she said. "I don't know who it is, but you might."

Something hot and scared went through Crystal, and for a minute she was frozen, her hand hard on the foot of the baby. Her breath had sailed away, and she couldn't quite get it back. Louise looked at her. "Come look."

Crystal eased up to the window, afraid to see, afraid not to. Robert's truck was parked in front, and she saw him get out on the driver's side and stretch, followed by Marissa. The passenger door opened, and out stepped a figure with dark hair. No, not just dark.

Her heart caught. It was the blackest hair she'd ever seen, shining the way it always did in the sunlight. He wore his leather jacket, the one his mother had saved to buy him for Christmas, and it made him look strong. With a noise she wasn't even sure came from her, Crystal turned and bolted for the door, yanking it open, running down the walk, tears streaming out of her eyes. It felt like her heart was exploding, burning up her chest, and she had to stop, just short of him, to cover her mouth, try to pull it together.

It was only then that she remembered that he had not seen her pregnant, and might not like it, and she put her hands on her belly, hiding it, looking up to see how he would take it. He was standing very still, only a few feet away, and his chest was moving hard like he'd been running. One hand covered the side of his face, and he looked scared and sad all at once. "Mario?" she said.

He held out a hand, his mouth moving, but no words came out. And she catapulted forward, touching the damage that made his eye crooked, damage from a beating that had nearly killed him. It marred his face, dragged his eye down, but he was still her Mario, her only only one, and she couldn't stop the wild swell of emotions in her any longer. She took that precious face in her hands and kissed it, kissed the mouth and the nose and last the ruined place.

He made a harsh, deep noise, and she knew he was trying not to cry as he crushed her to him. "I was in the hospital a long time," he said. "And when I got out, I couldn't find you."

And they were both crying. Laughing, crying, kissing. His hand on her tummy, questioning, and she nodded, and more tears. And then they just slumped together, her head on his shoulder, and she knew everything would be all right.

All three adults were misty-eyed to varying degrees, Marissa noticed, trying to blink away her own tears. Louise was unabashedly weeping at the window, blowing her nose on a blue tissue as she watched, and as Robert and Marissa came in, she gave them a beneficent smile. "They're gonna be just fine," she said.

They all three watched the pair at the foot of the drive. The young couple touched each other's heads, as if to ascertain the reality of the other body, their hands tangling. Crystal pulled him down to sit beside her, and held his hand in both of hers, listening intently as he talked. Her face blazed with such happiness, Marissa could hardly believe it was the same girl. "Her knight in shining armor," she said, thinking of the way Crystal had always stared out the windows at school.

"Where'd you find him?" Louise asked.

Marissa stiffened a little. Robert looked at her and said, "Denver. We looked in Albuquerque, but his mother hustled him out of there after some gangbangers nearly beat him to death." His mouth went grim. "Literally."

"I have a few connections in Denver," Marissa supplied mildly. "They helped us find him very quickly."

"A few connections," Robert echoed quietly, not meeting her eyes.

Her mouth tightened. "I'm beat. Need to get home. Can you take a few minutes and drop me off?"

He nodded. "Be right back," he said to Louise.

On her way to the truck, Marissa paused to hug Crystal. "Come see me as soon as you can, okay?"

Crystal caught her hand. "Will you come to dinner?

Please please please? Not today. But…Saturday, maybe?''

Marissa looked at Robert, who gave a dense little shrug. "Sure," Marissa said. "Take care, Mario."

The boy stood to shake her hand. "Thank you, Ms. Pierce. I don't know how I'll ever repay you."

"No need," she said. "Just take good care of them."

"I will," he promised.

She waved and climbed into the truck with Robert. The former ease between them, fostered by a meeting of hearts that took place away from the world, had shattered once the world intruded, but it seemed desperately unfair to her now.

Marissa had seen the walls going up, shooting up, the whole time they were in the offices. And there had been nothing she could do to stop them.

Now she said, "I guess I can safely assume that whatever we discovered back there in Albuquerque is going to stay there, huh?"

He dipped his head, sighed. "Marissa, it's just ridiculous for us to even think about a real relationship. Even if it's never true, the only thing anyone's going to see when they look at me is a man using you for your money." He shot her a dark look. "And I'm not entirely convinced that you aren't slumming to some degree. It just doesn't make any sense—why would you keep dating guys like me, when the whole world is open to you?"

"Guys like you?" she echoed. "I don't date anyone like anyone else. I've had one simple rule from the beginning—a man had to see me. Not the money, not the fat, not anything external. Me."

That stopped him for a minute. Then he shook his

head. "It doesn't matter. It's not about you, it's about me. It's too much. It makes me uncomfortable."

She shook her head. "No," she said. "You're afraid. You're afraid that it can't be real if we're from such different worlds." She paused. "You're afraid that I'll betray you."

He swallowed, staring hard out of the window, and she knew she'd struck the truth. And how could she possibly address that? Defeated, she said only, "Fine." As he came to a stop outside her house, she let herself out of the truck and slammed the door, stomping up the walk, wishing for the yards of hair she used to have so she could flip it haughtily.

"Hey, princess," he called.

She turned, eyes narrowed. "What?"

"Thanks for your help." He lifted a hand and drove away.

She wanted to throw something at him. "Aaargggghhh!" she cried, and Victoria came out of the house, her mouth quirked. "Told you."

"I know," she said darkly, and raised her miserable eyes to her sister's face. "Don't you get sick of it, Victoria?"

"Yeah, sweetie. I really do."

# Chapter 15

Over the next few days, Robert kept his mind off Marissa by staying busy. He told Tyler he'd attempt the window, pay suspended until it was finished, and Tyler was gratifyingly pleased. They ordered the materials straight away, and Tyler insisted upon turning over a studio area in the Forrest Construction complex for him to work on it. He spent his evenings working out small representations at the kitchen table, a piece here and there, tiny replicas of this corner or that section.

It gave him room to think about Mario and Crystal. After dinner the first night, the two had presented their case: hands laced together for courage, they asked Robert to help them get married. It floored him at first, and he'd not been able to give them a definitive answer. He needed to think about it. They were disappointed, but respectful. A point in their favor, actually.

Now that he'd had a chance to observe them, it was plain they were more than teenage lovers who'd grown infatuated with each other and thought it was the real thing. No Romeo and Juliet here. They talked all the time, about all kinds of things. He heard them murmuring, laughingly arguing, planning, dreaming. They watched movies together, took short walks when Mario discovered Crystal needed to build up her strength. He helped her with her homework, and together they designed and carried out a science experiment in the kitchen so that she could pass her class.

But Robert remained torn. Crystal was only sixteen. Mario was eighteen and a high school graduate, and he'd been working to help support his mother while he saved money toward college. If they got married now, chances were very good neither one could afford to go to college, and that would be a tragedy.

But how much worse a tragedy if the family was torn asunder? He wanted to talk about it. Wanted, specifically to talk to Marissa about it. She'd have good insights. He trusted her judgment.

He did not, however, trust his will to be aloof with her. Not yet. In time he'd get over this hormonal overload, forget about her and find someone appropriate. Whatever shook out with Crystal and Mario, it was plain to Robert that he was taking on more of a family than he'd ever anticipated. It gave him a wild, stunned sense of happiness, but Marissa had so much more going for her. She could do anything, go anywhere. Why would she even want to be here with them?

Louise was just heartsick. All her planning and scheming had come to nothing—and just when she was so close. There was a small victory in getting Mario back to his Crystal. As devoted a pair of young lovers as she'd ever seen, and they had plenty of good sense to see what they had, unlike some adults she knew. If more adults had that kind of sense, Louise would not be required to meddle nearly as much.

But Crystal told her that Robert and Marissa had not even spoken on the telephone since they'd returned last week, and in fact, Marissa had called at the last minute to cancel dinner plans Saturday night, saying she had a cold.

Too much pride. Both of them.

She'd just see about that.

Marissa did have a cold. A miserable, headachy, dismal virus that kept her in bed for three days. It was almost welcome, since it reflected her internal misery so well. She took an almost gleeful satisfaction in it, and let Victoria take care of her with chicken soup made from scratch and endless cups of herb tea. The two of them hibernated together in her bedroom, safe from the outside world, in a way they hadn't done in years and years. Victoria spilled the tale of her disastrous love affair with an actor whose name was very familiar. Marissa spilled her woes over Robert. They shared the little things that had formed the past couple of years—Marissa's crusades for programs to benefit the poor, her drive to get into the high school as a teacher, the excitement of owning her first home. Victoria shared her travels, her process of creation and the possibility of one of her screenplays being directed by a very hot director.

It was soothing and peaceful. "Why don't we do this more often?" Marissa asked late Sunday evening. "Just plan a retreat and meet every few months, so we can heal and rejuvenate? There's no one in the world who understands me the way you do."

"We should," Victoria said. "It's true for me, too.

Maybe that's part of what makes it so hard to find the right guy. It's hard to measure up to a twin.''

Marissa nodded, but her heart yelped. She'd found the right guy. He just wouldn't let himself be that man.

The phone rang—Louise calling to invite them both to a dinner at the country club, in honor of Crystal and Mario's reunion. ''I have a couple of real nice fellas lined up for you both to meet.''

''Louise,'' Marissa warned, ''don't do it. You know better. I'll tell Alonzo.''

''Pish,'' she said dismissively. ''He only minds when I do it in an underhanded way, and I'm not. I'm being very up-front with you. There are two nice, young, single men with excellent credentials and I'm hoping one or the other of you will hit it off with one or another of them.''

Marissa grinned. ''All right. I guess that's legal.''

''Tuesday, seven o'clock. Black tie.''

''Black tie?'' Marissa said. ''What are you going to do about Crystal and Mario and Robert?''

''Don't you worry about that. I've got them covered.''

''Okay.'' She put the receiver down and fell back on the bed. ''We are summoned,'' she said to Victoria. The phone rang again and a stab of knowledge, awareness, *heat* blistered through her. She picked up the phone. ''Robert!'' she said, and then tried to smooth it, but her voice just dropped to a smoky register. ''Hi.''

''How did you know it was me? Caller ID?''

Marissa closed her eyes, focusing everything on that voice, touching her ear, and felt the purest, most pointed longing she'd ever experienced in her life just to be standing next to him for five minutes.

And then she realized what he'd said, and her gaze flew to Victoria in alarm. ''Uh, yeah,'' she said, distracted by the sorrow in her sister's face. But even that couldn't pull her away from the sound of Robert on the phone. Him. The one. "How are you?"

"All right. You?"

"Bad. I have a terrible cold. It only seems fair that you should have it, too."

He laughed, the sound coming out before he could stop himself, she was sure. "Sturdy stock, I guess." A pause. "Listen, I don't want to intrude, but I'd really like to talk to you about Crystal and Mario. Friend to friend."

Liar, she thought. But she said, "Sure. When?"

"Whenever is convenient for you."

"Now is good." She heard Victoria sigh heavily behind her. "Want to get a latte or something?"

"That'd be great."

When she hung up after arranging the details, Victoria was standing by the window, her back to Marissa. "Your heart is going to be shattered in this, Reesy." The childhood nickname only came out at dire moments. "I feel it."

"You feel the danger of that possibility," Marissa said, getting out of bed. "And I won't deny that exists. But I'm not willing to throw away the possibility of joy because there also exists a possibility of pain."

Victoria still didn't turn. "You knew it was him."

Marissa paused, thinking of the night he'd come to her house and she'd run down the stairs thinking that Victoria had come. "I know." And in spite of herself, she felt a flutter of terror. "It happened before, too."

"The first day, when I called you and you had just talked to him at school, I was scared enough that I knew I needed to come visit." At last, Victoria turned, her arms crossed over her belly. "I'm scared I'll lose you to him," she said, and a tear shone in her eyes. "And then I won't find anyone to match you."

Marissa flew across the room and threw her arms around her sister. "Oh, honey! This is different from what you and I have. It feels really good. You'll see, I promise."

"If he hurts you, I'll kill him," she said.

"No, you won't," Marissa said with a smile. "You'll be too busy feeding me chicken soup."

Robert waited for her at the café they'd agreed upon. It was a bright spring afternoon, the ground sloppy and wet from recent snow, but promising verdant green any second. He ordered his latte and sat by the window, tapping a spoon against the table, peering out anxiously for a glimpse of her. The woman in front of him turned around at the noise he was making, and he put the spoon down. "Sorry."

At last she arrived, one minute not there, the next standing in the doorway, slightly windblown, looking for him. Her cheeks were flushed, as if she'd hurried, and she wore a simple white shirt with jeans—an outfit that doomed him as she caught sight of him and waved, then started toward him, her breasts moving seductively beneath—

He winced and wiped his face. Not that it helped all that much. He smelled her before she sat down, a soft greeny note that made him think of pines and margaritas and sex. It was earthy, he realized, not the rich-cosmetic smell he'd always thought. Not perfume and lotions and potions, just the essence of Marissa—charismatic, quirky, sexy, strong.

His heart ached.

"Hi," he said, and there was roughness at the edges.

"Hi," She sat down and folded her hands in front of her, those bottle-blue eyes bright. Her nose was red and she was stopped up, her voice a little croaky. "What did you order?"

"I got you a real latte, not-skinny, since you've been sick. Do you mind?"

She smiled, flashing those perfect rich-girl teeth. "Thank you." She sipped it. "So, what's going on with Crystal and Mario?"

He took a breath and just said it straight out. "They want to get married."

"Ah. I see." Her face sobered, taking in all the implications. "And what do you think?"

"I don't know. I can't make up my mind. They're so young—they hardly know anything about themselves yet. How can they know they'll still love each other twenty, thirty years down the line?"

She nodded seriously.

"On the other hand, people used to do it all the time, didn't they? Love, make the commitment and then stick with it, through thick and thin. They have a baby coming."

"That's true."

He looked at her across the table, at the light falling over her poreless skin, casting white crescents over her glossy hair, and his entire world narrowed. He didn't hear the other patrons or the noise of the espresso machines, couldn't smell the rich aromas of chocolate and coffee, only Marissa. Only her eyes, burning blue like a bottle he'd found at a Salvation Army store and put on a window for some tiny touch of beauty in his life. "I don't know what to do," he said, and wasn't sure which dilemma he was talking about.

She placed her hand over his. "Do you want me to just listen, or do you want my opinion?"

"I want—I trust—your opinion, your insight."

A flicker of sadness there in her eyes, quickly doused. She leaned forward, meeting his eyes earnestly. "I keep thinking about the way they greeted each other. It was—" she looked around, as if the word she sought was in the air above them "—like everything you ever dream about romance, but also about love. They weren't seeing the flaws. They were seeing each other, totally, and they were so grateful to have that one thing in their lives that was right."

He felt a tightness in his throat and he nodded.

"They are young. But their innocence was stolen a long time ago, and I think they're always going to be each other's helpmates, married or not. So you might as well let them make that public commitment, let their baby be born to parents who are married and love each other and have said they're going to stay together forever."

He ducked his head, hiding emotions that just roared out from somewhere. Her hand was still over his, and he moved his thumb to touch her fingers, seeking the refuge, the strength he'd found with her that cold, sad night in Albuquerque. And somehow it gave him the space he needed to take a breath, raise his head and smile. "Very wise." He hesitated, then let the rest come out. He didn't talk about his mother, not ever, but it seemed germane here. Important. "When my mother was pregnant with me, she was madly in love with a guy who just left her to fend for herself. What kind of difference would there have been in her life, in my life, in Alicia's and Crystal's lives if there'd been a kid like Mario, standing there—" He cleared his throat, looked out the window, continued. "Just standing there, loving them?"

She didn't reply. Knew even that—knew that he needed the moment of her silence to reassemble his control. Her hand stayed steady on his own.

"Thanks," he said at last.

She smiled gently. "Sure."

For one long, aching moment, he looked at her across the table and wanted to just put everything right. All he would have to do was lean over the table and kiss that precious, sweetly flavored mouth. He felt his mouth parting, felt the yearning for it like a grasping hand, but he didn't have the courage to do it. In his imagination, he saw Jake Forrest standing on a cliff and the land giving way beneath it. He saw the promise of order and honor in the army disintegrate under the force of a war that punished the innocent. He saw his mother—

"I'm sure," he said quietly, "that Crystal will want to tell you herself."

"Okay."

He drained the rest of his latte in a single gulp and put the cup down, realizing she was just gravely looking at him, a sad smile on her face.

"What?" he said.

"You just don't get it, do you?" she said, and stood. "Never mind. Don't answer that." And she left, swinging those bodacious hips as naturally as some siren. More than one male head turned to watch, and Robert wanted to sock every last one of them with a solid right to the jaw. They didn't know her. They had no right.

Sadly, neither did he.

# Chapter 16

Tuesday evening, Marissa and Victoria dressed separately—Marissa at home, Victoria in the ski lodge—and arranged to meet at the doors of the country club a little before seven. Marissa, in a last-ditch bid to convince Robert Martinez that he was the stupidest man in the world if he let her get away, was wearing the blue dress—altered a little to avoid the gaping problem—that had slain him that night he first kissed her.

To both of their amusement, Victoria showed up in exactly the same dress in red. "No way!" Victoria cried. "I just bought this dress a few weeks ago!"

"So did I." Marissa laughed. At least the accessories were different. Victoria had flung a huge, antique piano scarf with fringe around her shoulders, while Marissa had on a little black jacket. The gifts they carried for Crystal and Mario were suspiciously close to the same size. "Maybe we need to compare notes," Marissa said as they walked in. "I bought a layette, in green."

"Movie scripts," Victoria said, grinning. "The girl's a natural. I want to start priming her to be my successor now."

"Oh, that's great!"

The party was in a large room near the back of the building, and they heard the voices of many people laughing and talking before they went in. Marissa took a breath, bracing herself.

Victoria took her arm. "Chins up."

But even Victoria had to suck in her breath at the magnificence of one devastatingly sexy male when they walked in. He stood by a cloth-covered table, drinking red punch from a crystal cup, making polite conversation with a woman in a low-cut black dress who was doing everything but falling down in a dead swoon.

Marissa made an annoyed sound, but Victoria said, "Well, I can't say that I blame her."

Nor could Marissa. As always in public, the long hair was smoothed into a tight, glossy braid that fell down his back. As always, his lean, strong body carried his clothes as neatly, perfectly as if he were a model. But she'd never seen him in a tuxedo before, and she could see it was custom tailored. He looked exotic, flirtatious and absolutely devastating in the hushed and elegant room.

"What a rat," she said, and, in a sudden, irrational impulse, ignored him. "Let's find Louise and her suitable suitors, shall we?"

But before they'd even moved, Louise was on them, smelling of Chanel No. 5, her hair coiffed and upswept. "Come on, girls. I've got people for you to meet."

The people were, of course, young men. Several of them Marissa already knew and did not find impressive. One in particular had been a thorn in her side for years;

the son of a business associate of her father's, he had everything: money, breeding, good looks. He was a vigorous sportsman and had always nagged Marissa to "work her body" more so she could get some of her weight off. It was very irritating to discover he'd been right.

She had not seen him in some time, and his eyes widened. "Marissa?" he said with a flattering look of amazement. "You look great!"

She smiled. It wasn't his fault he was nauseatingly normal. "Thanks."

He grinned. "And you're as gorgeous as I always suspected. What did you do? Wait—" He looked at her body frankly, but without offense. It was just the way he did things. "Walk. You walk, right?"

"Louise told you."

"No. Those calves are a dead giveaway."

"Really?" She looked down to see what he saw, and realized she did have very buff calves. She smiled at him, genuinely this time. "Good guess."

Crystal fretted when Marissa came in. "Look, there she is," she hissed to Mario. "We have to do something."

He lifted his eyebrows. "It's not our business. They're adults. They can figure it out."

"*No,* Mario." She scowled when Louise dragged Marissa and her sister over to a bunch of young rich guys standing by the windows, and they all started talking. Crystal wondered if Robert noticed. She glanced at him, and saw him raising his glass to drink some punch like he didn't have a care in the world.

What was wrong with these two?

And what was Louise doing, anyway? Mr. Chacon

was sitting across the table from her, smiling beneath his bushy mustache, his eyes twinkling as he watched his wife. "What is she doing, Mr. Chacon?" Crystal said urgently.

He made a gesture with his hand that meant more or less to settle down. "She's matchmaking, *hija*. Watch and see what she does by the end of this night." He chuckled.

"But I—"

"Watch," he said again, and winked.

Crystal decided to give it through supper, due to be served by buffet in a half hour. If things weren't looking better by then, she'd take matters into her own hands.

She didn't even look his way when she came in, Robert noticed, despite the fact that he'd been unable to keep himself from paying attention to every detail as he dressed tonight. The tux he'd had for more than five years, purchased for a song just before he got out of the army. The cuff links were from a trip to Italy. The earring in his pierced ear was a ruby he'd purchased in the Middle East, the heavy ring a memento from Brussels.

And she didn't even notice. Louise hustled her over to the corner with those three guys, and they were hovering like a bunch of bees, laughing too loudly at her jokes, trying to curry favor by bringing her champagne or pulling out a chair.

One in particular grated on Robert's nerves, and it was a little thing. Marissa reached for a morsel of cheese on the tray that graced the middle of each table, and he grinned and took it away from her. Marissa's face bled of expression for a single instant, but then she was smiling again.

"Idiot," he murmured under his breath.

They called for dinner and they all filled plates with the robust offerings. Robert told himself to get over it, and immersed himself in the very solid attention of the young woman in a black dress who'd attached herself to him. It was amusing more than arousing. She had to be fifteen years his junior, with a kind of fresh-faced earnestness that spoke of travels to beleaguered places. She was so pleased to have a real Native American to talk to that he was even tempted to make up some reservation stories.

The second little incident happened during dinner. Marissa had piled her plate with melons and veggies, and when she was finished, she stood up to return to the buffet. The man beside her, laughing, gestured at her chair and took her plate out of her hands.

Marissa blinked, stood up and walked back to the buffet, where she chose meat and a sliver of pie. Robert found himself waiting for the familiar gesture—and grinned when she cut the pie in half lengthwise and put it on another plate, which she carried back to her sister.

At the end of dinner, Crystal leaned over with a hard look on her face. "Uncle, if you let that woman walk away, you're really a lot stupider than I thought."

He narrowed his eyes. "What do you mean?"

She rolled her eyes. "Oh, I guess you don't know that she's wearing a green dress."

"Blue."

She gave him a hard look. "Exactly."

But he couldn't seem to do anything about it, even then. There were toasts to Crystal and Mario. Sweet toasts, really, with Jake and Ramona in the lead. And then, finally, there was dancing.

Robert thought maybe then he'd have a chance to talk, at least a little, to Marissa. But she was a popular partner,

and something about the whole aspect of the evening
made him remember her from years before. When she
and Lance, Louise's middle son, would tear up the floor
at the Wild Moose Inn while Jake and Red Dog drank
their shots and watched.

He was an imposter, and he knew it. He wondered
why she didn't know.

Because she really didn't. Every so often, he caught
her glancing his way, then glancing quickly away when
he looked up. He wondered if that blue dress had been
fixed and if that was why the dude with the teeth was
hovering, and the idea gave him a shock of intense jeal-
ousy.

Enough to propel him across the room finally, and
bend over close to her ear. "Want to dance, beautiful?"

She raised her eyes. "Yes. Very much."

The man next to her said, "Sorry, man, she's with
me."

Marissa made a noise. "Wrongo, buddy."

The man leaned over and said, loudly enough for only
Marissa and Robert to hear, "You don't have to go
slumming like that anymore, babe. Have a little self-
respect."

Marissa stood up without a word and headed out toward the dance floor. She looked over her shoulder at
Robert. "Coming?"

He gave her a rueful smile as he put his arms around
her. "Senator's son?"

"Close enough," she said. "I really think I need to
marry him immediately."

Oh, God, she felt good. Their bodies were just somehow perfectly aligned, shoulder to chest to hip to knee,
so there was a simple alignment. "Absolutely."

He moved his hands on her sides, feeling the slippery

heat of her flesh beneath the dress. Her breasts brushed his chest. Her hips moved a little closer as she met his eyes. "Maybe this was a bad idea," he said.

"Only if you're still chicken."

"Chicken!"

"Yeah. Like yellow. Like a big fat coward." The deep blue eyes narrowed. "I dare you. Double dare you. Double triple dare you to kiss me like you mean it, right now."

He went still, feeling terror and desire in equal measures. This world was not his world. And his world, or at least the world he'd once known, was not hers. "And then what?"

"Whatever you want." Her lips quirked. "I bet you can think of something."

He thought of her Tiffany screen, the shards of individual glass burning with light, thought of her standing with him in a pueblo in New Mexico admiring a work of art with tears in her eyes. He thought of her laughing, her joy, and the agony of loss he'd felt these past few days.

"I love you," he said suddenly.

"I know you do," she said.

And there really wasn't anything left to do. He stopped dancing and pulled her close and kissed her, that same electric, blistering kind of kiss they shared the first time. A deep kiss. Then a tender one. "I'm scared to death," he whispered against her neck.

"Me, too," she said. "But I'm a lot more terrified of what happens if I don't grab you now."

"What are *you* afraid of?" he said, surprised.

"Oh, about a million things. That you only want me now because I'm thin." A ruefulness in the words, but genuine sorrow, too.

"I don't care about your body, Marissa," he said gruffly. "I mean I like it, but I've known zillions of bodies. It's not about that."

She swallowed hard and he could see she didn't believe him. "What about you? What are you so afraid of?"

"That you'll wake up one day and see that you've married an ex-runaway nobody with nothing to offer."

"Marry?"

"You're the one who said it. With Crystal and Mario." He lifted a shoulder. "If you don't want the whole gig, I can't play."

She was utterly still, and he was suddenly sick with apprehension, thinking of a moment when they'd made perfect love and Marissa had panicked. His pride couldn't take that now, not in front of all these people.

"I'm amazed, that's all. I didn't expect it," she said.

"Stop torturing me, Marissa. I'll bring you a prenuptial agreement, all that. I know I come with a lot of baggage—the kids and their family, but you knew that, too."

"Yes," she said.

"Yes," he echoed, frowning.

"I knew it was you on the phone," she said, and leaned close, putting her head on his shoulder with a sigh of relief.

"I don't understand."

"I'll explain later." She raised her hands around his neck. "Just kiss me again, in front of everybody. I love them being jealous."

He laughed. "So do I," he said, and kissed her.

She put her arms around his neck and held him tight, so tight. "I see you, Robert," she said quietly. "Just you."

"I see you, Marissa," he whispered. "You and me."

Across the table from Crystal, Mr. Chacon let go of a low, deep laugh when Robert and Marissa kissed on the dance floor. "See?" he said. "My wife, she's real good at this."

Crystal put her hand in Mario's and grinned. "I guess she is."

# *Epilogue*

Louise loved weddings more than any other single thing on the planet. Loved every teeny little thing about them—churches or open places, flowers, the music, the dresses, the various litanies of commitment.

And there had never been a finer day for a wedding than this early-June afternoon. Sunlight streamed in the windows to the pews filled with people in their Sunday best. The organist was one of the best in the world, and she played a hymn of joy and celebration as the two grooms edged into the room. Robert wore his tuxedo, but he'd left his hair down today, a glory of gleaming hair that made him look devilish and mysterious. He folded his hands in front of him, and looked toward the back of the church calmly.

Next to him, Mario was slighter, but no less straight and proud. He looked to Robert and folded his hands in front of him, too.

The wedding march began—*bum bum be bum*. Louise

reached for Alonzo's hand and sang softly, "Here comes the bride…" He lifted her fingers and kissed them. It hadn't been all that long since their own wedding, after all.

Louise loved weddings. And this was a part she loved a lot: when the bride, or in this case, the brides, came through the doors in their finery. What a fine pair of brides they were, too—Crystal, tiny and delicate, wearing a replica of a 1912 wedding dress Marissa had helped her to find. It draped sweetly over the mound of her belly. Marissa's gown was white and low-cut, displaying her creamy shoulders and a dazzling abundance of cleavage. Alonzo whistled softly and murmured something in Spanish. Louise chuckled. "Amen."

But this, now, this was her favorite part of any wedding. She turned to look at the men on the altar, waiting for those brides, watched their angular faces go radiant with light and anticipation. Everyone talked about the radiance of brides, but it was the grooms Louise liked to see. Nothing like the right woman to make a good man better.

As the grooms and brides joined hands and bowed their heads, Louise smiled in satisfaction. Oh, she was so good at this. Her three sons and their wives and various children sat scattered around the room, their own faces alight with the pleasure of anticipation that happily married people brought to a wedding.

Happy marriages could do a lot to heal the world of a whole lot of evil, she thought, idly rubbing the thumb of the man who'd made her a happy wife after so many years of being an unhappy one.

A teeny little sniffle caught her attention. Victoria, glorious in orange, caught her cry in a linen handkerchief. She sat alone, her long legs crossed, her arms anchored around her middle.

Louise smiled. There was work to do yet.

And she was good. Very, very good.

\* \* \* \* \*

*Look for Victoria's story*
*when Ruth Wind continues*
**THE LAST ROUNDUP** *series.*
*Coming soon!*

INTIMATE MOMENTS®

Silhouette®

# COMING NEXT MONTH

**#1015 EGAN CASSIDY'S KID—Beverly Barton**
*The Protectors*
Kidnapped! Mercenary Egan Cassidy only discovered he had a son when the boy was stolen from the school playground. Now nothing would stop him from rescuing his kid—or claiming the boy's beautiful mother, Maggie Douglas, once and for all!

**#1016 MISSION: IRRESISTIBLE—Sharon Sala**
*A Year of Loving Dangerously*
For seven long years, Easton Kirby had been living in self-imposed isolation. So when SPEAR agent Alicia Corbin asked him for help in tracking down a deadly traitor, Easton wanted more than anything to say no—to her pleas *and* her sensual curves. Was Easton ready to put his heart—and his life—on the line once again?

**#1017 THE ONCE AND FUTURE FATHER—Marie Ferrarella**
*The Baby of the Month Club*
After delivering heartbreaking news *and* Lucinda Alvarez's baby, detective Dylan McMorrow realized that he couldn't get Lucinda off his mind—or out of his heart. But with an elusive killer watching Lucinda's every move, Dylan had to do whatever it took to keep her safe—even once he discovered her well-kept secret....

**#1018 IMMINENT DANGER—Carla Cassidy**
*Mustang, Montana*
Temporarily blinded after witnessing a violent crime, Allison Welch was taken to quiet Mustang, Montana, and placed under the protection of strapping Sheriff Jesse Wilder. Jesse was drawn to the vulnerable beauty from the moment she arrived, but with her dangerous past not far behind, Jesse vowed to protect her at all costs—and then claim her as his beloved bride.

**#1019 THE DETECTIVE'S UNDOING—Jill Shalvis**
*The Heirs to the Triple M*
Rancher Delia Scanlon was determined to gain custody of the brother she'd never known existed. And thanks to sexy private investigator Cade McKnight, she already had a worthy ally. But could Cade convince Delia he would gladly stand by her not only in the courtroom but in life?

**#1020 WHO'S BEEN SLEEPING IN HER BED?—Pamela Dalton**
Amnesiac Katerina Reeves desperately wanted to remember her life—and the handsome stranger who claimed to be her husband. Unfortunately, nothing Mitch did seemed to help. But when her past caught up with her and a little boy's life was threatened, could Katerina trust in Mitch's love and the bond they still shared?

CMN0600

# SILHOUETTE'S 20ᵀᴴ ANNIVERSARY CONTEST
## OFFICIAL RULES
### NO PURCHASE NECESSARY TO ENTER

1. To enter, follow directions published in the offer to which you are responding. Contest begins 1/1/00 and ends on 8/24/00 (the "Promotion Period"). Method of entry may vary. Mailed entries must be postmarked by 8/24/00, and received by 8/31/00.

2. During the Promotion Period, the Contest may be presented via the Internet. Entry via the Internet may be restricted to residents of certain geographic areas that are disclosed on the Web site. To enter via the Internet, if you are a resident of a geographic area in which Internet entry is permissible, follow the directions displayed on-line, including typing your essay of 100 words or fewer telling us "Where In The World Your Love Will Come Alive." On-line entries must be received by 11:59 p.m. Eastern Standard time on 8/24/00. Limit one e-mail entry per person, household and e-mail address per day, presentation. If you are a resident of a geographic area in which entry via the Internet is permissible, you may, in lieu of submitting an entry on-line, enter by mail, by hand-printing your name, address, telephone number and contest number/name on an 8"x 11" plain piece of paper and telling us in 100 words or fewer "Where In The World Your Love Will Come Alive," and mailing via first-class mail to: Silhouette 20ᵗʰ Anniversary Contest, (in the U.S.) P.O. Box 9069, Buffalo, NY 14269-9069; (In Canada) P.O. Box 637, Fort Erie, Ontario, Canada L2A 5X3. Limit one 8"x 11" mailed entry per person, household and e-mail address per day. On-line and/or 8"x 11" mailed entries received from persons residing in geographic areas in which Internet entry is not permissible will be disqualified. No liability is assumed for lost, late, incomplete, inaccurate, nondelivered or misdirected mail, or misdirected e-mail, for technical, hardware or software failures of any kind, lost or unavailable network connection, or failed, incomplete, garbled or delayed computer transmission or any human error which may occur in the receipt or processing of the entries in the contest.

3. Essays will be judged by a panel of members of the Silhouette editorial and marketing staff based on the following criteria:

   Sincerity (believability, credibility)—50%

   Originality (freshness, creativity)—30%

   Aptness (appropriateness to contest ideas)—20%

   Purchase or acceptance of a product offer does not improve your chances of winning. In the event of a tie, duplicate prizes will be awarded.

4. All entries become the property of Harlequin Enterprises Ltd., and will not be returned. Winner will be determined no later than 10/31/00 and will be notified by mail. Grand Prize winner will be required to sign and return Affidavit of Eligibility within 15 days of receipt of notification. Noncompliance within the time period may result in disqualification and an alternative winner may be selected. All municipal, provincial, federal, state and local laws and regulations apply. Contest open only to residents of the U.S. and Canada who are 18 years of age or older, and is void wherever prohibited by law. Internet entry is restricted solely to residents of those geographical areas in which Internet entry is permissible. Employees of Torstar Corp., their affiliates, agents and members of their immediate families are not eligible. Taxes on the prizes are the sole responsibility of winners. Entry and acceptance of any prize offered constitutes permission to use winner's name, photograph or other likeness for the purposes of advertising, trade and promotion on behalf of Torstar Corp. without further compensation to the winner, unless prohibited by law. Torstar Corp and D.L. Blair, Inc., their parents, affiliates and subsidiaries, are not responsible for errors in printing or electronic presentation of contest or entries. In the event of printing or other errors which may result in unintended prize values or duplication of prizes, all affected contest materials or entries shall be null and void. If for any reason the Internet portion of the contest is not capable of running as planned, including infection by computer virus, bugs, tampering, unauthorized intervention, fraud, technical failures, or any other causes beyond the control of Torstar Corp. which corrupt or affect the administration, secrecy, fairness, integrity or proper conduct of the contest, Torstar Corp. reserves the right, at its sole discretion, to disqualify any individual who tampers with the entry process and to cancel, terminate, modify or suspend the contest or the Internet portion thereof. In the event of a dispute regarding an on-line entry, the entry will be deemed submitted by the authorized holder of the e-mail account submitted at the time of entry. Authorized account holder is defined as the natural person who is assigned to an e-mail address by an Internet access provider, on-line service provider or other organization that is responsible for arranging e-mail address for the domain associated with the submitted e-mail address.

5. Prizes: Grand Prize—a $10,000 vacation to anywhere in the world. Travelers (at least one must be 18 years of age or older) or parent or guardian if one traveler is a minor, must sign and return a Release of Liability prior to departure. Travel must be completed by December 31, 2001, and is subject to space and accommodations availability. Two hundred (200) Second Prizes—a two-book limited edition autographed collector set from one of the Silhouette Anniversary authors: Nora Roberts, Diana Palmer, Linda Howard or Annette Broadrick (value $10.00 each set). All prizes are valued in U.S. dollars.

6. For a list of winners (available after 10/31/00), send a self-addressed, stamped envelope to: Harlequin Silhouette 20ᵗʰ Anniversary Winners, P.O. Box 4200, Blair, NE 68009-4200.

Contest sponsored by Torstar Corp., P.O. Box 9042, Buffalo, NY 14269-9042.

# ENTER FOR
# A CHANCE TO WIN*

## Silhouette's 20th Anniversary Contest

### Tell Us Where in the World
### You Would Like *Your* Love To Come Alive...
### And We'll Send the Lucky Winner There!

Silhouette wants to take you wherever
your happy ending can come true.

Here's how to enter: Tell us, in 100 words or less,
where you want to go to make your love come alive!

In addition to the grand prize, there will be 200
runner-up prizes, collector's-edition book sets
autographed by one of the Silhouette anniversary
authors: **Nora Roberts, Diana Palmer,
Linda Howard** or **Annette Broadrick**.

## DON'T MISS YOUR CHANCE TO WIN!
## ENTER NOW! No Purchase Necessary

*Where love comes alive*™

Visit Silhouette at www.eHarlequin.com to enter, starting this summer.

Name: _____

Address: _____

City: _____  State/Province: _____

Zip/Postal Code: _____

Mail to Harlequin Books: **In the U.S.**: P.O. Box 9069, Buffalo, NY
14269-9069; **In Canada**: P.O. Box 637, Fort Erie, Ontario, L4A 5X3